The W[illegible]
Master's Promise to
a New Life

STAND-ALONE NOVEL

A Western Historical Romance Book

by

Sally M. Ross

Disclaimer & Copyright

This is a work of fiction. Names, characters, places and incidents either are products of the author's imagination or are used fictitiously. Any resemblance to actual events or locales or persons, living or dead, is entirely coincidental.

Table of Contents

Letter from Sally M. Ross

"There are two kinds of people in the world those with guns and those that dig."

This iconic sentence from the "*Good the Bad and the Ugly*" was meant to change my life once and for all. I chose to be the one to hold the gun and, in my case…the pen!

I started writing as soon as I learned the alphabet. At first, it was some little fairytales, but I knew that this undimmed passion was my life's purpose.

I share the same love with my husband for the classic western movies, and we moved together to Texas to leave the dream on our little farm with Daisy, our lovely lab.

I'm a literary junkie reading everything that comes into my hands, with a bit of weakness on heartwarming romances and poetry.

If you choose to follow me on this journey, I can guarantee you characters that you would love to befriend, romances that will make your heart beat faster, and wholesome, genuine stories that will make you dream again!

Until next time,

Sally M. Ross

Prologue

Dusty Creek, Kansas, Spring 1849

15 years later

A fly buzzed noisily against the kitchen window glass as Sarah ran a hand over the back of her neck, beads of perspiration running down the arch of her spine. A sudden flutter in the pit of her stomach caused her to lower her hands, pressing it against her slightly swollen belly.

Sarah hadn't told her husband that she was with child again. She was afraid of how Robert would react.

Sarah turned away from the stove and looked out the window. The late afternoon sun beat down mercilessly upon the parched earth, casting long shadows across the barren landscape. It was spring, but the air hung heavy with the oppressive heat, suffocating and unrelenting. Not a whisper of breeze stirred the dust that swirled in lazy spirals, coating everything in a fine layer of grit.

Through the window, Sarah surveyed the remnants of what was once a thriving community, now reduced to a dusty relic of its former self. The once vibrant town lay nestled amidst the sun-scorched plains, its wooden structures weathered and worn by years of relentless sun and unforgiving winds. The Great Drought was still upon them, and the creek, once a lifeline for the town's residents, lay dormant and dry, a mere memory of the life-giving waters that once flowed freely.

In the distance, the skeletal remains of last year's crops stood as silent sentinels, their wilted leaves drooping in defeat under the relentless onslaught of the sun. The landscape stretched out before her, a vast expanse of cracked earth and faded dreams, the harsh reality of life in the heart of the Dust Creek.

Sarah sighed as she turned her attention back to the pots on the stove. It was too hot for cooked food, but she knew Robert would complain if she served a cold supper. She and Robert had been married for four years, ever since Sarah was eighteen years old.

Sarah had been forced to marry Robert Turner, a man ten years her senior. Her father, a poor farmer, had traded her for a piece of the last fertile land in the town. Sarah could still remember the day her father had come home with the news. She'd thought he was joking at first, a sick, cruel joke, but she quickly realized he wasn't joking. He'd traded her life as if she were no better than a heifer or broodmare. She'd thought about running away, but she had nothing. Her family was as poor as the dirt that coated their boots.

The night before her wedding, Sarah had cried bitterly into her pillow, but when the dawn light peeked in through the gap in the threadbare curtains, she'd washed her face and decided that it might not be all bad. Perhaps Robert Turner would be kind to her, give her a better life than the one she had, stuck in a decaying house with her father, who'd given up living the day her mother had passed away.

She'd married Robert Turner almost four years ago to the day, and not a day had passed that she'd wished she'd run away despite having nothing to her name. That tiny glimmer of hope she'd had on the morning of her wedding faded into nothing but shadow only hours after they said their vows.

On the night of their wedding, Robert had gotten stinking drunk and crawled into their marriage bed. That night had been the start of the rest of Sarah's life.

Lost in her thoughts, Sarah reached for the spoon handle and gasped, pulling her hand away and cradling it against her chest for a moment. Then she opened it, wincing as she looked down at the scorched, red, and inflamed skin. She walked over to the sink and put her hand into the basin of cool water, wincing slightly.

She looked out of the window again, blinking back tears. The baby growing inside her belly should be something that made her full of joy and gratitude, but instead, it only instilled in her a deep sense of fear and regret. Over the past four years, she'd been with child three times. The first baby died before it was even three months old; the second and third were both stillborn. The pain of losing her babies was something that weighed heavily on Sarah's chest. Sometimes, her grief was so great that it crushed her, making it impossible to think or breathe, as if it were pulling her under the water, deeper and deeper, until the daylight above her grew paler and paler, vanishing altogether into suffocating darkness.

Equivalent to her grief was Robert's anger. With every child they lost, he grew more and more resentful, as if it were Sarah's fault, as if she wasn't trying hard enough or doing something wrong. Did he not understand how it felt as a mother? To carry life inside of you only to see it taken away in a second? Yet that was Robert; he had a way of always choosing his words, a way that cast doubt upon Sarah's perceptions, eroding her sense of self. She was trapped in her marriage, and each day that passed, she struggled to discern truth from fiction and reclaim her own agency in a world of his making.

Another flutter in her stomach, and Sarah looked down at her stomach, her long, dark-blonde plait falling over her right shoulder. She'd always longed for a family and children, but how could she bring them into this world? A world full of cruelty and pain? How could she protect her unborn child from their father when she couldn't even protect herself?

Sarah turned as she heard the front porch creak under Robert's weight. The knots in her stomach tightened uncomfortably. She quickly smoothed the crease in her white apron and plastered a smile onto her pale face as she turned to the door.

Robert stumbled into the kitchen moments later. He held onto the door frame as he looked around the kitchen. Sarah held her breath as she looked at him. Robert was a tall man with a head of thick, black curls and a dark beard. He had dark blue eyes and a crooked nose, broken during a brawl as a younger man. When Sarah had first laid eyes on him, she'd thought he was handsome, but now she only saw the rottenness inside him.

"What's for supper?" he barked as he walked across the kitchen, almost losing his balance as he sat at the small table.

"Roast chicken and potatoes," Sarah said automatically.

Robert squinted his eyes at her as Sarah chewed the inside of her cheek nervously. It was not unusual for Robert to come back drunk; however, today, there was something in his eyes, a darkness that scared Sarah, leaving her frozen to the spot.

"Well, hurry up," he snapped.

Sarah jumped before she quickly turned to the stove. She picked up the roasting dish, doing her best to steady her shaking hands. She carried the roast chicken to the table and set it down before fetching the potatoes.

Sarah sat opposite Robert as he carved the chicken, her hands clasped tightly in her lap. She kept her head down, worried that she might look at Robert in a way that irritated or angered him.

They ate in silence for a long while. Sarah kept her eyes glued to her plate. The chicken tasted like sawdust in her mouth as she struggled to swallow. The air in the kitchen was tense.

"Chicken's dry," Robert said, pushing his plate back in disgust.

Sarah said nothing, her throat dry.

"Look at me when I am talking to you," Robert commanded.

Sarah looked up at him under her long lashes.

"A man works hard all day, and this is what he comes home to?" Robert said, his eyes glowering. "I reckon even a dog wouldn't touch this sorry excuse for a meal. Do you even know the first thing about cooking? It's a wonder I haven't withered away to nothing with the slop you serve up on this table. A man expects a decent meal after a hard day's work, not this sorry excuse for food."

"I-I-I am sorry," she stammered.

"A lot of good that is going to do now."

"I will do better tomorrow," Sarah promised him.

Robert scoffed as he pushed back his chair. "I am going to bed."

Sarah lowered her gaze as Robert left the kitchen. As soon as he was gone, she took a deep breath, her shoulders dropping. She sat at the table for a while longer before she got up and cleared the table.

By the time she had finished washing the dishes, it was dark outside, and the moon was rising over the horizon.

Sarah left the kitchen and went to bed, where Robert snored loudly. She got undressed and into bed, careful not to make a sound in case she woke him.

Sarah lay in bed staring at the ceiling for a long time, wishing for the sweet release of sleep. Yet her mind was racing. Perhaps she could leave, pack up her things and go. Robert worked at the farm store in town all day, so if she left right after he went to work, she'd be a whole day away by the time he realized she was gone. Leaving was the only way she could have this baby. She could not raise them in this home. The idea of leaving Robert filled Sarah with as much fear as it did hope. It was not the first time she'd considered leaving him, but she'd always hoped things would improve. Maybe Robert would change if they had a child, but now she knew she'd been a fool to think so.

Sarah rolled over in her, her mind racing. She'd been stashing away some extra money every week, but it wasn't enough to leave yet. Maybe it would be in a week or two.

The next morning, Sarah took great care in preparing Robert's breakfast exactly as he liked it. However, morning came and went, and Robert did not come out of the bedroom. Sarah thought about waking him; she did not want him to be late for work, but she was afraid.

Around midmorning, Robert entered the kitchen, his skin ashen and eyes bloodshot. His breakfast was now cold, the eggs rubbery.

"Coffee," Robert ordered.

Sarah fetched the pot of coffee and poured him a mug, handing it to him with trembling hands. He took it without a word of thanks.

"I wonder if I should perhaps wake you..." Sarah said, her voice trailing off.

Robert took a long sip from the mug.

"I'm not working at the farm store anymore," Robert said, putting his mug on the table a little too firmly.

Sarah's eyes widened. "Oh?" she said cautiously.

"I ain't going to work for a swine who treats his employers like dogs," Robert said, his voice rising in anger, and his fists balled up so tightly that Sarah could see the whites of his knuckles.

Sarah said nothing. Mr. Harriet, the farm store owner, was a kind and generous man. Everyone in Dust Creek liked him, and he'd given Robert numerous warnings about coming to work drunk. There had been an incident a few months back when some of the supplies had gone missing. Sarah had heard from several sources in town that Robert and his younger brother, Jacob, were involved, yet Mr. Harriet had never been able to prove it.

Sarah wanted to know what had happened, but she dared not ask. Her heart was in her throat.

Just then, Jacob appeared in the back doorway, and Sarah turned to him. He held her gaze for a moment before Sarah looked away. Jacob looked much like his older brother, with the same dark hair and blue eyes. He was a few years younger, closer to Sarah's age. Sarah didn't like Jacob; he had a way of looking at her that made her stomach squirm.

"Jacob," Robert said. "What are you doing here?"

"I wanted to see if you want to go down to the saloon?" Jacob asked.

"Why not?" Robert said. "Ain't got no place better to be."

Robert pulled himself up from his seat and walked over to the back door, not giving Sarah a second glance. Jacob tipped his hat to her before following his older brother outside and leaving Sarah alone.

She watched them disappear around the side of the house and out of sight. As soon as they were gone, she exhaled shakily. What was she going to do now? If Robert had lost his job, it meant there would be no more money. With his reputation, there was no way anyone else in town would hire him, and even without his poor reputation, jobs were scarce in Dusty Creek. The two-year-long drought had gutted their town.

Sarah pressed her hands to her stomach as she blinked back tears. If there was no more money, how could she leave? And with Robert home all day, her only escape now seemed impossible.

Chapter One

Dusty Creek, Kansas, Summer 1849

Sarah stood in the doorway, wishing for the slightest hint of a breeze. Her lips were dried and cracked, and her skin felt like sandpaper. How long would they have to endure this drought?

The sun beat down on the small porch as Sarah turned and walked back into the house. As she did, she caught sight of her reflection in the dusty glass.

Her cheeks hollowed, and her brown eyes sunken with fatigue. The lines of worry etched upon her brow. Her clothing hung loosely upon her emaciated frame, the fabric worn thin. Her dark-blonde hair was tousled, strands hanging loosely over her shoulders and back. Sarah barely recognized herself anymore.

Sarah quickly looked away, bowing her head as she walked back into the house.

Robert was asleep in a chair in the sitting room, an empty bottle at his feet. His legs were stretched out in front of him, and his mouth hung open, a thin trail of saliva running down his chin.

Two months had passed since Robert had lost his job, and Sarah's life had become unbearable. If she'd thought things were bad before now, they were much worse. Not a day went by when Sarah prayed for some respite from this torture, to be free of Robert and his hold on her.

Sarah walked into the kitchen and into the pantry, where the air was slightly cooler. She looked around, but the shelves were bare. She had no idea what she would make for supper; they had no meat and barely enough flour to make bread. Yet Robert expected food on the table as if Sarah were some kind of magician who could fashion food out of thin air.

She pressed her back against the cool wall and sighed. She had not told Robert about the baby yet, and he barely paid her enough attention to notice. Yet it wouldn't be too long before she started to show. Sarah knew she had to tell him, but something held her back. It was as if she kept it a secret, then there was still a chance she could escape.

After a few moments, Sarah left the pantry, fetching a wicker basket from the floor beside the door. She went out the back door to the small vegetable garden. Sarah kneeled, shifting uncomfortably as she searched in vain for something to salvage, but the vegetable garden was nothing but cracked soil and wilted foliage. The tomatoes and cucumbers that had survived the heat were all a sickly shade of brown, with shriveled skins. Still, there was nothing else, so Sarah picked them up and placed them in the basket. She then got up, and as she did, she suddenly felt faint.

Sarah rocked on the heels of her boots for a moment, closing her eyes as she took deep breaths. But the air was heavy and thick, alive with the scent of rotting vegetation. Sarah exhaled shakily as the world moved in and out of focus.

Just then, she felt a pair of hands on her waist, and she turned to find Jacob, Robert's younger brother, standing behind her. He was so close that she could smell the whiskey on his breath and the sweet, sickly sweat on his skin.

Instinctively, Sarah pushed his hand off her and stepped back. Jacob's blue eyes were fixed on her as she quickly reached down and picked up the basket. Without a word, she headed back to the house.

Sarah stood beside the sink as Jacob entered the kitchen. He sat at the table and watched her as she peeled off the wrinkled skins of the tomatoes. She was painfully aware of his eyes on her, traveling the curves and arches of her body, and she was terrified he would notice her growing belly.

Just then, Sarah heard boots in the hallway and turned to see Robert entering the kitchen. He did not look at her as he walked to the table and sat beside his brother.

"You," he said, looking at Sarah now. "Fetch us a drink."

Sarah wiped her hands on her apron before reaching under the sink and fetching a bottle of whiskey. She then got two glasses from the dresser and carried them to the table before putting them down.

Robert uncorked the bottle with his teeth and poured amber liquid into two glasses, filling them to the brim.

Sarah returned to the sink, keeping her head down as the brothers spoke.

"So?" Robert said. "Is it sorted?"

"Yup," Jacob said, sitting forward in his chair. "We leave at dawn for Westport."

Sarah frowned. Where were they going? Perhaps this would be her chance to get away.

"Woman," Robert said sharply.

She turned away from the sink and looked at him. His eyes, as usual, were bloodshot.

"Start packin'," he said. "We leave at first light."

Sarah stared at him, her heart racing. "W-where are we going?"

"California," Robert said shortly.

Sarah continued to stare at him, frozen to the spot. She couldn't go to California, not in her condition.

"There's a group leaving tomorrow," Jacob explained. "We're joining."

Sarah glanced at Jacob. She had heard stories of the California Trail—they all had. Two thousand miles of unforgiving terrain stretched on without an end, a crucible of adversity testing the limits of human endurance with each passing mile. She had heard the whispers of fierce storms that descend without warning, lashing out with fury upon the hapless travelers below, their wagons swallowed whole by the raging torrents of rain and wind.

And amidst the chaos of the elements, other dangers lurked in the shadows—bandits and outlaws, preying upon the vulnerable and unsuspecting. Wild animals roamed the untamed wilderness, their primal instincts honed by centuries of survival in the unforgiving landscape. Not to mention the disease and petulance that swept through camps without mercy. She would never survive such a trip, but what was more, there was no way her unborn baby would survive it.

"No," Sarah said, shaking her head. "I-I-I can't."

A shadow passed over Robert's face as he pressed his lips into a hard line.

"There are no ifs, ands, or buts about it," he said sharply. "I've made up my mind, and that's the end of it. We're headin' west, and you're comin' along whether you like it or not. So quit your fussin' and start packin'."

Sarah opened her mouth and then closed it again, her mind racing. She had to tell him now; it might be the only way.

“I am with child,” Sarah blurted as she moved her hands instinctively over her stomach.

Robert raised his eyebrows, glancing at her belly before he turned away, draining his glass.

"Well, ain’t that just peachy?” he said bitterly. “Another mouth to feed on this fool’s errand of yours. We’re fixin’ to trek across the country, and now you reckon it’s a grand idea to saddle us with another burden? Three children gone to the dirt already, and you think this one’s gonna fare any better?”

Sarah’s mouth turned dry as she blinked back tears.

Robert filled his glass again and took another sip, shaking his head.

"You know, for all these years, I’ve been waitin’ on you to do your part as a wife, to give me children to carry on my name, but there’s something wrong with you, and I ain’t stayin’ here just ‘cause you’re with child. I ain’t puttin’ my faith in you to keep this one alive. We’re takin’ our chances on that trail.”

Sarah’s face burned as the little life growing inside of her fluttered. She loved the little person so much already. She had to do everything she could to protect the baby, even if it meant standing up against Robert. She had to try.

“Go without me,” she said.

Robert’s shoulders tensed, and he got up so quickly that his chair crashed to the floor behind him. He marched across the kitchen to Sarah and grabbed her wrists, twisting the skin painfully as she cried out in pain.

"You think I'd leave you behind?" he hissed, his blue eyes glinting dangerously. "You're mine."

"Please," Sarah begged. "You're hurting me."

Robert tightened his grip on her wrists. "You're pathetic," he spat. "If your pa were still alive, I'd give you back to him. It's no wonder he was so eager to be rid of you."

"Please—"

Robert held her gaze for a moment longer, and then he let go of her wrists, pushing her against the sink. Sarah gulped, unable to swallow over the lump in her throat. Her hands were shaking.

"Now, get packin'," he said dismissively. "We're leavin' at first light, whether you like it or not."

Sarah rushed across the kitchen, tears now rolling down her cheeks. As she reached the doorway, Robert cleared his throat.

"Sarah."

She hesitated, not turning to look at him.

"If you think of running away, I'll kill you myself," he said.

Sarah rushed down the hallway and to their bedroom. As soon as she was inside, she collapsed onto the floor in a crumpled heap. A strangled sob escaped her throat as she pressed her cheek against the floor. She closed her eyes for a long moment, trying to slow her heart, which was threatening to beat right out of her chest.

As she lay on the hard floor, the walls of their small home started to close in around her. She'd been so desperate to escape this place, to escape Robert, but this? Did he hope that she would die on the Trail? Sarah had lost count of the number of times Robert had threatened to kill her over the years, and yet he'd never done it. Despite his hatred and threats of violence, she could not shake the unsettling realization that he relished in the power he had over her.

It was not love that bound them together, but something darker and more sinister—a twisted desire to control and dominate every aspect of her life. He may despise her, threaten her, even wish her dead, but he would never let her go. In his eyes, she was not a wife to be cherished and loved but a possession to be owned and controlled. She could try to run, but he would come after her.

Sarah exhaled heavily as she pulled herself up off the floor. She walked over to the dresser and reached up, removing the suitcase from the top. She carried it over to the bed and opened it.

Sarah's hands trembled as she folded a dress and placed it in the worn leather suitcase on her bed. She had to pack as Robert told her to. Obedience had been ingrained in her through years of harsh lessons, and she knew better than to defy him. But as she moved mechanically, her mind raced, trying to think of a way out of this.

Suddenly, the floorboards creaked. Sarah froze, her heart pounding in her chest. She turned slowly, her eyes widening as she saw Jacob standing in the doorway, watching her through the crack in the bedroom door. She had no idea how long he had been there, silently observing. Neither of them moved, locked in a tense, unspoken moment.

"Jacob," she whispered, her voice barely audible.

She took a cautious step toward the door, her mind racing with a desperate plan. If anyone could stop Robert, it might be Jacob. He was the only one who ever seemed to get through to him, even if just a little.

"Can you... can you talk to Robert?" she asked, keeping her voice low, almost pleading. "Can you stop this? Please, Jacob. I don't want to go. The baby..."

Jacob's expression remained unreadable, but there was a flicker of something in his eyes—sympathy, perhaps. He shook his head slowly. "I can't, Sarah. Robert's made up his mind. Once he's decided on something, there's no changing it."

Sarah felt a wave of despair wash over her. "Please, Jacob," she begged, her voice cracking. "You have to try. For the baby's sake. I can't... I can't do this."

Jacob looked away, a muscle in his jaw tightening. "You know how he is," he said quietly. "He won't be persuaded. Not by me, not by anyone."

A lump rose in Sarah's throat.

"But maybe it won't be so bad," Jacob said, his expression softening. "We'll all be together."

Sarah said nothing. His words, which she assumed meant to bring comfort, did the exact opposite. Not only was she to be trapped on a two-thousand-mile-long journey with Robert, but Jacob, too.

Just then, they heard Robert's voice, harsh and commanding, bark Jacob's name from down the hall. Jacob stiffened, casting a glance over his shoulder. He gave Sarah one last lingering look, then disappeared.

Sarah stood there, feeling utterly defeated. Her last hope had vanished with Jacob's retreating form. She closed her eyes, fighting back tears. She had to stay strong for the baby. But the future felt darker and more uncertain than ever.

She returned to her packing, her movements slow and heavy with resignation. As she folded another dress, her thoughts drifted to what lay ahead. The Trail was fraught with dangers—disease, harsh weather, and the ever-present threat of attack. But the thought of Robert's wrath if she disobeyed was even more frightening.

Tomorrow, they would leave Dusty Creek, and before them stood a journey of uncertainty and hardship. Sarah was no stranger to hardships, so it was not herself she was fearful for but for the fate of her unborn baby.

Chapter Two

Westport, Missouri River, Summer 1849

Nathaniel Jameson stood at the front of the barn, his green eyes traveling over the sea of faces before him. He saw fear and apprehension in their eyes, but he also saw hope. Hope for a better life, a better future.

"Thank you all for coming," Nate said, clearing his throat. "Tomorrow morning, we embark on a journey that will test our mettle, our resolve, and our spirit like never before. For some, this may be your first time setting foot on the Trail, while it's a familiar path well-trodden for others. But make no mistake—each and every one of us will be tested in ways we cannot yet imagine."

The pioneers' faces grew more somber as Nate paused. Again, he looked around at the people he would soon lead across the great American frontier. Young and old, men, women, children, they would soon be under his care, their trust placed in him to safely get them to their destination. It was a responsibility that Nate had grown accustomed to over many years, but it was not one he had ever taken lightly.

"The California Trail stretches before us like an uncharted wilderness," Nate continued. "Its twists and turns are shrouded in uncertainty. We'll face challenges—fierce storms, treacherous terrain, and dangers lurking in the shadows. But know this: we do not embark on this journey alone. We are bound together by a common purpose, united in our quest for a better life on the western frontier."

A sudden movement caught Nate's eye, and he turned to see two tall men with dark features standing in the barn doorway.

Nate raised an eyebrow as the men came inside, not bothering to apologize for their tardiness. Behind them was a pretty young woman whose face was thin and ashen. As she walked, she cradled her belly in her hands. She did not look well, certainly not well enough for the journey she was about to embark on. As Nate's eyes lingered on her, she looked up for a moment and then bowed her head.

Nate turned back to the crowd. "From here, we will follow the Santa Fe Trail westward before joining the California Trail. After we cross into Nebraska, we will follow the Platte River, continuing through Wyoming and into Utah. After that, we enter Nevada, passing through the Humboldt River Valley before crossing the Sierra Nevada Mountains and descending into California."

Nate turned to find the new newcomers whispering to one another, and he shot them a stern look. The taller man met his gaze, his eyes full of arrogance and defiance. After all the years on the Trail, Nate had gained the ability to read people. He could see beyond the surface to the heart of who they were, and he could tell immediately that this man was going to give him trouble.

"Our journey will take us through some of the toughest country you've ever seen," Nate continued. "But all things going well, we will arrive in California in four to six months."

Nate looked around, and he saw the young woman turn paler. Despite not knowing her, he felt a peculiar curiosity about her.

"Now, before we depart, I want to make sure we're all on the same page," Nate said. "First things first, we need to make sure we're packin' smart. When loadin' up your wagons, remember—every inch of space counts. Pack the essentials first—food, water, ammunition, and spare parts for the wagons. Then, and only then, can you start thinkin' about luxuries."

Some of the group nodded, their focus on Nate as they listened intently.

"Water's scarce out on the Trail, so make sure you've got enough to last between the supply depots. When it comes to food, there will be chances to hunt and forage, but you can't rely only on the land. Make sure to pack non-perishable, durable foods that will sustain you on the trip. Things like cornmeal, salted meat, hardtack, canned goods, pickled vegetables, and dried fruits."

"What feed and supplies do we need for our livestock?" a man near the front asked, taking a step forward.

"Good question," Nate said approvingly. "There is plenty of grazing land on the Trail, but bring extra feed, including salt blocks."

The man nodded.

"How can we protect our children from coyotes and mountain lions?" a woman asked, her voice rising in agitation.

"Believe it or not, but the animals out on the Trail are more scared of you than you are of them," Nate said, smiling slightly. "But, each night, we'll set up camp in a safe and secure location near water sources whenever possible. We'll establish a perimeter and take turns keeping watch to ensure our safety while resting. It's a good idea to keep your guns handy for protection, but use them responsibly and only as a last resort."

The tall, dark-haired man scoffed, and Nate turned to him, his eyebrows raised.

"Ain't no man telling me when I can use my gun," he said. "It's my right."

"What's your name?" Nate asked, a hint of irritation in his voice.

"Robert Turner," the man said.

Nate nodded. "Well, Mr. Turner, it is your right to bear arms. But out there, on the Trail, I make the rules, and no man uses his gun without my say-so."

Robert's eyes glinted dangerously as he gritted his teeth, his thick arms folded across his chest.

"I've been down this road more times than I can count, and I've seen the dangers," Nate said, looking around the group again. "One little mistake can tear a wagon train apart. So if you are joining this trail, you are agreeing to follow my lead, and if you don't like it, well, there's the door."

He fixed his steely gaze on Robert again, daring him to challenge his authority. For a moment, he thought he just might, but then he dropped his arms.

"Right," Nate said. "Well, are there any more questions?"

It was late afternoon by the time Nate had answered all of the pioneers' questions, and the atmosphere in the barn was less tense as they all felt more reassured now. Of course, no one could predict what kind of challenges or dangers they would face on the road, but Nate had prepared them as best he could and had enough experience to navigate most of whatever the Trail threw at them.

"Right," Nate said. "Well, get an early night; we ride out at dawn."

The group began to disperse, and Nate hung back in case anyone wanted to talk with him. As he did, he watched the two men leaving, Robert and the other one. They were talking between themselves. The young woman was a few feet behind them, her gaze fixed on the floor. As they left the barn, Nate stepped forward, reaching out his hand.

"Excuse me?" he said as the young woman flinched.

"I am sorry," Nate said. "I didn't mean to frighten you."

The young woman said nothing as she looked up at him, meeting his gaze. She had soft brown eyes, and her long, dark-blonde hair hung in a long plait over her shoulder. Yet there was something in her face, a quiet desperation that worried Nate. She was frail, fragile.

"Are you all right?" he asked.

"I-I'm fine," the woman said.

Nate pressed his lips together. "That man, Robert Turner, is he your husband?"

She nodded.

"Well, Mrs. Turner," Nate said. "I know it may not be my place to say, but I've seen firsthand how unforgiving this journey can be, especially for someone in your condition."

She said nothing, her cheeks flushing.

"It ain't my place to tell you what to do, but I reckon you oughta consider whether this journey's worth the risk, both for you and the little one you're carryin'."

Nate looked at the young woman with genuine concern. He knew the decision ultimately rested with her, but he wouldn't feel right not saying his piece, making sure she was fully aware of the challenges ahead.

She opened her mouth to say something, but before she could, Robert appeared in the doorway, his expression as dark as thunder as he looked between them.

"What's goin' on here?" he barked.

Nate exhaled as he turned to Robert. "The Trail is a hard place for a woman in your wife's condition."

"What business is that of yours?" Robert demanded, squinting his eyes.

"It's not my business," Nate agreed. "But I wouldn't feel right not giving you fair warning—"

"Well, we don't need you sticking your nose where it don't belong," Robert seethed. "We paid good money just like everyone else, so why don't you stop worrying about my wife and do your job."

"I am doing my job," Nate argued, a muscle in his jaw tensing.

Robert glowered at him as he grabbed the woman's arm roughly.

"Come on," he said.

Before Nate could say anything else, Robert dragged her out of the barn. As he watched them go, Nate felt a gnawing sensation in the pit of his stomach. He was sure right from the outset that man would be trouble, and now he was certain of it.

***

Nate sat in the dimly lit dining room of the boarding house, the wooden floorboards creaking under the weight of the patrons moving about. The room was filled with the soft murmur of conversation, the clinking of cutlery against plates, and the occasional scrape of chairs. Oil lamps hung from the walls, casting a warm, flickering glow that created a sense of intimacy and coziness despite the high ceilings and sparse furnishings. The long communal tables were made of sturdy oak, their surfaces worn smooth by years of use. Simple white curtains framed the windows, providing a modest attempt at decoration.

Mary sat across from Nate, her sharp eyes observing him with concern and curiosity. Her plate was nearly empty, save for a few crumbs, but Nate's food remained largely untouched.

Nate had met Mary Williams almost ten years earlier after she'd just lost her husband to dysentery. Mary was from Scotland and had no other family. She and her husband, Angus, had spent years on the Trail before he died, and when she offered to join him and be their camp cook, Nate had readily accepted. Since then, they'd grown close, and to Nate, she had become something of a surrogate mother. She was kind and compassionate and looked after everyone. Yet she wasn't a pushover; in fact, she was one of the strongest women Nate had ever met.

"Ye've barely touched yer food, lad," she said, her voice gentle yet firm. "What's botherin' ye?"

Nate sighed, pushing his plate away slightly. "I can't stop thinking about that young woman, Mrs. Turner, and her husband."

Mary raised an eyebrow, leaning back in her chair. "It's no' the first time a woman wi' child has made the journey, ye ken. Sometimes folks dinna have another choice."

"I know," Nate replied, rubbing a hand over his face. "But something about Mr. Turner doesn't sit right with me. I get a bad feeling from him."

Mary pursed her lips thoughtfully, her expression softening. “We've had all sorts on the Trail, Nathaniel. Ye know that as well as I do. Desperate times make desperate men."

Nate nodded, but his unease didn't dissipate. “I just... I don't know. I can't shake this feelin’.”

Mary's eyes softened with understanding. “Aye, well, I'll keep an eye on her for ye. We womenfolk have our ways of lookin' out for each other.”

Nate managed a small, grateful smile. “I appreciate it,” he said. “But I doubt Mr. Turner will let anyone near her.”

After dinner, they retired early, knowing they had an early start in the morning. The boarding house provided modest but clean accommodations. Nate's room was small, with a single bed covered in a patchwork quilt, a wooden dresser, and a washbasin on a stand. The walls were bare except for a small mirror and a single candle providing the only light.

Nate changed into his nightclothes, the simple cotton garments a welcome relief after a long day of preparations. As he lay on the bed, the mattress creaking beneath his weight, his thoughts kept drifting back to Sarah Turner. Her face, pale and strained, lingered in his mind. He had seen fear in her eyes, a silent plea for help that he couldn't ignore.

He turned onto his side, staring at the flickering shadows on the wall. The journey ahead would be long and arduous, and he knew they would face many challenges. But the feeling of unease about the Turners gnawed at him, making it difficult to find peace.

As he finally drifted off to sleep, Nate resolved to keep a close eye on Mrs. Turner, to do what he could to ensure her safety. It was the least he could do for her and for the unborn child she carried. The Trail was often a harsh and unforgiving place.

Chapter Three

Sarah stood behind the wagon as another wave of nausea swept over her. Her stomach cramped painfully as bile rose in her throat. She crouched over, whimpering. Although it was early, it was already hot, and her dark hair clung to the back of her neck. Her skin was clammy, and she was slightly feverish.

"Sarah?" Robert barked.

She quickly stood up, wiping her mouth with the back of her hand. She felt dizzy and unsteady on her feet.

"There you are," Robert said, coming around the side of the wagon. "I thought I told you to fetch me my breakfast?"

Sarah said nothing as she clutched the wagon wheel to steady herself. They'd been on the Trail for just over a week, and she was barely surviving it. Sarah did not know if it was the movement of the wagon or the pregnancy, but she'd been unable to stop throwing up. She couldn't keep food down, and with each passing hour, she felt herself growing weaker. She worried about her unborn baby and how her deteriorating condition would impact them. Yet she could not ignore that niggling feeling at the back of her mind that told her maybe it would be better if she lost the baby.

"Well, don't just stand there," Robert snapped.

Sarah did her best to ignore her cramping stomach and walked around the wagon. The rest of the camp were gathered around the fire, talking and laughing amongst themselves. Seated together were Mr. Samuel Hawkins, a retired soldier who'd joined the Trail to see the West one last time. He was with Elijah Carter, a scout and hunter who worked on the Trail beside Nate, and the blacksmith, Mr.

Thomas Reid. Emma Johnson, a nurse with a taste for adventure, was gathered around the pots and pans of food. She was talking with Clara Thompson, a young bride whose husband was already in California working in the gold mines. She was on her way to join him.

As Sarah approached the group, some of the others looked at her sympathetically, but she kept her head down. Robert had instructed her to stay away from the others, and they'd eaten all their meals separately from the group.

"Mrs. Turner?"

Sarah looked up to see the camp cook, Mrs. Mary Williams, smiling at her. She was an older woman with a sturdy figure that commanded both respect and affection. She was of medium height but built solidly, her broad shoulders and muscular arms evidence of a life spent working hard. Her auburn hair, streaked with the first hints of gray, was usually tied back in a practical bun, but a few stubborn strands always managed to escape and frame her face. Her face was round and weathered, with a multitude of laugh lines radiating from the corners of her brown eyes. Her cheeks were ruddy from a combination of sun exposure and spending so much time cooking over a hot campfire.

"Why dinnae ye take a seat an' let me brew ye a wee cup o' peppermint tea?" she offered.

"No," Sarah said. "Thank you, but I must fetch Mr. Turner his breakfast—"

"Aye, I'm sure Mr. Turner's is capable o' fetchin' his own breakfast," Mrs. Williams said. "Now, come on."

Sarah opened her mouth to refuse, but Mrs. Williams wrapped an arm around her waist and led her to the campfire, where she sat her down. As Sarah sat, she caught Nathaniel's eye, and he smiled at her. Sarah quickly looked away. Mr. Jameson had been kind to her that day when they had the meeting in the barn, and she'd caught him watching her sometimes, but he had not approached her again. Sarah was grateful for that. Robert had vocalized his dislike for the Wagon Master more than once since their first meeting. Of course, Sarah did not agree, but she had not dared to say so. Still, it was best if Mr. Jameson kept his distance.

"Here we go," Mrs. Williams said, handing Sarah a cup of tea. "That should help soothe yer stomach."

“Thank you,” Sarah said gratefully, taking the cup from her.

Mrs. Williams smiled as she sat beside Sarah. “I can fetch ye somethin’ to eat?” she offered.

“No, thank you,” Sarah said, sipping the tea.

“Ye have to eat,” Mrs. Williams said. “For the wee bairn.”

Sarah said nothing, but she had no appetite. The tea was helping to soothe her nausea, but her stomach was still tied up in knots.

"Ye ken, it’d do ye good to sit up front on the wagon," she said. "Get some fresh air in yer lungs rather than stayin’ cooped up inside."

Again, Sarah stayed silent. She’d spent the better part of the week lying in the wagon between all the supplies while Robert and Jacob sat on the seat out front.

“Ye could sit with me?” Mrs. Williams offered.

“No,” Sarah said. “Mr. Turner wouldn’t like that.”

Mrs. Williams pursed her lips in disapproval.

“Sarah,” she said. “May I call you Sarah?”

She nodded, but her heart leaped into her throat just then as she turned to see Robert standing a few feet away. She quickly stood up and hurried to make him a plate of breakfast. As she did, she could feel his cold gaze on her.

Sarah fumbled with the spatula as she spooned scrambled eggs onto the tin plate; her hands were shaking so badly that she was worried she might drop it. She fetched two pieces of salted pork out of the saucepan and a spoonful of baked beans.

Sarah then carried the plate to Robert; however, as she offered it, he slapped it out of her hands. Scrambled eggs and beans rained down on her as the plate hit the ground.

"It's cold," Robert said stiffly.

Sarah stood frozen to the spot for a moment, aware that everyone's eyes were on her. Her cheeks burned as she fell to her knees to retrieve the plate.

"Mrs. Turner?"

Sarah looked up to see Nate standing in front of her. His green eyes were full of sympathy.

"I'm fine," Sarah said, quickly looking down again.

"Let me help—"

"I said I am fine," Sarah insisted, her face flushed.

Without another word, she got up and carried the plate over to the large basin of water. She washed it and, after returning it to the pile of plates, hurried back to the wagon. She climbed up inside and sat, blinking back tears. Her hair and face were covered in eggs and beans, but the food did not bother her; it was the humiliation. Robert had humiliated her in front of the whole camp.

The canvas flap opened, and Robert stuck his head inside the wagon. He looked at Sarah for a long moment.

"Next time I tell you to fetch my breakfast, you'll do it," he said, his tone dangerous.

Sarah nodded, her eyes down

"Now clean yourself up," he said.

Sarah said nothing as Robert disappeared.

A short while later, the wagon began to roll forward, and Sarah wrapped her arms tightly around her body as if doing her best to hold herself together. She did not know how much more of this she could take.

Sarah fell in and out of sleep as the wagon rolled on. When lunchtime came, she did not leave the wagon but stayed inside. As the afternoon passed, the air inside the wagon grew stifling, pressing down like a suffocating blanket. Beads of sweat trickled down her temples as she tried in vain to find relief from the oppressive heat.

The rhythmic sway of the wagon only served to exacerbate her queasiness, and each jostle and bump sent a wave of nausea churning through her stomach.

Despite her best efforts to find a comfortable position, Sarah could not escape the relentless discomfort. The wooden slats of the wagon bed offer little respite from the unforgiving heat.

Sighing wearily, Sarah closed her eyes and leaned back against the rough-hewn boards, her hand resting gently upon her swollen abdomen. She longed for nothing more than a cool breeze to wash over her, soothe her aching muscles, and ease the burden of her weary bones.

Sarah fell into a listless sleep, but when she woke, she realized she was not alone. Jacob was sitting beside her, his eyes fixed in a way that made her stomach squirm.

"Jacob," Sarah said, sitting up. "What are you doing?"

"Robert shouldn't have done what he did this morning," Jacob said, the smell of whiskey thick on his breath.

Sarah said nothing. In all the years she'd been married to Robert, Jacob had never come to her defense. He'd witnessed Robert's cruelty toward her and stood back, watching in silence. She did not know why he was coming to her now.

"Sarah," Jacob said, reaching out to touch her face.

She recoiled from his touch, but there was nowhere to go.

"Jacob?"

Sarah froze as Jacob quickly turned and left the wagon. Only once the canvas flat was closed again did she breathe again. What had Jacob been doing? Had he been watching her sleep? She'd never felt comfortable around him or liked how he watched her.

Just then, Robert's head appeared through the canvas flaps again.

"Get up, woman!" he barked.

With great effort, Sarah crawled out of the wagon and outside. The air was cooler, and she took a deep breath.

"Fetch us our supper," Robert instructed.

Sarah did as she was asked, but this time, she did not look at anyone or talk to anyone. She could feel everyone's eyes on her, sympathetic eyes and pitying eyes, but she did not want a repeat of that morning.

Sarah sat on the floor, with her back pressed against the wagon wheel, as Robert and Jacob ate supper and drank whiskey. Eventually, they stumbled over to their bedrolls and fell asleep.

She stayed seated on the ground for a long time, long after everyone had gone to bed. As she sat there, Sarah looked up at the stars. A cool breeze rustled the prairie grasses, and an owl hooted softly in the distance. Sarah sighed to herself. How was it that here, with an endless sky of stars above her head and a never-ending prairie at her feet, with all this freedom around her, she still felt entirely trapped?

Just then, the baby kicked, and Sarah gasped softly as she pressed her hands to her stomach. There was something indescribable about that feeling, but the feeling was fleeting as a shadow of dread that tugged at the corners of her mind. Sarah could not ignore the pang of guilt in her stomach, the pang that felt so much stronger than the kick of her unborn child.

"Are you all right?" a gentle voice asked, breaking through her thoughts.

Sarah looked up to see a woman standing nearby; it was Emma Johnson. She was a slender woman with an air of quiet grace about her. She moved with a fluidity that seemed almost effortless, her steps light and purposeful. Her long, chestnut hair was usually pulled back into a loose braid that hung over one shoulder. She had a gentle face, with soft, expressive eyes that were a deep shade of brown, warm and inviting. They were the kind of eyes that made people feel safe and understood, capable of conveying empathy and kindness with just a glance.

"Yes, I'm fine," Sarah replied, her voice low.

The woman stepped closer. "We haven't had a chance to be introduced. I'm Emma Johnson."

"Sarah Turner," she replied, instinctively glancing over at Robert, who was snoring loudly.

Sarah had been watching Emma from afar since they'd joined the Trail. She admired how she carried herself with a quiet confidence, her posture straight and her chin held high.

"How far along are you?" Emma asked, her tone soft and caring.

Sarah hesitated, unsure of the exact answer. "I'm not really sure," she admitted.

Emma took another step closer as Sarah's eyes flicked nervously to Robert again.

"Your husband keeps you on a tight leash, doesn't he?" she joked, trying to lighten the mood.

Sarah grimaced, and Emma's face fell as she realized her mistake.

"I'm sorry," Emma quickly apologized.

Sarah shook her head. "It's all right," she whispered. "The truth is that when he's passed out from the drink, well, it's the only time I can breathe freely."

To Sarah's surprise, Emma kneeled beside her and took her hand, her touch gentle and reassuring. "We should be friends," Emma said softly, her eyes full of empathy.

Sarah managed a small, grateful smile but knew deep down that Robert would never allow such a thing. The idea of having a friend, someone to confide in, was a distant dream.

"I don't think so," Sarah said sadly.

“Well, I am sure your husband wouldn’t argue with a nurse keeping an eye on you and the baby, would he?" Emma suggested, her tone hopeful.

Sarah said nothing, her eyes flicking back to Robert, who mumbled in his sleep and rolled over. The fear of his wrath was ever present, a constant shadow over her thoughts.

“You should go,” Sarah said quietly. “Before he wakes up.”

Emma squeezed her hand gently before standing up. Then, without another word, she turned and disappeared around the side of the wagon.

Alone in the darkness, Sarah’s heart ached with the weight of her silent struggle, torn between her love for her child and the overwhelming fear of the future. She knew the dangers that lay ahead, the risks of raising a child in a world poisoned by violence and cruelty. She did not want her child to suffer, and she did not know how to protect them from Robert.

She blinked back tears as she closed her eyes, resting her head against the wood of the wagon wheel. When she opened her eyes again, a star streaked across the sky, its arc cutting through the velvety expanse of the night. Sarah stared at it, transfixed. Then, just when everything seemed lost, a tiny flicker of hope ignited in her chest. The star was an unexpected reminder that even in the darkest of nights, there are still moments of light to be found.

Sarah stared up at the spot in the sky where the star had disappeared and wondered. After everything, did she dare to hope again? Hope was dangerous; she’d learned that a long time ago.

***

The next day, Sarah woke as the wagon bumped down the road. She had overslept and missed breakfast, but that didn't matter; she wasn't hungry anyway.

From the driver's seat, she could hear Robert and Jacob talking. Robert's voice was slurred, and she guessed he was still drunk from the night before.

Sarah crawled to the back of the wagon for some fresh air, but as she did, the wagon swerved and lurched forward. Sarah clung tightly to the wagon bed.

Suddenly, there was a loud crack, and the wagon jolted forward violently, throwing Sarah across the floor. She landed on her right arm with a painful thud. The world seemed to spin for a moment as she lay there, dazed and breathless. The sharp, acrid smell of the dust that had been kicked up filled her nose, making her cough.

She heard a loud thump followed by a groan from outside, a sound that sent a jolt of fear through her chest.

"Robert!" Jacob cried, his voice high and panicked.

Sarah pulled herself to her knees, her arm aching as she pushed open the canvas flap. The harsh sunlight hit her eyes, making her squint. She saw Robert lying on the ground, his face twisted in pain and rage. As she climbed down from the wagon, her legs wobbled, barely supporting her weight. Her breath came in shallow, painful gasps, and her heart pounded.

Jacob rushed to his brother's aid, kneeling in the dirt beside Robert. The sun glared down mercilessly.

"Are you all right?" Jacob asked, his voice edged with worry.

"I am fine," Robert spat, his face bright red with anger and embarrassment. He got to his feet unsteadily, dusting himself off with quick, sharp movements. His eyes flashed with irritation as he glanced around, clearly humiliated by his fall.

Just as he straightened up, Mr. Hawkins, Mr. Reid, and some others arrived, their faces etched with concern and curiosity, eager to see the holdup. The men murmured among themselves, their eyes flicking between Robert and the wagon, trying to piece together what had happened.

Sarah looked around frantically for Nate but saw him still making his way down the road, unaware of the commotion unfolding behind him.

The wagon sat at an awkward angle, one of its wheels having hit a large rock that now lay partially buried in the dirt. The horses snorted and stomped nervously, sensing the tension in the air. Sarah's heart ached with a mix of fear and helplessness. She knew Robert's temper could flare up any moment, making an already bad situation worse.

"What happened?" Mr. Samuel Hawkins asked.

Robert grumbled something unintelligible. Despite his best efforts, he was covered in dust from head to toe.

Mr. Hawkins walked over to the wagon. "Axle's broken," he said.

Sarah glanced at Robert, who was still bright red in the face, his eyes flashing.

"Well, why are you just standing there?" he said, turning to the blacksmith. "Fix it."

Thomas Reid folded his arms across his chest as he raised his pale eyebrows. He was a few years older than Robert and as tall, but more muscular.

"Sorry," Mr. Reid shrugged, not sounding the least bit sorry.

"What do you mean 'sorry?'" Robert snapped. "You're the blacksmith; your job is to fix it."

Thomas Reid said nothing as Robert turned a deeper shade of puce. He walked up to him, pointing his finger at his chest.

"Fix it," he said.

But Thomas did not move a muscle, and the air crackled with tension.

"How about I fix your wagon when you and your deadweight brother do something around this place other than get drunk and act like fools?"

Robert balled his hands into fists at his sides, and Sarah could see the whites of his knuckles. She clutched the threadbare shawl closer to her shoulders, her eyes wide and fixed on the growing quarrel between Robert and the blacksmith. With their old life now firmly behind them, Robert's temper threatened to strip away the last vestige of security they had. If they were cast out from the wagon train, where would they go? The wilderness was unforgiving; solitude here could mean death. They were no survivalists—Robert's skills lay in his fists and foul words, not in navigating the unyielding terrain or coaxing the stubborn earth to yield its meager bounties.

"I should tan your hide right here in front of everyone," Robert threatened, his voice now dangerously low.

"I'd like to see you try," Mr. Reid said, not blinking.

Robert took a step forward, and Sarah held her breath. She was scared, scared of the wilderness, scared of being alone, scared of what Robert might become if left unchecked by the laws of civilized men.

"All right, fellas," Mr. Hawkins said, suddenly stepping between them. "No need to get riled."

Just then, Sarah heard horse hooves and saw Nate riding up toward them, his hat pulled down low over his eyes. A wave of relief washed over her at the sight of him.

"What's going on?" he asked.

"Turner broke the axle," Mr. Reid said. "Driving drunk, again."

Nate glanced at the wagon, frowning as Robert eyed the blacksmith hatefully.

"Can you fix it?" Nate asked.

"I can," Mr. Reid said. "But not if Turner is going to go and break it again tomorrow."

Nate sighed. "Please, Tom."

Mr. Reid pressed his lips together begrudgingly. "Fine."

Nate gave him a grateful nod.

Sarah looked at Robert again to see him smiling smugly. No one else was smiling; in fact, everyone looked annoyed and disgusted by the situation.

Mr. Reid worked on the axle all morning. While he worked, everyone else was forced to wait. Robert and Jacob made no effort to appear sorry for the delay and did nothing to aid the blacksmith. Instead, they sat in the shade, drinking whiskey.

By lunchtime, both Robert and Jacob had passed out on the grass, so Sarah decided to go for a walk.

She'd only gone half a mile when she came to a small creek. She took off her boots and waded into the cool water, which soothed her swollen feet.

"Mrs. Turner?"

She turned to find Nate standing on the bank.

"Is everything all right?" she asked.

"Fine," Nate said. "Mr. Reid is almost finished with the wagon."

"That's good," Sarah said. "I am sorry for all the trouble."

"It's not your fault," Nate said, his green eyes softening.

Sarah nodded but said nothing. She was so used to everything being her fault that it felt good to hear these words.

"Can I walk you back?" Nate offered. "We'll be back on the road as soon as the axle is fixed."

Sarah waded out of the water and put on her boots. Then she and Nate walked back to camp. Neither spoke, but Sarah could sense Nate's eyes on her every now and then.

"Are you all right?" he asked.

Sarah's eyes widened in surprise.

"You're clutching your arm," he said.

Sarah looked down to see that Nate was right; she was holding her right arm to her left.

"I am fine," Sarah said. "I just bumped it when the axle broke."

"Let me see," Nate said.

Sarah hesitated a moment before she extended her arm. Nate carefully rolled back her sleeve, and Sarah inhaled as his rough fingers brushed against her skin.

"Sorry," Nate said, looking across at her under his dark eyelashes. "Does that hurt?"

"No," Sarah lied, her cheeks flushing.

Nate looked down again and frowned. "Are these bruises from today?"

Sarah said nothing, not knowing what to say. She couldn't tell him where those bruises really came from.

"Sarah?" he said tenderly.

She quickly pulled her arm from his grasp. "I said I am fine."

Nate opened his mouth, but before he could say anything else, Sarah turned and hurried back to camp, her heart in her throat.

Chapter Four

"We have to do somethin'," Mary insisted.

Nate ran his hand through his short, dark hair. The sun was rising over the horizon, and they sat together drinking hot coffee, their empty breakfast plates on the ground beside them.

"I know," Nate sighed. "But I am not sure what I am supposed to do? He's her husband..."

Nate's voice trailed off as he shook his head.

"That man is a beastie," Mary said in disgust. "And ye ken I've seen all types of men on the Trail, but he takes the cake."

Nate did not disagree. Robert Turner was not a good man. It had been hard for all of them to watch how he treated his wife, and Nate could not forget about the bruises he'd seen on Sarah's arm. Yet Nate had not been able to come up with a solution. In the world they lived in, wives were subject to the authority of their husbands. Moreover, there was a prevailing belief in the sanctity and privacy of marriage. Robert Turner had already made it clear to Nate that he did not appreciate his involvement in his marriage, and yet, as much as Nate wished he could stay out of it, he knew he couldn't. He'd never been able to tolerate cruelty, and he could not spend the next few months watching Sarah wither away under her husband's thumb.

"It has to be dealt with gently," Nate said. "He's bound to fly off the handle as soon as I open my mouth."

"Aye," Mary agreed.

Nate sighed. He wished there was a straightforward solution, but deep down, he knew that if he confronted Robert Turner, it would end in a fight.

“That poor lass,” Mary said. “I’d be surprised if she and the wee bairn lasted a month.”

A lump rose in Nate’s throat as he looked around the campfire. As usual, neither of the Turner brothers nor Sarah were there.

“If we can just convince him that his wife’s in dire need of tendin’ to," Mary suggested. "We need to get her away from him before there’s not a speck of her left."

Nate sighed, and they fell silent for a moment.

“Aye, well, I’d better get everything packed up,” Mary said.

She pushed herself to her feet, and Nate watched her go.

Nate stayed seated on the ground for a few moments longer. The truth was that the whole situation with the Turners was upsetting the rest of the group. It wasn’t just how Robert treated his wife that disturbed them all; it was their general attitude. From the first day on the Trail, Robert and his brother Jacob had separated themselves from the rest of the group. They did nothing to help, refusing to get involved with cooking, guarding, or helping out other pioneers in need. They were surly and unapproachable at the best of times and spent most of the evening drinking, waking up still drunk most mornings. Nate was surprised they hadn’t driven their wagon off a cliff already.

Robert had gotten into various arguments with some of the others. Thomas Reid was not the first. Robert was aggressive to the point of being threatening. His brother Jacob was quieter, but Nate sensed something below the surface, a quiet anger that was no less dangerous. He knew they could not go on like this; he would have to speak to Robert and his brother, although he had no great desire to do so. These people were his responsibility, including Sarah and her unborn baby.

Nate sighed as he got up from the floor. He would go and speak to Robert now. He would tell him he needed to pull his weight and stop treating Sarah so poorly. If he refused, Nate would have no choice but to give back his money and tell him to go.

Nate found Robert on top of his bedroll, snoring loudly. Jacob was nowhere to be seen. Nate considered waking him up but then decided against it. They needed to get back on the road; he would talk with Robert when they stopped for lunch.

As Nate led the wagons, the landscape unfolded before them. Rolling prairies stretched as far as the eye could see, their golden grasses swaying gently in the breeze. Here and there, clusters of wildflowers dotted the landscape, splashing vibrant purple, yellow, and blue hues against the backdrop of green. Every now and then, Nate spotted a lone buffalo or antelope grazing in the distance, silhouetted against the horizon.

As he held the reins, Nate sighed softly to himself. No matter how many times he rode this Trail, he never got tired of it. The vastness of the wilderness was as exhilarating as it was intimidating. At the back of his mind, Nate was always aware of the challenges and dangers ahead. Still, there was also a profound sense of freedom and possibility in the open expanse of the frontier, a feeling that anything was possible beneath the endless sky.

The morning rolled by without incident, and as the sun moved above them in the sky, Nate brought the wagons to a halt on the banks of the Missouri River. The wagons creaked and groaned to a stop, and the oxen snorted and stamped their feet, eager for a rest. Nate climbed off his wagon, his boots crunching on the gravelly riverbank. He walked over to the water's edge, squinting in the bright midday sun.

The river was a churning mass of muddy water, swollen from the recent rains. It rushed past with a fierce, relentless energy, carrying branches and debris along its current. The water was a murky brown, its surface broken by swirling eddies and the occasional whitecap. The sound of the river was a constant roar, a reminder of the power and unpredictability of nature. Nate could see the water lapping aggressively against the banks, the wet earth crumbling and falling into the river.

He'd intended to cross here, but the sight of the swollen river gave him pause. Nate had done trickier crossings before, guiding the wagons through treacherous waters and across unstable terrain. He knew the risks all too well: the danger of the wagons tipping over, the possibility of losing valuable supplies, and the threat to the lives of the pioneers and their animals. The thought of Sarah and the other women and children made his chest tighten with concern.

Nate removed his hat and wiped the sweat from his brow, scanning the river's width. He estimated it had swelled to nearly twice its normal size, the banks on the far side barely visible through the shimmering heat haze. He could see where the water had carved out new paths, creating shallows and deep channels that would make crossing even more unpredictable.

“What are you thinking?” Elijah said.

Nate turned to the younger man, whose light-brown hair was tied in a ponytail at the back of his neck. Elijah was a tall, lean man, his frame wiry. His skin was deeply tanned from years spent under the relentless sun. His face was angular, with high cheekbones and a strong jawline, often shadowed by a day's growth of stubble. A thin scar ran from the corner of his left eye to his jaw. Despite his rugged appearance, there was an intelligence and a calm, calculated demeanor in his eyes.

"Too risky," Nate said.

"I'll ride a few miles upstream," Elijah said. "See if there is a safer point."

Nate nodded as he turned, putting his hand on Elijah's shoulder for a moment.

He'd met Elijah almost six years ago. He had grown up in a small frontier town on the outskirts of Westport, where life was harsh and opportunities were scarce. Orphaned at a young age, he never had a home or a family. Then, one night before they were to embark on the Trail, Elijah had snuck into the wagon train under cover of darkness. Nate had discovered him the following day, and he had initially been wary of the stowaway. However, as an orphan with no family, Nate chose to give him a chance, and It quickly became clear to him that Elijah was very much like himself. He learned the skills of navigation, survival, and wilderness as if they were second nature to him.

While Elijah went off to scout a safer point to cross the river, Nate directed the wagons off the Trail and lined them up beside one another. The weary travelers dismounted, and as they did, Nate kept an eye out for Sarah, but she was nowhere to be seen.

They set up camp on the bank under the shade of a large willow tree, its long, sweeping branches providing a much-needed respite from the relentless sun. The air was thick with the earthy scent of the river and the sweet fragrance of blooming wildflowers nearby. The willow's leaves rustled gently in the breeze, creating a soothing, whispering sound that mingled with the soft murmur of the water flowing over rocks.

Nate and the others worked quickly to establish their temporary haven. The pioneers moved with practiced efficiency, each person knowing their role. The oxen were unhitched and led to the water to drink, their heavy, contented breaths mixing with the river's sounds. The wagons were arranged in a semi-circle.

Mary, ever the organizer, directed the women as they prepared the meal. Pots and pans clanged softly as they were unpacked and set over the fire. The smell of cooking food soon filled the air, a comforting aroma of stewed vegetables and cornbread. The scent of the smoke mingled with the fragrance of the river and the flora, creating a uniquely rustic bouquet.

Nate lit a small fire near the center of the camp, the flames crackling and popping as they took hold of the dry kindling. He straightened up, dusting his hands off on his trousers, and glanced around, his eyes taking in the scene. He looked around for Sarah, but she was nowhere to be seen. She mostly kept to her wagon, and Nate could not help but think about what a lonely existence she must live. He had a mind to go and find her but suddenly heard raised voices. He turned sharply to see Robert and Jacob near the water's edge, their figures tense and animated. Robert's face was flushed with anger, his fists clenched at his sides, while Jacob's expression was one of frustration, his hands gesturing wildly as he spoke. They were with one of the other travelers, an older bachelor named Mr. Fields.

"What now?" Nate grumbled to himself.

He put down the stick he held in his left hand and exhaled deeply as he walked over to them.

"What is going on?" he asked.

"I saw this man going through my wagon," Mr. Fields said, pointing at Jacob.

Nate frowned as he glanced at Jacob, but Robert stepped forward before he could say anything.

"Are you callin' my brother a thief?" Robert demanded.

"Yes," Mr. Fields said, his voice wavering. "I am missing two bottles of whiskey, my pocket knife, and my coin purse."

Robert's blue eyes gleamed dangerously. "It wasn't him, all right?"

"I saw him," Mr. Fields insisted.

"You're mistaken," Robert said between gritted teeth.

Mr. Fields glanced helplessly at Nate.

"I think everyone just needs to calm down," Nate said. "I am sure we can get to the bottom of this—"

"I ain't lettin' anyone accuse my brother of being a thief," Robert yelled, cutting Nate off.

"No one is accusing anyone," Nate said.

"I saw him sneaking out the back of my wagon," Mr. Fields said firmly. "I saw him with my own eyes."

Robert gritted his teeth as he raised his hands. He was poised to fight, and Nate stepped in between them.

"Mr. Turner," Nate said. "Walk away."

"Not while he's spoutin' hot air about my brother," Robert yelled.

"Why would Mr. Fields lie?" Nate asked.

Robert's expression hardened. "You takin' his side?"

"I am not taking sides," Nate said, trying to keep his voice level. "But if your brother had nothing to hide, let me search your wagon."

Robert's eyes widened. "You're not searchin' anything. You ain't got no right."

"Like I said, if your brother has nothing to hide—"

"You ain't searching our wagon!" Robert cried.

Just then, Nate caught a movement out of the corner of his eye and turned to see Sarah. She stood just a few feet away from them, her brown eyes wide and her thin face pale.

"What is going on?" she asked.

"Stay out of it, woman," Robert snapped.

"Don't talk to her like that," Nate said without thinking.

"She's my wife, and I'll talk to her however I want to—"

"She deserves to be treated with more respect," Nate said, his voice rising.

"It's none of your business," Robert said, the air crackling with animosity. "She's *my* wife!"

"Precisely," Nate said. "And yet you treat her as if she is your property—"

In an instant, Robert's fist connected with Nate's jaw, and there was a dull cracking sound. Nate staggered back, his face aching.

"Robert!" Sarah cried.

However, he did not seem to hear her as he launched himself at Nate again, his fist flying. Nate dodged the second punch, catching Robert in the stomach with his shoulder as the ground beneath them gave way.

Both the men tumbled toward the river's edge. With a desperate lunge, Nate managed to regain his footing and looked up just in time to see Robert stumbling backward, his arms windmilling as he toppled over the edge and into the churning waters.

For a moment, time seemed to stand still as Nate watched Robert flailing around in the river, his panic-stricken cries lost in the roar of the current. With a final, desperate gasp, Robert disappears beneath the surface, swallowed by the relentless flow.

"Someone help him!" Jacob screamed. "He can't swim!"

As Jacob's cries pierced the air, Nate spurred into action. He pulled off his boots, but just as he was about to jump into the river, a hand grabbed his arm. He turned to see Mr. Hawkins., his withered face set into a grim mask.

"It's too dangerous," he said. "The current is too strong."

He turned toward the river again and knew Sam was right—the current was too strong. He'd never reach Robert in time, and if he tried, he risked drowning himself.

As Nate looked down into the murky depths, a tumult of emotions washed over him. Guilt and regret. He'd never intended for this to happen.

After a moment, he turned to Sarah, who was standing in the exact same spot, staring at where Robert had vanished. Her face was expressionless, but her eyes betrayed her; they were full of relief.

Chapter Five

Sarah stood on the river bank, a whirlwind of emotions rushing over her, leaving her numb and overwhelmed. Shock coursed through her veins like ice, paralyzing her as she struggled to comprehend the reality of what she'd just witnessed.

"Sarah?"

She felt a hand on the small of her back and turned to see Mrs. Williams, her eyes full of concern.

"Come away, dear," she said softly.

Sarah allowed the older woman to lead her away from the water's edge. She moved as if she were sleepwalking, and the faces around her blurred. Mrs. Williams led her to the small fire and sat her on an overturned wooden crate. Sarah stared into the flames, which danced and crackled, licking at the air, so alive.

"Here," Mrs. Williams said. "Sweet tea for the nerves."

Sarah took the cup from her without a word, and as she did, Mr. Hawkins appeared.

"We are going to follow the river," he said. "See if we can recover the body."

Mrs. William put a hand on Sarah's shoulder as she nodded.

Sarah clutched the mug tightly as she watched the men—Nate, Jacob, Mr. Hawkins, and a few others—prepare to leave. Jacob, who'd not said a word since his brother fell into the water, was watching Sarah now, his eyes burning into her, but Sarah kept her gaze averted.

"I should go with them," Sarah said suddenly.

"No," Mrs. Williams said. "You don't need to see that."

But Mrs. Williams was wrong; Sarah needed to see it. She needed to see it to believe that it was true, that Robert was really and truly gone.

Without a word, Sarah got up and walked over to the men. Nate turned to her.

"I want to go with you," she said.

Nate shook his head. "Not in your condition."

"But I need to see it," Sarah insisted. "I need to see him."

Nate sighed, his eyes full of remorse.

"We'll bring him back if we find him," Nate said. "You have my word."

Sarah pressed her lips together and then nodded.

She stood watching as the men left, her heart in her stomach. Would they find Robert's body, or had he already sunk to the bottom of some watery grave? A part of Sarah could not help but wonder if he'd survived; perhaps he'd managed to catch onto a low-hanging branch and pull himself out. The truth was that she didn't know what would be worse—if they came back with his body or came back with him alive.

Sarah returned to her seat beside the fire, her arms wrapped around her belly. Time passed slowly as they waited, and as the sun began to sink, it cast long shadows across the long prairie grasses.

She was painfully aware of the others watching her and didn't know how she was supposed to behave. Was she sad? Shocked, most certainly, but she also felt numb.

Each passing moment felt like an eternity, each second stretching out into an agonizing eternity as Sarah wrestled with her conflicting emotions.

"They're back," Mrs. William said.

Sarah got up from her seat just as the men appeared. Robert's lifeless body had been placed across the saddle of the horse. A solemn silence descended upon the camp, broken only by the soft shuffle of hooves against the earth. Robert's limbs dangled limply, swaying gently with the horse's rhythmic gait. His clothes clung to his body like a shroud, sodden and heavy with the weight of the water. Strands of dark hair plastered to his face, obscuring his features with a mask of tangled strands. His skin, once bronzed by the sun, was now drained of color.

Sarah raised her hand to her mouth and whimpered, but even at that moment, she did not know if she whimpered out of sorrow or relief. Yet she could not ignore the small voice buried deep within, cheering in celebration. For years, she had endured Robert's tyranny, his cruel words, and violent outbursts, and now, she was unexpectedly untethered, free from the shackles of his oppression.

Jacob stood beside the horse, his face puffy and tear-stained, and after a moment, Nate walked over to Sarah.

"I am so sorry," he said.

"It was an accident," Sarah said, not tearing her eyes away from Robert's body.

Nate nodded, his face grim as he turned back to the others.

"Fetch your shovels," he said to the others.

Jacob frowned, taking a step forward. "You can't bury him here."

Nate turned to him. "We can't take him with us."

Jacob opened his mouth to argue, but Nate turned back to Sarah. He held her gaze for a long moment before he tipped his hat to her before he walked over to the wagon to fetch his shovel.

Sarah stood beside the wagon as she watched as the men dug Robert's grave a short distance from where he had fallen. As she watched, she wrestled with shame for feeling relieved by his passing, yet she couldn't deny the freedom that came with the knowledge that she was no longer bound to him.

When the grave was dug, the camp gathered around, but as Sarah looked around, she knew that only one person was truly mourning Robert's passing: Jacob. He'd not been there to dig the grave, but he was there now, a bottle of whiskey in his hand as he watched the other men lower Robert's body into the ground.

Sarah stayed until the earth had been patted down over her husband's body, and only then did she turn away. She walked back to the wagon, her face dry of tears.

"Mrs. Turner?"

She turned to see Nate.

"May I have a word?" he asked, removing his hat.

Sarah nodded.

"I just wanted to apologize again," he said, his eyes guilt-ridden. "I didn't mean for any of this to happen."

"I don't blame you," Sarah said.

Nate's shoulders dropped in relief as he stepped closer.

"I hope you know you are still very welcome here," he said. "On the Trail. I know it hasn't been easy for you, but I want to help."

Sarah could see that despite her words, Nate still blamed himself for Robert's death. But no one was responsible except Robert. He had been getting into fights all his life, and they'd finally caught up with him. Nate had been willing to jump into the water after Robert; Sarah would not forget that. He'd been willing to risk his own life to save Robert.

"Mrs. Williams has offered to take you under her wing," Nate continued. "You have a place here if that is what you want."

His gesture touched Sarah, but she didn't know if she would stay on the Trail now that Robert was gone.

"Thank you," Sarah said genuinely. "But I do not know if I can continue to California in my current condition."

Nate nodded. "I understand," he said. "But if you do change your mind, things will be different. Life on the Trail can be challenging, but things would be easier for you now..."

Nate's voice trailed off, and Sarah knew what he meant. Things would be easier now that Robert was dead. But she'd never wanted to come on the Trail to begin with.

"If you decide to continue with us, I will do everything in my power to keep you and your baby safe," Nate said. "However, if you decide you do not wish to come with us, we will arrive in Independence in a few days."

Sarah nodded as Nate gave her a small smile. Then he turned to go, and just as he did, Jacob came around the side of the wagon.

“Jacob,” Sarah said, frowning slightly.

He lifted the whiskey bottle to his lips and took a long sip.

“I can’t believe he’s gone,” Jacob said, shaking his head.

Sarah said nothing as he took another swig.

“I am sorry, Jacob,” Sarah said. “I know you loved your brother.”

“I did love him,” Jacob agreed. “Which is more than can be said for you.”

Jacob pointed his finger at her playfully. Sarah said nothing. What was the point in lying now? She had never loved Robert, not even for a single second.

Jacob took a step toward her, the whiskey sloshing in its bottle.

“No one on this Trail liked him,” Jacob slurred, frowning. “They all just stood back and watched him drown.”

“Jacob,” Sarah said. “Don’t you think you’ve had enough to drink?”

Sarah reached for the bottle, but Jacob jerked it away. He took another sip as he looked Sarah up and down; the corners of his mouth turned up.

“We should get married,” he said suddenly.

“What?” Sarah said, her mouth dropping open in surprise.

“It makes sense,” Jacob said, smiling. “You’re carrying my brother’s baby. It’s what Robert would have wanted.”

Sarah stared at him, quite sure this was *not* what Robert would have wanted.

Jacob reached for Sarah's hand, but she pulled it away; his skin was clammy.

"Come on, Sarah," Jacob pressed, his smile faltering slightly as a hint of impatience crept into his voice. "We could get off at Independence and raise the baby together as if it were our own. I never wanted to go to California to be a miner."

"No, Jacob," Sarah said, shaking her head. "I do not want to marry you."

Jacob's expression hardened, and a shiver ran down Sarah's back. Jacob had always been quieter than his brother, but it was his quietness that had unsettled Sarah. She always felt like something was seething just below the surface, something dangerous.

"So what are you going to do?" he challenged.

"I don't know," Sarah admitted.

"You think you will survive on your own?" Jacob scoffed.

Sarah said nothing, and Jacob's expression softened again.

"I am sorry I never stood up for you," he said. "I wanted to, but you know what my brother was like—"

"I am not going to marry you, Jacob," Sarah said firmly.

Jacob gritted his teeth. "Why won't you let me do what's right? With my brother gone, you are left vulnerable and alone."

With your brother, I was vulnerable and alone, Sarah thought to herself. She also knew that for all his words,

Jacob didn't want to marry her for her sake but rather for his own. Yet what Jacob said was true; she was now vulnerable and alone. She needed protection, but she also required room to discover who she was now that she was free of Robert's shadow.

Sarah suddenly made up her mind. She would stay on the Trail and help Mrs. Williams. Here, she would have Mr. Jameson's protection, and when they finally arrived in California, she would get a fresh start.

"Mr. Jameson had offered me a place here on the Trail," Sarah said.

Jacob raised an eyebrow. "You're not serious?"

"I am," Sarah said.

"But you're not built for this life, Sarah," Jacob argued. "I mean, look at you."

Sarah said nothing. She hadn't found it easy, that was true, but now that Robert was gone, things could be different. She'd have the opportunity to make friends, help around the camp, and build something of her own.

"I think it might be best if you get off at Independence," Sarah said.

Without another word, she turned to go, but as she did, Jacob caught her by the wrist.

"Let go of me," Sarah insisted.

"You're making a mistake," Jacob hissed.

"No," Sarah said, pulling herself free from his grip. "For the first time in a long time, I am doing something for me and my baby."

Sarah turned and walked away from Jacob, and as she did, she found a glimmer of her old self, the girl she'd once been. Sarah had been so sure she was gone, extinguished by Robert's darkness, but at that moment, she knew she was still in there somewhere, desperate to get out.

Chapter Six

Nate was grooming his horse when he heard a twig snap behind him. He turned to find Sarah walking toward him, her posture tentative.

"Mrs. Turner," he said.

"I wanted to tell you that I accept your offer to stay on the Trail," Sarah said.

Nate said nothing for a moment. The truth was that his guilt was weighing heavy upon his conscience. He played a role in the death of her husband, and although the circumstances were beyond his control, he couldn't shake the feeling that he failed in his role as Wagon Master. This guilt was the reason he'd asked Sarah to stay, the reason he'd offered her his protection.

Yet a nagging doubt gnawed at the edges of his consciousness. Sarah was frail and pregnant, and with months of travel still ahead of them, how could he keep her safe from all the possible dangers that lay ahead? Still, he had made a promise, and now he must do whatever it took to ensure her safety and shield her from harm to the best of his abilities.

"Good," Nate said, trying to smile. "I know Mrs. Williams will be glad to have another chick to mother."

Sarah pressed her lips into a tight smile, and they fell silent for a moment.

"I am going to bed," she said.

"Goodnight, Mrs. Turner," Nate said.

Sarah hesitated. "I think it would be all right if you called me Sarah."

"All right," Nate agreed. "Goodnight then, Sarah."

She turned, and Nate watched her go, and he could not help but notice that she looked lighter, taller, as if a heavy burden had been lifted from her shoulders.

Nate returned to grooming his horse; the light was fading now, the last rays of sunlight slipping away behind the distant horizon. As he moved the brush over the horse's hindquarters, he heard footsteps and turned, expecting to see Sarah again, but it was Jacob Turner.

"Mr. Turner," Nate said as he glanced down at the almost empty bottle of whiskey in the man's hand.

"You didn't even try to save him," Jacob said, his words slurring angrily.

Nate sighed. "I am sorry for your loss. But the current was too strong."

"How convenient," Jacob said.

Nate frowned but said nothing.

"You didn't like my brother," Jacob said, stepping forward. "None of you did."

Again, Nate chose to remain silent. What good would it do to bring it up now? Robert was gone.

"Is there something I can do for you, Mr. Turner?" Nate asked.

"You can stay away from Sarah," Jacob said.

Nate raised an eyebrow. “Mrs. Turner wants to remain on the Trail; that is her choice.”

Jacob narrowed his eyes but said nothing.

“It’s getting late, Mr. Turner,” Nate said. “And we have an early start tomorrow.”

Without another word, Nate walked over to his saddlebag and slipped the brush inside. As he did, he could sense Jacob watching him. However, he did not turn around.

***

Nate stood on the riverbank. Robert, his features contorted in anguish, teetered on the edge as the current churned violently below. His heart pounded in his chest as he reached out in vain, his voice a desperate plea lost in the roar of the rushing waters. And then, in an instant, Robert disappeared from view.

As the dream faded into darkness, Nate jolted awake, his body drenched in a cold sweat, his heart racing. In the distance, he saw the first rays of dawn light creeping over the horizon, and he pushed himself to his feet.

Nate dressed quickly and rolled up his bedroll.

As he approached the camp, he found Mary boiling water over the fire.

“You’re up early,” Nate noted.

“I could say the same for ye,” she said.

“Couldn’t sleep,” Nate said, stifling a yawn.

“Aye,” Mary said. “I’ll make you a cuppa.”

Nate smiled gratefully as he watched Mary make them a cup of coffee. Often, they were the first ones away in the morning, and Nate liked having his first cup of coffee with her.

"Here you go," she said.

"Thanks," Nate replied, taking the cup from her.

Mary sat beside him.

"How's Sarah?" Nate asked, taking a sip of the strong, bitter liquid.

Nate had suggested to Mary the night before that she invite Sarah to come and stay with her.

"She was still asleep when I left her," Mary said. "It's a bonnie relief for her, and the wee bairn, that they're no longer cooped up in that wagon from morn till night."

Nate nodded. It was also better for her to be away from Jacob.

"D'ye reckon the brother'll be takin' his leave o' us when we reach Independence?" Mary asked.

"I don't know," Nate sighed. "I hope so."

"Aye," Mary agreed. "He's fair quiet, that one. It sets my nerves on edge."

Nate agreed after their brief conversation the evening before that they would all be better off if Jacob stayed behind in Independence.

Just then, Nate turned to see Sarah approaching them, her long blonde hair loose over her shoulders and back. She looked well-rested, the dark rings under her eyes less pronounced.

"Good mornin', dear," Mary said brightly.

Sarah smiled. "Is there anything I can help with?"

"Ach, dinnae fash yerself, lass. Come an' take a seat, I'll brew ye a cup o' tea."

Sarah glanced at Nate, who chuckled. "Don't worry," he said. "I didn't understand half of the things she said at first, but you'll get used to it."

Mary swatted Nate playfully with her hand as she got up, offering Sarah her seat. She sat, and for a moment, neither of them spoke.

"How did you sleep?" Nate asked.

"Well," Sarah admitted.

Nate nodded as he glanced over at her, and she flushed.

"I am sorry," Sarah said.

"You have nothing to apologize for," Nate said.

"I hope you don't think I am uncaring," she said, lowering her gaze.

"I don't," Nate said.

"It's all just been such a shock," Sarah confessed. "I am not sure how I am supposed to feel or act..."

Her voice trailed off, and Nate fought the inclination to reach out and take her hand. He did not judge Sarah. He could not imagine what she must be feeling. Relief, mingled with fear of the unknown, and perhaps even a lingering sense of guilt for feeling anything other than sorrow for Robert's passing.

Just then, Mary handed Sarah a cup of tea, and she sipped it delicately.

The rest of the camp began to emerge, and Mary prepared breakfast with Sarah's help. Nate watched them for a while and could not help but smile. Mary had a way of putting people at ease and was the ideal person for Sarah to be around right now. She'd keep her busy enough to keep her mind off Robert and the journey. He was sure they would figure things out if they took one day at a time.

The rest of the day passed without incident. Nate kept an eye on Jacob, but he was silent and sullen, keeping to himself. Nate caught him glowering at him a few times, but he ignored him.

Nate was relieved to see Sarah eating dinner with them that night. She'd need to put some meat on her bones to keep up her strength for the coming months.

That night, they all went to bed early in preparation for their arrival at Independence the following day.

***

Nate led the train of wagons into the town of Independence, where wooden buildings lined the dusty streets, their weathered facades bearing the marks of years of sun, wind, rain, and snow. The wagons creaked as they trundled along the thoroughfares, and Nate turned to see the others craning their necks to get a good look around. It was their first encounter with the civilized world in almost three weeks.

Nate led them into the town square, which served as the heart of Independence. Market stalls were dotted around, offering a colorful array of goods and provisions for sale, from dried meats and canned goods to tools and clothing for the journey ahead. Merchants hawked their wares in loud voices and friendly banter, vying for the attention of passing pioneers.

Amidst the square's hustle and bustle, the sounds of hammering and sawing echoed from the nearby blacksmith and carpentry shops. Skilled craftsmen were fashioning and repairing wagons and equipment for the journey westward. The scent of freshly sawn timber and burning wood mingled with the tang of smoke from the nearby hearths.

He brought his wagon to a stop, and the others followed suit. Nate jumped down, gravel crunching beneath his feet.

"All right," Nate said as the others gathered around. "We will be here for two days, so make sure you check your supplies and stock up on anything low."

The group nodded before they broke apart.

Nate went off to find Sarah, but as he walked around the wagon's side, he heard raised voices and stopped to listen.

"I've already told you, Jacob," Sarah insisted. "I am staying on the Trail."

"Then you are a fool," Jacob said. "You won't make it to California, nor will the baby. Robert wouldn't have wanted this."

"Robert never wanted this baby," Sarah said, her voice rising. "He didn't care about either of us."

"That's not true," Jacob said. "He loved you."

Sarah scoffed.

"Please, Sarah," Jacob pressed. "Let us stay here in Independence together, if not for ourselves, then for the baby."

"No, Jacob," Sarah said. "I don't want to be with you. I am going to California—"

Just then, Nate heard a scuffle, and he walked around the back of the wagon to see Jacob with his hand on Sarah's arm. They both turned to him, and he saw the frustration in Jacob's blue eyes and the fear in Sarah's.

"Let her go," Nate commanded.

"Stay out of it," Jacob said between gritted teeth. "It's none of your business."

"I've offered Sarah my protection," Nate said, stepping forward.

Jacob smiled humorlessly. "Is that so?"

"Yes," Nate said firmly. "Let her go, Mr. Turner. I won't ask you again."

A muscle in Jacob's jaw tensed, and for a moment, Nate wondered if he had another fight on his hands, but then Jacob dropped his arm.

"I am going to the saloon," he said before he turned, stalking off.

Nate waited until he was out of earshot and then turned to Sarah.

"Are you all right?" he asked, his brows knitted in concern.

Sarah nodded, her bottom lip trembling.

Nate wanted to reach out to her, to comfort her, but he stopped himself. She'd just lost her husband; it wasn't appropriate, and he did not wish to give her the wrong idea.

"Do you think I am making a mistake?" Sarah asked. "Staying on the Trail?"

"I think it is the harder path," Nate admitted. "But we will do everything we can to help you."

Sarah nodded as she wrapped her arms around her stomach. Suddenly, Nate had an idea.

"Come on," Nate said. "There is something I want to show you."

Nate led Sarah through the bustling streets toward the historic courthouse square. The air was alive with the sound of hoofbeats and the chatter of passersby.

A short while later, they stepped into the courthouse square, where the famous Santa Fe Trail Tracks lay preserved. Nate paused beside the deeply etched ruts in the earth, his eyes tracing their path for a moment.

"What are they?" Sarah asked.

"The Santa Fe Trail Tracks," Nate replied, stepping forward as he gestured toward the tracks. "They were created as wagon wheels repeatedly traveled the same path. They gradually wore down the earth, leaving these indentations behind."

Nate paused as he watched Sarah trace her fingers along their weathered surface.

"They are a reminder now," he continued, "of those first pioneers who first set out from Independence on the Santa Fe Trail, seeking fortune and adventure."

The air fell silent between them momentarily, and Nate glanced at Sarah.

"You know, none of those first pioneers knew what difficulties they would face on their journey," he said. "They didn't know they were brave until they faced the toughest challenges. It's like they say: courage isn't about being fearless; it's about facing your fears head-on, even when it seems impossible."

Sarah turned to him, her brown eyes misty.

"But those first pioneers, they kept going, one step at a time, because they believed in something bigger than themselves."

Sarah pressed her lips together. "Do you really think I am like them, those first pioneers?"

"Everyone who chooses to come on the Trail is like them," Nate said. "And everyone is scared, but it's only when we let our fears conquer us that we are truly lost."

Just then, Sarah reached out and put her hand on Nate's hand, but he did not pull away.

"I don't want to be afraid anymore," she said, her voice barely above a whisper. "I've spent so long being afraid."

"Maybe it's time to stop letting your fear hold you back," Nate said. "Perhaps it's time to embrace it; let it be the thing that fuels you and gives you the determination you need to carve out a better future for you and your baby. Because, as hard as it might be to see it now, there's a life waiting for you at the end of this Trail."

"Do you really believe that?"

"I do," Nate said. "And I promise I'll be right beside you every step of the way."

Sarah said nothing as she turned and looked at the tracks again, and for a long moment, they stood together in silence, holding hands.

Nate would do what he promised; he would look after Sarah and do everything he could to get her and the baby safely to California. But he knew he had to be careful. Ever since he first met her in the barn, he'd found himself inexplicably drawn to Sarah, like a moth to a flame, yet he couldn't quite understand why. Something about her, a warmth in her eyes, a hint of vulnerability in her smile, tugged at his heartstrings in a way he couldn't explain.

But as much as he felt himself pulled toward her, he also wanted to pull back. He had built a life for himself as a Wagon Master and cherished the freedom and independence that came with his life on the Trail. He loved waking up every morning to the open road stretching out before him like an endless horizon. He didn't want to lose that, and he feared that if he got too close to Sarah, he just might.

Chapter Seven

Sarah exhaled slowly as the cramps began to ease. She was lying on the wagon floor as Emma moved her hands in circular motions over her stomach.

"How does that feel?" Emma asked.

"Better," Sarah said.

"Good," Emma said, sitting back on her haunches.

Sarah had been hesitant at first when Mary had suggested she let Emma help her, but she'd woken up that morning with such bad cramps that she could hardly sit up. So eventually, she'd agreed.

Emma kneeled on the floor of the wagon at her side. She was older than Emma by a few years. The nurse was a short woman, petite, with a heart-shaped face and kind eyes.

"Have you been with child before?" Emma asked.

Sarah hesitated. She did not like to talk about the babies that she'd lost. It was her greatest shame.

"Sorry," Emma said. "Being nosey comes with the territory."

"It's all right," Sarah sighed. "Yes, I have been with child before, three times, but I lost all of them."

Sarah's cheeks burned as Emma's expression softened.

"I am so sorry that happened to you," she said. "I can imagine there is no greater pain than losing a child."

Sarah swallowed a lump in her throat. There was no judgment in Emma's eyes, only sympathy.

“Was there a midwife or doctor with you?” Emma asked.

Sarah shook her head, and Emma frowned.

“My husband, Robert, did not like other people getting involved in his business,” Sarah explained.

“But surely he wouldn’t have expected you to give birth on your own?” Emma asked in disbelief.

He had, and she did. Sarah had given birth to two stillborn babies on her own.

“Oh, Sarah,” Emma said, her face falling.

Sarah said nothing, blinking back tears.

Emma leaned over Sarah and put her arms around her, hugging her tightly before she sat back again, meeting Sarah’s eye.

"Sarah,” she said firmly. “You are not to blame for what happened to your babies. Childbirth can be unpredictable, and sometimes, despite our best efforts, things don’t go as planned. You did everything you could to care for your babies and loved them deeply. Sometimes, these things happen through no fault of our own, okay?”

Sarah nodded, a tear rolling down her cheek. Robert had always blamed Sarah for their lost children, and over the years, she’d begun to believe that he was right, that it was her fault.

The wagon flap opened, and Mary stuck her head inside.

“Is everything...”

Her voice trailed off as she looked at Sarah, who quickly wiped away her tears with the back of her hand.

"I am fine," she said, clearing her throat. "Emma has magic hands."

Mary's expression softened. "Good," she said. "Then, if you are all done, we are ready to get back on the road."

Sarah nodded as she got up and followed Emma out of the wagon.

They'd been in Independence for two days, and it was time to continue their journey. Sarah had not seen much of Nate since their visit to the Santa Fe Trail Tracks, but she had thought a lot about what he said to her, and he was right. Sarah had let her fear control her for too long, but no more. Robert was gone, and she was free. She had the chance for a fresh start and intended to make the most of it.

Sarah walked over to Mary's wagon and was about to climb onto the front seat when she suddenly spotted Jacob, who was tightening the rope of the wagon canvas. Sarah hadn't seen much of Jacob over the past few days. Word was that he'd been holed up in the saloon all this time.

"Jacob?" Sarah said as she walked up to him. "What are you doing?"

He turned to her, a slight smirk on his lips. He stank of stale sweat and whiskey. "What does it look like I am doing?"

"But you are not coming with us?" Sarah said. "You said you wanted to stay in Independence."

"I said I wanted to stay in Independence with *you,*" Jacob corrected.

Sarah's brow furrowed. She didn't want Jacob to go with them. She wanted a fresh start, a life away from her past, from the Turners.

"But you don't want to be a miner," she insisted.

Jacob shrugged. "I'll do something else."

"Jacob," Sarah said firmly. "If you think I will change my mind, I won't. I am determined to make a new life for myself and my baby."

Jacob's smirk widened. "Who knew you had a bit of fire in you? I like it; it looks good on you."

"Jacob," Sarah pressed. "Why are you really coming to California?"

Jacob said nothing for a moment, a flicker of annoyance in his eyes now. Sarah did not trust his motivations for coming with them.

"I think you should stay," she said.

"Sorry to disappoint you," Jacob said. "But I am coming."

Just then, Nate gave them a signal to start moving.

"Ride with me?" Jacob offered.

"No, thanks," Sarah said, crossing her arms.

"Suit yourself."

Jacob turned away from her, and Sarah hesitated a moment longer before walking back to Mary's wagon.

"He's comin', then?" Mary said, a crease in her wrinkled brow.

Sarah nodded as she climbed up beside her.

Mary sighed softly as she took the reins. She clicked her tongue, and the wagon lurched forward. Sarah glanced over her shoulder at Jacob, who smiled at her, but it was a smile that made the hairs on her arms stand up.

As the town of Independence disappeared behind them, the rolling prairies of Missouri gradually began to give way to a more rugged terrain. Hills and valleys undulated beneath a vast expanse of open sky, which was a pale cornflower blue. In the distance, rocky outcrops and jagged cliffs rose from the earth.

Dust rose from the ground in the wake of their passing wagon wheels, mingling with the scent of sagebrush that perfumed the air, and Sarah sighed softly to herself.

"How are you feeling?" Mary asked, glancing at her.

"Better," Sarah said.

"Aye," Mary nodded sagely. "Nothing like a wee bit o' fresh air. Clears the mind and soothes the soul, it does."

Sarah smiled. She liked Mrs. Williams very much. She was easy to talk to and made Sarah feel at ease. Yet she did not know much about the older woman or how she'd become a camp cook on the Wagon Trails.

"Mrs. Williams," Sarah said. "How did you come here, to America?"

"Call me Mary, dear," she said. "And tis quite a long tale."

"I don't mind," Sarah said. "And we have the time."

Mary chuckled. "Aye," she agreed. "That we do."

Sarah smiled as Mary began to tell her story.

"I was born and bred in the bonnie highlands o' Scotland," she began. "But from a young age, I dreamt of far-off lands and grand adventures, the kind ye read about in stories. But life in the glens wasnae always easy, and I kent that if I wanted to see the world, I'd have to go out and find it meself."

"So you left?"

"Aye," Mary said. "I was just a lass o' eighteen when I decided to leave Scotland and seek me fortune in the New World. It was a bold move, to be sure, but I was determined to make me mark on the world."

Sarah looked at the older woman in awe. To leave her home and her family behind was indeed a bold move.

"When I finally set foot on American soil, I felt a thrill like no other. The air was different here, charged wi' promise and adventure. I kent that I'd made the right choice, and I was ready to embrace whatever lay in store for me. As luck would have it, I met my future husband, a strappin' young lad by the name o' Angus Williams, not long after arrivin' in America. He was a bold and adventurous soul, much like meself, and we hit it off right from the start."

Sarah smiled, picturing a younger Mary in her head.

"Together, we journeyed westward, seekin' our fortunes on the wagon trails o' the American West," Mary continued. "It was a hard life, but we faced it together, hand in hand, wi' nae but each other tae rely on. Angus was a skilled hunter and tracker, while I discovered me talent for cookin' along the way. Together, we made a formidable team, helpin' tae keep the wagon train fed and movin' forward."

"So you've been on the Trail since you were eighteen?" Sarah asked in amazement.

"Aye," Mary said. "Give or take a year or two."

"What happened to Angus?"

"He died," Mary said. "Taken from me too soon, a victim o' the harsh realities o' life on the frontier. His loss was a blow from which I thought I'd never recover, but then I met Nathaniel."

"How did you two meet?" Sarah asked curiously.

"After I lost my Angus, I kent not where to turn or what to do next, feelin' like a leaf blown about by the wind, wi' nae direction or purpose," Mary explained. "Then, as fate would have it, I met Nathaniel at Fort Bridger, and we got talkin'. He was only a boy then, just startin' out, and as green as the grass, he was."

Sarah could not imagine Nate any other way than the way he was now.

"Aye, I told him me tale, and he shared his own," Mary said. "When I offered tae join him and tend tae the camp's hearth, he welcomed me with open arms. Since that day, I've been by his side. He's become the son I never had."

The emotion in Mary's voice was palpable. Sarah had seen more and more over the past couple of days how the people on the Trail could become your family. Nathaniel and Mary were close; Sarah had seen that, and she couldn't help but feel envious.

"Aye, Nathaniel's a fine lad, no doubt about it. But the Trail has a way of grippin' on ye like a Highland mist, consuming yer days wi' danger and hardship. Ye can lose sight o' what truly matters, forgettin' what it means to find joy in life's simple pleasures. I fear for him, I do, afraid that he'll grow old without ever knowin' the warmth of love's embrace, the sweetness of bein' loved in return. True happiness is a rare treasure on the Trail, and I pray he finds it afore it's too late."

Sarah's heart was in her throat as she glanced at Mary, whose eyes were misty.

"Now look at me, chatterin' away like a babblin' brook," she said, smiling faintly. "Dinna fash yerself, lass, I'm just like an old mother hen, cluckin' about."

"I think it's nice," Sarah said. "That you have each other."

"Aye," Mary agreed. "Out here, there's not much that's certain. So ye cling to the folk you ken and trust, countin' on them to see you through the rough patches."

Sarah smiled, and silence fell between the two women.

It struck a chord within Sarah, this notion of forging connections with those around her, of creating a family where none existed before. After years of enduring abuse and isolation, she longed for the warmth of companionship, for the sense of belonging that came from being part of something greater than herself.

At that moment, Sarah resolved to do her best to open herself up to her fellow travelers, get to know each of them, and become a part of this Trail family she envied so much, even if for only a time. She understood that the road ahead would be fraught with challenges, but she could face them knowing she was not alone.

Chapter Eight

Nate stood at the river's edge, his arms folded across his chest as he surveyed the area. In the distance, thunder rumbled, and he looked up to see dark clouds on the horizon.

"The water's high," Elijah noted.

"I know," Nate sighed. "But we need to get across before the storm, or it'll be harder."

The summer rains had come early and were heavier than expected. They'd been lucky until now. Elijah had managed to scout several shallow areas for them to cross safely, but this time, it would be risky. Still, Nate had done it before.

"I'll take the rear," Elijah said.

Nate nodded.

"All right, listen up, folks," Nate cried, cupping his hands around his mouth. "We're about to cross this river, and it ain't gonna be easy. Remember, stay calm and follow my lead."

He climbed onto his wagon and took the reins, exhaling deeply as he mentally prepared himself for the crossing. After a moment, he clicked his tongue, and the wagon lurched forward.

With Nate in the lead, the wagon train approached the swollen river; his heart rate quickened as he entered the churning and frothing waters. The river's surface glistened under the midday sun, reflecting the ominous clouds that loomed overhead.

"Keep your reins steady!" Nate cried over his shoulder. "We need to maintain control as we enter the water. Easy does it now, no sudden movements."

Nate urged his oxen forward, leading them into the river's embrace. His heart raced as he fought to maintain control, his muscles straining against the powerful current.

"Watch your spacing!" Nate cried. "We don't want the wagons bunching up. Keep a safe distance between each one, and we'll avoid any collisions."

Inch by agonizing inch, they pressed forward, the water swirling around them in a dizzying frenzy. Nate did his best to concentrate, not allowing himself to give in to the river's unforgiving force, which would sweep them away in the blink of an eye.

And then, after what seemed like an eternity, Nate emerged on the other side, battered but unbroken. He let out a breath he hadn't realized he'd been holding, relief flooding through him.

Nate jumped down from his wagon and turned to see the other wagons emerging from the water. However, one wagon had not made it through and was drifting dangerously against the current. It was Jacob Turner's wagon.

"Jacob!" Nate yelled, rushing to the water's edge. "Keep those reins steady and try to steer toward the shore."

Jacob's face was pale, and his eyes unfocused. The oxen pulling the wagon bellowed as they struggled to hold their footing. Nate wasn't sure if he'd heard him, but he did not try to tighten his hands on the reins, and the wagon continued to drift. Nate needed to do something before another Turner was sent to a watery grave.

"Elijah?" Nate cried.

Elijah appeared at his side.

"I need your horse," Nate instructed.

Elijah dismounted, and Nate quickly pulled himself up into the saddle. He rode into the water, grateful that Elijah had trained his horse so well.

The cold water splashed against Nate's legs as they waded deeper into the current, the force of the river tugging at them relentlessly. He gripped the reins firmly and guided the horse toward the struggling wagon.

With each powerful stride, the horse fought against the surging water, its muscles straining with the effort. Nate fixed his eyes on the wagon ahead, focused solely on reaching it before it was too late.

As they drew closer, Nate could see the panic on Jacob's face. With great effort, he reached into his back pocket and cut through the rawhide, securing the oxen to the wagon. Now free, the oxen scrambled for the shore, struggling against the whirling current.

Nate turned the horse toward Jacob, who was clinging to his seat.

"Give me your hand," Nate instructed.

Jacob stretched out his arm, and Nate pulled him off the wagon. He scrambled onto the back of the horse. As he did, the wagon creaked and then began to tip over, giving in to the force of the water, the contents spilling over the side.

"The wagon!" Jacob cried.

"It's too late," Nate said.

He turned the horse and steered it back toward the shore. The rest of the camp lined up on the bank, watching in concern and apprehension.

As the horse climbed out of the river, Nate exhaled, sweat dripping down his back. He climbed down off the horse.

"Are you all right?" Mary asked, hurrying to him.

Nate nodded, out of breath.

He turned back to Jacob, who was sliding off the side of the horse, but as he did, he lost his footing and fell. Nate walked up to him and offered him his hand, and as he pulled Jacob to his feet, he rocked on the balls of his feet. Nate looked into his face and saw that his eyes were bloodshot, and his breath smelled of whiskey.

"You're drunk," Nate said in disgust.

"I'm not," Jacob lied.

"That's why you couldn't steer the wagon," Nate said, his tone hard.

"It's not my fault you led us through that!" Jacob argued, his words slurring. "We should have found somewhere else to cross."

"There was nowhere else to cross," Nate said.

"It's your fault," Jacob said, gritting his teeth. "And now I've lost my wagon."

It took every ounce of self-control Nate possessed not to grab him by the collar and shake some sense into him. Instead, he turned to Elijah and Mr. Hawkins.

"We'll set up camp here," Nate said. "Let's see if anything from the wagon washes to shore and can be salvaged."

The men nodded as Nate turned back to Jacob.

"You owe me a wagon," Jacob said, his eyes gleaming.

"I owe you nothing," Nate said. "You knew the risks, and you chose to drive drunk."

"You're supposed to be the Wagon Master," Jacob cried, his voice rising.

"Jacob," Sarah said. "You need to go and sleep this off."

"I am not going anywhere," Jacob insisted. "Not until he apologizes."

"Apologize?" Nate said, his eyes widening in disbelief. "In case you haven't noticed, I just saved your life."

"I wouldn't have needed saving if you hadn't made us cross that river," Jacob spluttered.

"I don't need to listen to this," Nate said, suddenly exhausted. "Sarah's right, go and sleep it off."

Nate turned away, but as he did, Jacob grabbed his arm. Acting on instinct, Nate whirled around and punched him on the chin. Jacob dropped like a stone, landing on the hard ground in a heap.

Despite his frustrations with the man, Nate immediately felt guilty.

"I'm sorry," he said, offering Jacob his hand.

"I don't need your help," Jacob said, slapping his hand away as he got up, his face bright red.

Without another word, Jacob stalked off, disappearing from view behind the wagons. Nate exhaled deeply, running a hand through his hair.

“All right,” he said. “Show’s over; everyone start setting up camp.”

The group broke apart, and Nate returned to the water’s edge.

“Nate?”

He turned to find Sarah, her expression concerned.

“Are you all right?” she asked.

“I shouldn’t have hit him,” Nate sighed. “I didn’t intend to.”

“Well, some might argue that he deserved it,” Sarah said, the corners of her mouth lifting in amusement.

“Has he always been like that?” Nate asked.

“As long as I’ve known him,” Sarah said. “He was always quieter and more reserved than my husband, but...”

Sarah’s voice trailed off.

“But what?” Nate asked.

She took a deep breath, as if searching for the right words. “Robert never liked to talk about his childhood much,” she began, her voice soft but steady. “But when he had too much to drink, sometimes he’d let things slip. He’d talk about their father, who was a hard man and a mean drunk.”

Sarah paused for a moment.

“Their mother died in childbirth, giving birth to Jacob,” she continued. “Robert said their father always blamed Jacob for it and never forgave him.”

Nate listened intently, feeling an unexpected pang of sympathy for the boys he’d only known as men.

"Robert also once said that he was his father's favorite, but all that meant was he got beaten less than Jacob."

A knot formed in Nate's stomach. During the years on the Trail, he had seen the effects of such brutal upbringings before, the way they twisted people and turned them into something they might never have become otherwise.

"That's... that's tough," he said quietly, not sure what else to say.

Sarah nodded, her expression sad. "I've often wondered if they would have turned out to be different men if they'd had a decent father and if their mother had survived."

Nate sighed, looking down at the ground. "They probably would have," he agreed. "It's hard to break free from that kind of past. It shapes you in ways you can't always see until it's too late."

"Do you think people can change?" Sarah asked. "Even after all they've been through?"

He considered her question carefully. "I think it's possible," he said slowly. "But it takes a lot of strength and the right reasons. Some people never find that strength or those reasons. Others do, but it's never easy."

"I hope Jacob can find that strength," she said softly. "For his sake and everyone around him.

Nate said nothing, but he felt a surge of admiration for Sarah, for her ability to look for hope in people where perhaps hope no longer existed. Yet, from what he'd experienced of Jacob Turner, he did not know if he had the strength to be a better man.

"May I ask you something?" Sarah said.

Nate nodded.

"Why didn't you leave Jacob in Independence?" Sarah asked.

"Truthfully?" Nate asked.

Sarah nodded.

"I've never left anyone behind before."

Sarah took a step forward, and for a few moments, neither spoke as they stared at the abandoned wagon like a shipwreck at sea.

"How are you doing?" he asked, changing the subject. "Are you managing the long days?"

"Yes," Sarah said. "Mary entertained me with the story of how she came to America."

Nate chuckled. "Ahh," he said, nodding. "Mary loves telling that story."

Sarah smiled. "It is a pretty good story."

"It is," Nate agreed.

They fell silent again, and Nate glanced at Sarah. He could not help but notice how much better she looked. She was still too thin, but her skin was no longer ashen, and her eyes were brighter. He'd never noticed the gentle arch of her lips before, but now he could not stop tracing the curves, and as he did, his heart began to race.

Sarah met his gaze, and Nate quickly bowed his head.

"Sorry," he said, clearing his throat.

Sarah said nothing.

"Well, I'd better get back and help the others set up," Nate said. "Excuse me."

Nate turned to go, leaving Sarah on the bank of the river. He could feel her eyes on him, but he did not turn around. He'd slipped, only for a moment, one decadent moment, but he couldn't let it happen again.

Chapter Nine

"Why don't ye ride wi' Nate today?" Mary suggested, her voice encouraging.

They were all seated around the campfire eating breakfast. Jacob was there, glowering at Sarah over the fire. Nate had already eaten and had gone to check the oxen.

"Oh no," Sarah said. "I wouldn't want to impose."

"Aye, he could do with a bit o' company," Mary insisted, her tone firm yet gentle. "And I reckon you're weary of hearin' my tales o'er and o'er again."

"I could never get tired of your stories," Sarah replied.

"Aye, but that drunken brother-in-law o' yours is ridin' wi' me now that his wagon's sunk," Mary remarked with a hint of wry amusement.

"He is?" Sarah said in surprise.

"Aye," Mary nodded. "Thought it better that he ride wi' me than Nathaniel. I can keep an eye on him."

Sarah chewed her bottom lip. After the incident yesterday, things were very tense with Jacob, so it was probably best that Mary kept a close eye on him.

"So you'll ride with Nathaniel," Mary said.

After breakfast, they cleared away the breakfast items and got ready to continue.

"Sarah?"

She turned to find Jacob, whose eyes were still bloodshot and his clothing disheveled.

"What is it?" she asked.

"I need to talk to you," Jacob insisted.

"Not now," Sarah replied. "I am busy."

Jacob took a step closer, but as he did, Mary appeared.

"Come on, you," she said. "Get on the wagon before I change my mind and leave you behind."

Jacob frowned, but before he had time to argue, Mary shooed him away and headed toward the wagon. Sarah finished packing the plates and tin cups and then headed to where Nate was waiting, her stomach in knots.

"Mary said I am to ride with you," Sarah said nervously.

"Did she now?" Nate replied, raising his eyebrows.

"Is that not all right?" Sarah said, her voice wavering. "I can go with someone else—"

"It's fine," Nate said. "Climb up."

She gave him a tight-lipped smile before climbing into the seat beside him.

Sarah sat atop the wagon, her gaze fixed on the horizon as the train moved steadily forward. Beside her, Nate guided the team of oxen with practiced ease, his eyes scanning the landscape ahead. She was aware of how close his arms were to her—so close, in fact, that she could feel the warmth of his skin beneath the material.

She glanced at him occasionally. His profile was striking, with his strong jaw and high brow.

"How are you this morning?" Nate asked.

"Fine," Sarah said. "Emma's been helping me."

"That's good," Nate said, nodding.

They fell silent again, and Sarah shifted uncomfortably on the hard wooden seat. She couldn't shake the feeling that she was intruding on his solitude, disrupting the quiet rhythm of his thoughts.

"I can really ride with someone else," She said.

"Am I such terrible company?" he asked.

"N-n-no, it's not that," Sarah stammered.

"I am only teasing," Nate said.

Sarah smiled, her cheeks warm.

"It's just that Mary said you like your solitude," Sarah explained.

"She's not wrong," Nate agreed. "I've been out here so long that I've grown accustomed to my own company."

"Then why did you agree to let me ride with you?" Sarah asked curiously.

Nate shrugged. "I promised to keep an eye on you," he said. "And it's a much easier task when you sit beside me."

"Right," Sarah said, nodding.

They fell silent again as the wagon creaked and the stones crunched under the rolling wheels. Sarah looked toward the horizon again just as a dark ridge rose above them.

"What is that?" Sarah asked, her gaze fixed on the horizon.

Nate followed her gaze, his eyes narrowing slightly as he surveyed the landscape.

"That's Thunderclap Ridge," he replied. "Named after a storm that rolled in one summer that was as loud as a cannon blast."

Sarah's eyes widened with interest, a spark of curiosity igniting within her. "Really? Were you there? What happened?"

"No," Nate said. "It happened long before I joined the Trail, but I've heard the story."

"Will you tell me?" Sarah asked.

"It was a summer's day much like this one," he began. "The sky was clear, not a cloud in sight, and the air was thick with heat. But as the afternoon wore on, a darkness crept over the horizon, swallowing the sun in its wake."

Sarah listened intently, her eyes wide with fascination.

"Suddenly, without warning, the heavens opened up, and the rain poured down in sheets," Nate continued, his voice rising dramatically. "But it wasn't just rain. No, it was as if the gods themselves were hurling thunderbolts from the sky, the thunder booming so loud it rattled the very earth beneath the pioneers' feet."

As Nate described the chaos of the storm, Sarah could almost feel the crackling energy in the air, the raw power of nature unleashed in all its glory.

"And then, just as quickly as it had begun, the storm passed, leaving behind a trail of destruction and awe," Nate concluded, his gaze distant. "And Thunderclap Ridge was born, a testament to the ferocity of nature and the resilience of those who call this land home, or so the story goes."

Sarah smiled, looking back at the ridge as she tried to imagine what it must have been like.

“You’re an excellent storyteller,” Sarah complimented.

“Thank you,” Nate said. “After a decade of living with Mary, I’ve picked up a few tips.”

Sarah smiled again, her shoulders relaxing. Nate’s story had broken the ice, and she no longer felt so uncomfortable.

As the morning wore on, Sarah was drawn into a world of wonder and discovery under Nate’s expert guidance. Before coming on the Trail, Sarah’s word had been so small, yet now it was unfolding before her very eyes—towering cliffs carved by ancient rivers, abandoned homesteads weathered by time, and delicate wildflowers swaying in the breeze.

“You know so much about everything,” Sarah marveled.

“I’ve spent most of my life on the Trail,” Nate said. “It’s my home.”

Sarah said nothing for a moment. She was curious about Nate and his past but did not want him to think she was prying.

“Do you have any family?” Sarah asked, hoping it was a safe enough question.

“Not anymore,” Nate said, stiffening suddenly.

“I am sorry,” Sarah said. “I shouldn’t have asked.”

“It’s fine,” Nate said. “They passed a long time ago, long before I became a Wagon Master.”

Sarah nodded but said nothing, and they fell silent. She wished she hadn’t said anything.

“What about you?” Nate asked. “Do you have any family other than Jacob?”

"No," Sarah said. "My mother passed away when I was just a girl, and my father, he never got over it."

"I am sorry," Nate said.

Sarah pressed her lips together. Sometimes, she wondered if she'd ever forgive her father for selling her to Robert. It still made her angry, and she hated it.

"Do you want to talk about it?" Nate offered.

The truth was that she didn't, but she'd also vowed to try and be more open and honest now that she had the opportunity to do so.

"My father gave me to Robert in exchange for land," Sarah admitted. "I was eighteen."

Nate turned to her, his eyes widening in horror and disbelief.

"I never spoke to him again after that," Sarah continued. "He died in the second year of our marriage."

"I am so sorry that happened to you," Nate said sincerely.

Sarah looked out at the horizon; as she did, her thoughts drifted back to her father's betrayal. The memory was a bitter knot in her chest, a wound that had never truly healed. She remembered the day he had made the deal, trading her off like a piece of livestock in exchange for a parcel of land. The sting of his betrayal still burned fresh in her mind, the sense of abandonment cutting deeper than any physical wound.

After her mother's passing, her father had become a stranger, his gaze filled with a mixture of grief and resentment whenever he looked at her. She had become a painful reminder of the woman he had loved and lost, a living embodiment of his guilt and regret. It was as if her presence alone was a constant reminder of his failures, his inability to protect his family from the hardships of life on the frontier.

Sarah's heart ached with the weight of her father's betrayal, the sense of betrayal and abandonment leaving her feeling adrift in a world that had once felt safe and secure. She had learned to fend for herself, to steel herself against the pain of rejection and betrayal, but the scars remained, a constant reminder of the wounds that had shaped her into the woman she had become. And as she sat beneath the endless blue sky, surrounded by the embrace of the wilderness, she couldn't help but wonder if her father ever regretted the choices he had made, if he ever looked back on the daughter he had forsaken with anything resembling remorse or sorrow.

"Sarah?"

She turned to Nate.

"If I've learned anything out here on the Trail all these years, it's that there is no better place to heal from the wounds of the past," he said. "Nature had a way of soothing the soul and teaching us about what is truly important."

Sarah believed him. Even sitting there now, she felt she could breathe easier. She did not know how she would ever fully recover from her past, from the trauma inflicted on her by the men in her life, but she wanted to. She wanted to be whole again, to look in the mirror and see someone she recognized, someone she liked. Sarah hoped this time on the Trail would allow her to become the woman she might have been had she not met Robert and spent the past four years being hurt and afraid.

Chapter Ten

Nate felt the wood of the wagon seat pressing into his back, each bump on the road sending a jolt through his spine, but he barely noticed. His mind was preoccupied. Sarah had been riding with him on his wagon for several days, and he'd never met someone who needed to be heard as much as she did. She'd been hesitant at first about opening up, but the more time passed, the more Sarah began to peel back the layers of her guarded self.

The more she revealed, the more Nate was drawn into her world, a feeling so unfamiliar that it left him both unsettled and intrigued.

Nate glanced over at Sarah, who sat beside him, her gaze fixed on the winding path ahead. She seemed different today; a tentative assertiveness replaced the timid air that usually clung to her. In fact, Nate had noticed a change in her; she was getting stronger, both physically and mentally. This morning, she even had a hint of color in her cheeks.

"How are you feeling today?" Nate asked.

"Fine," Sarah said, smiling faintly.

"That's good," Nate said.

They fell silent again, and Nate glanced behind him to see if everyone was following in line. As he did, he saw Jacob glowering from his seat beside Mary. Nate had done his best to avoid Jacob since the incident with the wagon.

As he turned back, he caught Sarah watching him.

"Nate," she said. "May I ask you something?"

"Sure," Nate said.

"How did you become a Wagon Master?" she asked. "I mean, it's just such a different way of life..."

Sarah's voice trailed off, and for a moment, Nate said nothing. He'd noticed how carefully she always chose her words as if she were scared of saying the wrong thing.

"I'm sorry," she said suddenly, pulling her thin cotton shawl around her shoulders. "I shouldn't pry."

"It's all right," Nate insisted.

They fell silent for a moment again. Nate had never liked to talk about his past, not with anyone. Yet he could understand why Sarah was curious. After all, she'd shared so much of her past with him.

"I didn't grow up imagining this life," Nate admitted. "As a boy, I lived in a small town in the Midwest. My pa was a farmer and a blacksmith, and my ma was a teacher at the local school. It was just me and my folks."

Nate paused for a moment, thinking back to those days. His childhood had been a tapestry of simple joys and everyday adventures. Even now, he could still recall the warmth of summer evenings, the scent of freshly turned earth in the fields, and the coolness of the shade under the apple tree in their backyard, where his mother would read to him.

"When I was around fifteen, our town fell on hard times," Nate continued. "The seasons grew harsher, and the rains were less predictable. Crops failed more often than not, and fields that once yielded waves of grain stood barren, their parched earth cracking under the relentless sun."

A lump rose in Nate's throat as he remembered how quickly everything had changed— how the apple tree had withered and died in the back garden and, along with it, the simple life he'd held so dear. As the months passed, his father spent long days in the smithy, waiting for customers who seldom came, and the ring of his hammer on the anvil echoed less frequently in the empty space. His mother found her schoolhouse quieter each day. Families unable to sustain themselves moved away in search of better opportunities, leaving behind empty homes and a town that seemed to be slowly folding in on itself.

"It was during this time that the notion of the West began to take hold in our community," Nate explained. "Stories of fertile lands, vast and untouched. My folks saw this as an opportunity not just to survive but to reclaim a sense of purpose and hope for our family. So they decided to join a wagon train headed for California."

Nate glanced at Sarah to see that she was listening intently.

"I was just a teenager, eager for adventure and to prove myself a man," Nate said. "We were all sad to say goodbye to our home, but my parents were ever the optimists, convinced that things would find a way of workin' themselves out."

Nate sighed. He wanted to skip this part of the story, but how could he? It was this part that had defined him. It was the very reason he was sitting here today.

"One afternoon, we were helping to secure the livestock and wagons against the fury of a storm," he said. "A sudden lightning bolt brought a tree branch down, spooking the oxen. They bolted..."

Nate exhaled shakily as the wagon creaked beneath his feet. He would never forget that day, not as long as he lived. It was a memory etched so deeply, a sharp, unyielding part of his consciousness. If Nate closed his eyes, he could still feel the sting of the dust, whipped into a frenzy by the howling wind, and hear the panicked cries of the oxen as they struggled against their restraints. The chaos had escalated so rapidly, the air thick with flying debris and blinding dust. Nate remembered his father's firm hand on his shoulder, the sharp crack of the branch as if yielded to the lightning's fury.

"Pa pushed me out of the way," Nate explained. "But he and Ma weren't so lucky. They fell under the oxen's hooves—"

Sarah reached out, her hand brushing against his arm in a gentle show of support. "I'm so sorry, Nate. I can't even imagine how hard that must have been."

Nate said nothing as he looked down at her hand. After the storm had passed, he'd found his parents lying together on the ground, broken beneath the oxen's hooves.

"It changed my life," he said. "I suddenly found myself alone, on a wagon train full of people who depended on each other to survive. Losing them made me realize how fragile life could be and how important it was to have someone who knew the way."

"So, you decided to stay?" Sarah asked softly.

Nate nodded. After losing his parents, Nate had been engulfed by a profound grief that threatened to consume him. He knew he needed to channel his pain into something meaningful.

"Yes," Nate said. "Becoming a Wagon Master felt like the best way to honor their memory. They'd died on the Trail searching for a better life but never had the chance to experience it. I thought if I could help others get the life my parents never did, well, then their deaths would mean somethin'."

Of course, when Nate looked back on those early years on the Trail, they had not been easy. Yet, as he grew into his role, his natural leadership abilities began to shine. The values his parents had nurtured in him—fairness, patience, and a protective instinct—were exactly what made him a good leader. He knew when to push the group hard, when to ease up, when to enforce discipline, and when to offer a listening ear. His leadership style wasn't just about getting to their destination; it was about ensuring everyone felt valued and safe, echoing how his parents had made him feel throughout his childhood.

Reflecting on those early years, Nate realized how integral they had been in shaping the man he had become.

Sarah sat quietly for a moment, processing his story. "You've turned your loss into a legacy, Nate," she said in awe. "That's really powerful."

Nate looked at her, a sincere gratitude in his eyes. "Thank you, Sarah."

Sarah pressed her lips together in a tight smile. They fell silent again, but Nate was very aware of Sarah, of the place on his arm where her hand had rested only moments before.

After the death of his parents, Nate had shut a part of himself down. This emotional distance became his shield, his survival strategy. It allowed him to make the hard decisions and to keep moving forward when the Trail demanded it. He quickly learned that building walls was the only way to survive in a time of constant threats. Grief was a luxury on the Trail; it left you vulnerable, and vulnerability could be fatal. Nate had seen too many lives lost. He knew he could not afford the weight of attachment, the pain of loss. So, he locked up that part of himself and threw away the key, or at least that's what he'd thought.

Yet now, having shared his past with Sarah and having allowed her into the guarded confines of his past, Nate felt the old barriers trembling. With Sarah, Nate found himself grappling with a new kind of fear—the fear of caring too much again, of having something real to lose. Part of him yearned to retreat into the safety of his emotional fortress to protect himself from the potential pain of loss once more. Yet another part, emboldened by Sarah's courage and her own story of resilience, wondered if he was brave enough to take this fork in the road, where might it lead?

As the morning progressed, the Trail took them through a dense forest, the trees towering around them. Light filtered through the canopy, casting dappled shadows on the ground. Yet, Nate kept his eyes straight ahead as the road grew increasingly treacherous. Roots snaked across the dirt, and thick mud clung stubbornly to the wheels.

As he led the group through the woods, Nate's attention was split between the path that wound through thick underbrush and the wagons behind them.

Then, without warning, a loud rustling from the underbrush spooked the oxen, their sudden, frantic bawling setting off a chain reaction down the wagon train.

Nate brought the wagon to a jolting halt and jumped from his seat, landing squarely on the soft earth. He looked around for the source of what spooked the oxen, but as far as the eye could see, there was nothing but dense underbrush.

"N-N-Nate," Sarah stammered.

He turned to her just as a giant bear emerged from the underbrush to their right. It was a grizzly, its fur a matted mix of dark browns and fleeting hints of silver. As Nate watched, the bear stood up on its hind legs. For a moment, Nate did not move. It was the biggest grizzly he'd ever seen. He must have been about eight hundred pounds and over eight feet tall.

"Don't move," Nate said under his breath.

Moving slowly, Nate reached for his rifle from its holder beside the wagon seat. He pointed it up in the air and set off a shot. The sound echoed through the forest as birds took flight, screeching in indignation and fear. Nate pinched the trigger, poised to fire again, when the bear suddenly grunted loudly and turned, disappearing back into the thick bush.

Nate's heart raced a million miles a minute as he watched it go. However, he was quickly pulled back into the present by the sound of the oxen, who were still bawling loudly, upset not only by the bear now but the gunshot.

"Elijah! Thomas! Help me calm these oxen down!" Nate called out.

Together, they approached the lead oxen, speaking in low, soothing tones.

"Easy there, easy," Nate murmured, his voice steady and reassuring. He moved slowly, deliberately, placing his hands on the massive shoulders of the nearest ox, feeling its muscle tense under his touch. Elijah did the same, their familiar presence serving to reassure the beasts.

"We should get out of here," Elijah said. "In case the bear comes back."

"You should have shot it," Jacob said from his seat beside Mary.

Nate frowned. "The bear's got more right to be here than we do."

Jacob squinted as Nate turned away from him. He walked back to his wagon, but as he did, he suddenly found that Sarah was gone. He climbed onto the wagon and looked under the canvas, but she wasn't there.

Nate climbed down from the wagon again, looking around, his stomach in knots. “Has anyone seen Sarah?”

“No,” Mary said, shaking her head.

Nate’s stomach sank to his feet. Where could she be?

“Sarah?” he called.

But there was no reply.

“Sarah?”

Still nothing.

Panic tightened its grip on his chest. He felt a surge of protectiveness, a fierce need to find her and ensure she was safe. The bear's appearance had rattled everyone, and the thought that she might have wandered off alone, possibly shocked or disoriented, was agonizing.

Just then, Sarah reappeared at the side of the wagon, her face pale.

“Where were you?” Nate demanded, his tone hard.

“I-I-I’m sorry,” Sarah said, flinching slightly. “I had a cramp in my leg…”

Nate exhaled, his shoulders dropping. “I thought you’d been eaten by the bear,” he said, his tone gentler. “Next time, tell me where you are going?”

“Okay,” Sarah agreed. “I’m sorry.”

“It’s all right,” Nate said. “Let’s get you back on the wagon.”

Nate helped Sarah back up into her seat. As he climbed up beside her, he could not help but feel guilty for snapping at her. As the Wagon Master, Nate was not easily rattled, but at that moment, when he thought something terrible had happened to her, he was scared.

Nate took the reins and led the group out of the woods. As the sun shined brightly overhead, he glanced at Sarah, his mind racing. The idea of losing Sarah, whether to the wild or to the distance he might reimpose between them out of fear, made him acutely aware of the stakes. If Nate continued to explore this connection between them, he risked bringing down the walls around his heart, letting them crumble at his feet. Nate did not know if he wanted to do that, but was he strong enough to stop something already in motion?

Chapter Eleven

Sarah stood with her arms wrapped around her stomach and her shawl pulled tightly over her shoulders. She'd never seen Nate rattled before, but that afternoon, in the woods, when he thought she was lost or hurt, Nate had been scared. She'd seen the fear in his eyes.

A pot clanged, and Sarah jumped in fright. She turned to see Mary crouching over the fire. Some of the others were gathered around, sitting in groups together. Jacob was there with some other men. He tried to catch Sarah's eye, but she looked away.

"Come here, lass," Mary beckoned with a friendly smile, gesturing to a pot simmering over the fire. "I'll show ye how tae make a hearty stew that'll warm yer bones. It's simple enough, but it takes a wee bit of know-how."

Sarah approached her, grateful for the distraction. She watched closely as Mary chopped some root vegetables with practiced ease, her hands sure and swift.

"Now, ye start with the hardest vegetables first, like yer carrots and potatoes. They take the longest, ye ken?" Mary explained, tossing them into the bubbling pot. "And here's a trick for ye—add a pinch of salt to the water. It'll help bring out the flavors."

Sarah nodded, following along, taking the knife Mary handed her to try her hand at dicing a turnip. The task was simple but grounding, helping her focus on the moment rather than on Jacob, who she could sense was watching her.

"So, how are ye gettin' on with Nate?" Mary asked, stirring the pot as she gave Sarah a knowing look.

Sarah paused, a small smile playing on her lips as she thought about Nate. "It's good," Sarah said. "He actually opened up to me today about his parents."

Mary's eyebrows shot up, her stirring slowing for a moment. "Is that so? Nate talkin' about his past? That's rare, that is. He doesn't let many people in."

Sarah said nothing as she thought back to their conversation that morning. She'd been hesitant to ask Nate about his past; he was such a private person. Yet, her desire to know more about him outweighed her hesitation.

"Ye must be having quite the effect on him if he's talkin'," Mary noted a slight tease in her tone, but her eyes were gentle.

Sarah blushed slightly, her hands busy with the vegetables as she considered Nate's actions in a new light. The idea that she might be someone special to Nate was both thrilling and terrifying. Was she even ready for something like that?

Mary chuckled softly, breaking Sarah's thoughts. "Now, don't let it stew in yer head too much, lass," she said. "Let's get these herbs in. Here, crush these with the side of yer knife. It'll release more flavor," she instructed, handing Sarah a handful of fresh herbs.

As Sarah followed the instructions, crushing the fragrant herbs and letting their oils coat her fingers, she felt mixed emotions. There was a budding joy at the connection growing between her and Nate, which seemed to deepen with each shared hardship and conversation. But there was also a fear, a hesitation to fully open her heart to what these feelings might mean. She'd only just been widowed. Surely, any kind of feelings for someone else would be wrong? Then again, she'd never loved Robert. The only things she'd ever felt for him were fear and anger.

A short while later, the stew was bubbling in the pot. Sarah sat beside Mary on an old wooden crate.

"He should have shot that bear," Jacob said, his voice rising.

There were murmurs of agreement from some of the other men he was seated with.

"Calls himself a Wagon Master," Jacob said, shaking his head bitterly. "He's put us in more danger than he's saved us from."

Sarah frowned. She did not like that Jacob was trying to stir up trouble.

"Dinnae mind him, dear," Mary said. "He's got a thistle in his breeks, that one."

Sarah pressed her lips together as Mary got up from the crate, her knees creaking. A moment later, Sarah turned as Mary clanged on the pot with the metal ladle.

"Grub's up," she called.

The camp gathered in an orderly line as they helped themselves to dinner. Sarah held back, waiting for everyone to serve.

"Here."

Sarah looked up to find Nate standing with a tin bowl outstretched in his hand.

"Thank you," Sarah said gratefully.

It was a small thing, Nate fetching her supper, but it made Sarah's heart somersault. It had been so long since someone had thought about her, about her needs.

Nate sat beside her, and they ate in silence for a while. The fire flickered behind them, casting a warm, reassuring glow around the circled wagons. In the distance, an owl hooted mournfully.

"Quite a day," Nate said after a few moments.

Sarah nodded in agreement as Nate turned to her, his spoon resting in his stew bowl.

"Sarah," Nate said. "I wanted to apologize for snapping at you earlier."

Sarah frowned.

"I feel bad about it," he continued. "I was just concerned something had happened to you."

"It's all right, Nate," Sarah said.

Nate nodded slowly. Sarah wanted to reach out and put her hand on his knee, but she stopped herself.

"What do ye think of Sarah's stew, then?" Mary asked as she walked over to them.

"You made this?" Nate asked.

"Not really," Sarah said, suddenly abashed. "I helped a little."

"Nonsense," Mary said warmly. "We'll make a trail cook out of ye yet."

Mary beamed at Sarah and Nate before she turned and bustled away.

"She likes you," Nate said fondly.

"I like her too," Sarah agreed.

They fell silent again as Sarah looked across the camp. Most people had finished eating and were heading off to bed. Jacob was still seated on the opposite side of the fire, glowering at them through the flames.

"I should probably get to bed," Sarah said.

"I'll walk with you," Nate said.

Just as Sarah got up, a sharp pain shot through her stomach, and she inhaled sharply, sitting back down.

"Are you all right?" Nate asked in concern.

"Just another cramp," Sarah panted.

"Do you want me to fetch Emma?" he asked. "Or Mary?"

"No," Sarah said, wincing. "It usually passes if I walk a bit."

"I'll walk with you," Nate volunteered, taking her hand and helping her back up.

As Sarah got to her feet, she could feel Jacob's eyes on them, his piercing blue eyes boring into her, but she did not turn to look at him.

Nate did not let go of Sarah's hand as he led her around the wagons. Sarah walked slowly, taking long, deep breaths as the pain started to subside some. She could feel Nate's eyes on her, and she looked over at him to find his expression tender and full of concern.

"I'll be all right, Nate," Sarah assured him.

Nate nodded, but the concern on his face did not disappear, making Sarah's throat swell. Robert had never shown even the slightest concern for her or the baby, yet Nate was there, holding her hand and not leaving her side.

They walked twice around the line of wagons before the cramp eased completely. By this time, Sarah was out of breath.

"Here," Nate said. "Sit."

Sarah sat on the fallen tree trunk, and Nate sat beside her. He was still holding her hand, but as they sat, he let go, clutching his hands in his lap.

They sat in silence for a while as Sarah moved her hands around her growing belly, and then suddenly, she felt a sharp kick against her skin.

"Oh!" she gasped.

"What is it?" Nate said. "Has the cramp returned?"

"No," Sarah said, smiling suddenly. "The baby is kicking."

Nate's shoulders dropped in relief.

"Do you want to feel?" Sarah asked.

Nate hesitated, and Sarah reached over and took his hand in hers. She placed it on her stomach and could feel the warmth of his skin beneath the thin material of her dress. The baby kicked again a moment or two later, and Nate jumped in fright. Sarah could not help but chuckle at the expression on his face.

"That's amazing," Nate said after a moment.

"No better feeling in the world," Sarah agreed.

Sarah suddenly looked away, a lump rising in her throat as tears stung her eyes. Nate's hand was still on her stomach.

"Sarah?" Nate said softly. "What is it?"

Sarah shook her head, words failing her for a moment.

"It's all right," Nate said. "You can tell me anythin'."

Sarah felt a sudden pull toward Nate, a need to share this part of herself that she had buried deep within. Ever since she'd started talking to him about her past trauma, Sarah had begun to feel lighter. The burden she'd carried for so many years eased.

Sarah turned slightly toward Nate, her gaze catching the glint of starlight in his eyes, a silent encouragement.

"There is something I've never told anyone," she whispered, her voice laden with a burden that, up until that point, she had borne in solitude.

Nate's attention was immediate, his body turning to face her more directly, a silent gesture of support.

"When Robert was still alive, I often found myself hoping that the child I carried wouldn't make it to birth," Sarah confessed, her voice shaking as the words left a bitter taste on her tongue. "I couldn't stand the thought of bringing a child into our world of fear and despair."

Nate's expression hardened, a flicker of anger passing through his eyes, quickly replaced by profound sadness.

"I hate myself for it now," Sarah said. "And I am so scared that something will happen to the baby. As if my thoughts have willed something into motion that I am now powerless to stop."

"No," Nate said, shaking his head as he reached for her hand and squeezed it tightly. "Your baby will be fine."

A tear rolled down Sarah's cheek as she looked up at the sky.

"There were other babies before... I lost them," Sarah said, her voice cracking in pain. "And each time, Robert made it feel like it was all my fault. It became my greatest shame, and it was as if each loss defined me, twisting me into this weak and pathetic person..."

Sarah's voice trailed off as Nate shifted closer toward her.

"Sarah, none of that was your fault. You know that, don't you?" His voice was a mix of fierceness and tenderness, battling the ghosts of her doubts that had haunted her for so long.

She nodded, more in hope than conviction, her eyes brimming with tears.

They fell silent momentarily as they looked up at the stars above them.

"You know, there's a Native American tribe called the Blackfoot," Nate said. "They believe the stars are not just lights in the sky but the spirits of their loved ones. They see them as ancestors, protecting and guiding them from above."

Just then, Nate gestured to the heavens, his hand sweeping across the star-studded sky. "Maybe your babies are among those stars," he said. "Maybe they're up there, watching over you, living in peace, away from any pain of this world."

Sarah kept her gaze fixed on the stars, each one suddenly seeming to hold a whisper of possibility, a hint of serene existence. "Do you really think that's possible?" she asked, her voice tinged with a gentle flicker of hope.

"I believe there's much more to this world than what we see," Nate responded, his eyes locked on hers, intense and sincere. "And yes, I believe they are out there, watching over you, proud of their mother's strength."

Sarah looked back at the stars for a moment longer and then looked down. Nate's face was so close to hers now that she could count the freckles across his cheekbones and the bridge of his nose. In an instant, the air between them changed, charged with a deep, shared connection, and they drew closer still, driven by an unspoken pull. Their faces were mere inches apart, their breath mingling in the cool night air. Then, the sharp snap of a twig echoed through the silence, and Sarah turned away, her heart thudding in her chest.

Jacob emerged from the shadows, his presence slicing through the moment.

"Everything all right here?" Jacob asked as his eyes darted between them, sharp and assessing.

Nate's body tensed, a protective edge to his posture.

Everything's fine, Jacob," Sarah said coolly. "We were just enjoying the stars."

Jacob's eyes narrowed as if he did not believe her. He looked as if he were about to say something before he turned and walked away. Sarah wrapped her shawl tighter around herself, feeling the warmth of the near moment fade into the chill of the night.

"We should get you to bed," Nate said as he got up and offered Sarah his hand.

As Sarah lay in her wagon that night, the stars still vivid in her mind, she felt a profound gratitude toward Nate. His story about the stars resonated deeply with her. It was as if he had gently taken the darkest pieces of her past, her deepest wounds, and reframed them in a light of hope and eternity. His words offered her a new perspective, a way to process her grief that didn't involve blame or shame but rather peace and release.

Nate's effort to find something to soothe her pain spoke volumes about his character. It was not just the story that touched Sarah, but the intent behind it—the desire to heal, to comfort, to protect.

This attempt to mend what was broken in her shifted something significant in Sarah's perception of Nate. He was no longer just a capable leader or a companion on this arduous journey; he was becoming her confidant, her solace, someone who saw her not as a victim of her past but as a survivor with a future. The fact that he had opened up about his own losses, sharing his vulnerabilities, only deepened her respect and affection for him.

As she reflected on his words under the quiet of the night, Sarah felt a stirring of something she had not anticipated—hope. Hope not just for healing but for new beginnings, for a life where she could feel whole again. And with Nate, she began to believe that it might be possible. His understanding and tenderness were slowly coaxing her heart open, awakening a part of her that she thought had been irreparably closed off.

The thought of this—of allowing herself to truly care for someone again, to possibly love and be loved in return—was both exhilarating and scary. Yet, as she nestled deeper into her blankets, the image of the stars etched in her mind, a peace settled over her. With Nate, she felt safe, understood, and valued. And as much as the idea of opening her heart again scared her, it also filled her with a sense that perhaps, together, they could navigate the trails of the wild and the pathways of each other's brokenness toward a healing neither had thought possible.

Chapter Twelve

Nate lay awake, the faint crackle of the dying campfire mingling with the whispers of the night wind. He couldn't shake the image of Sarah under the stars, her face awash with vulnerability and a dawning hope as she shared her heartache. Her story, her losses—they stirred in him deep-seated memories of his mother, Elizabeth, and the silent battles she had endured.

Nate's mother had always envisioned a bustling household, laughter echoing off the walls, a family table perpetually surrounded by many chairs. Yet, fate had carved a different path—harsh and unforgiving. Nate remembered the shadowed afternoons following each loss, the house cloaked in a somber, almost tangible quiet. His mother had lost several babies, each loss etching a deeper mark of sorrow into her gentle demeanor.

Despite the pain, his father, James, had been a pillar of strength and compassion. Nate had watched how each tragedy, rather than driving his parents apart, seemed to weave them closer together. James never let Elizabeth shoulder the grief alone; his presence was a constant reassurance, a balm to her aching soul. He'd often seen them by the fire, his father's arm around her, speaking words too soft for Nate to hear, but the tenderness unmistakable.

Reflecting on this, Nate felt a surge of anger toward Robert. How could a man blame his wife for such sorrows? The injustice of it burned within him. He recalled how Sarah's voice had trembled with the years of misplaced guilt she carried. It was a stark contrast to the shared grief and mutual support his parents had shown.

And yet, amid his anger, Nate was aware of a conflicting relief—that Robert was no longer there to inflict pain upon

Sarah. This relief, however, was tinged with guilt. To feel even indirectly grateful for another man's death was unsettling, yet he couldn't deny the truth of his feelings. Sarah was free now, free to heal and possibly to love again, to rediscover her strength away from the shadow of someone so cruel.

This mix of emotions—anger, relief, guilt—was complicated for Nate. He understood, perhaps better than he wanted to, the profound impact of loss and the deep scars it left behind. His heart ached for Sarah, not just for what she had endured but for the journey of healing ahead of her.

***

Nate awoke to the crisp morning air, the chill biting his skin. He sat up, rubbing the sleep from his eyes and feeling the familiar stiffness in his muscles. The predawn light cast a soft glow over the camp, illuminating the rolling fog that clung to the ground like a thin, damp blanket. The seasons were changing, he could feel it.

Nate reached for his clothes, neatly folded at the foot of his bedroll. The first layer was a woolen undershirt, its coarse fabric providing a barrier against the cold. He pulled it over his head, shivering as it touched his bare skin. Next, he grabbed his trousers—durable, brown canvas pants that had seen their share of wear and tear.

He stood up, quickly stepping into his trousers and fastening them with a leather belt. He reached for his socks, pulling the woolen material over his calves. His boots were next, sturdy leather with metal toe caps and thick soles. He laced them up tightly, ensuring they were snug and secure.

He shrugged into his cotton shirt, the fabric soft from many washes. It was a faded blue, the color reminiscent of the sky just before sunrise. Over the shirt, he donned a vest, its multiple pockets filled with small essentials like a pocket knife, a compass, and a few extra cartridges for his revolver.

The final layer was his coat—a heavy, knee-length duster made of oiled canvas designed to protect against wind and rain. The coat's deep brown hue blended seamlessly with the earth, making it both practical and inconspicuous. Nate fastened the brass buttons, the chill of the metal against his fingers reminding him of the morning's bite.

As dawn broke, casting a soft golden light across the camp, Nate found his way to the usual spot near the fire. Mary was already there, bustling about as she hummed softly under her breath. The air was filled with the scent of brewing coffee and the earthy aroma of the morning’s first fire.

As Nate approached her, Mary poured him a steaming cup and handed it to him with a knowing smile. Nate nodded his head in a silent gesture of thanks.

“Morning, Nathaniel,” she said. “Yer looking more broody than usual. Everythin’ all right?"

Nate accepted the coffee, his hands warming against the cup. "Mornin’, Mary. Just the usual thoughts, I suppose," he replied, settling on a nearby log.

Mary joined him, her keen eyes studying his expression. “And how are things going with our Sarah? You two were up quite late last night.”

“She needed someone to talk to,” Nate admitted.

Mary raised an eyebrow, and Nate sighed.

“We're friends, Mary. Just friends,” he stressed, his tone a mixture of conviction and hesitation.

Mary chuckled softly, shaking her head. "Aye, well, even the blind could see more brewin' there than just friendship. But ye sound like ye've convinced yerself otherwise."

Nate frowned, his gaze fixed on the dancing flames. "She's recently widowed, Mary. Carrying another man's child. I've enjoyed the solitude of my life; it's less complicated that way. I'm not looking for anything more than friendship."

Mary took a sip of her coffee, shaking her head. "Ye're not a young man anymore. Ye cannae spend the rest of your life alone because ye're afraid of a wee bit of complication. Life is complicated, love even more so. But it's also the part that makes livin' worthwhile."

Nate said nothing for a long moment. He knew Mary's feelings about love. As tough and worldly as she was, she was also a hopeless romantic.

"Mary, I know you mean well, but I like my life the way it is," he said.

"But nothin', Nate. I've seen the way ye look at her and how she looks at ye. It's rare, that kind of connection. Ye might not think ye want it now, but what about in ten years? Will ye be happy alone?" Mary's tone softened as she placed a hand over his. "Dinnae let fear decide your future, lad."

Nate remained silent as the camp stirred to life around them. He took another sip of his coffee, his mind wrestling with the possibilities Mary had laid before him. It wasn't as if he hadn't thought about it or felt Sarah's effects on him. But to admit it out loud? That was something entirely different.

After breakfast, Nate oversaw the process of packing up the camp with a practiced eye. Canvas tents were methodically folded, their waterproofed surfaces resisting the dew that had settled overnight. The heavy canvas, once the protection against the elements, now had to be secured atop wagons, their frames creaking under the weight. Women packed cooking utensils into wooden chests, the metal pots clanging softly as they were nestled with straw padding to prevent rattling during travel.

Children gathered the smaller livestock—chickens and the occasional goat—returning them to their travel cages or small penned areas within the wagons. The oxen, vital to the day's progress, were led from their grazing spots and yoked under the watchful eyes of their drivers. The animals' massive heads bowed, submitting to the familiar weight of the yokes, their hooves digging into the soft earth as they were prepared to pull the heavy Conestoga wagons.

As Nate walked among the wagons, inspecting the wheels and axles for any signs of wear or damage, he could not help but sense a change in the air. There was a tension, subtle but unmistakable. He noticed that not all the nods he received were friendly; some were curt, and others avoided his gaze altogether.

Nate approached Samuel, who was busily securing a tarp over his supplies. The older man was hunched with age, his shoulders curving like a question mark.

"Mornin', Samuel," Nate said. "Everything all right?"

Samuel glanced around before answering, his voice low. "Morning, Nate. Yes, all's in order here."

Nate nodded, but he saw a hint of concern in the man's pale eyes.

"Somethin' wrong?" Nate asked.

Samuel paused, scratching at his gray beard with his dirty nails.

"There's something you should know," he said.

Nate said nothing as he waited for Samuel to continue.

"Jacob's been stirring things up. Talking a lot about you, not in a good way, either."

Nate's brow furrowed, his hand pausing on the wagon's wooden frame. "What's he been saying?"

"It's nothing outright nasty, mind you. But he's planting doubts. Questions about your decisions, whispers about the paths you choose. He's got some folks wonderin' if you're really leading us right." Samuel's expression was apologetic, as if he disliked being the bearer of such news.

Nate clenched his jaw, his gaze hardening as he scanned the camp. Jacob had always been a thorn in his side, but this was something more. This was dangerous. "Thanks for letting me know, Samuel. I appreciate it," he said, keeping his voice even.

"No trouble, Nate. Just watch your back, eh? Not everyone's as blind to Jacob's games as he might hope," Samuel added, patting the wagon beside him before returning to his work.

As Nate continued his rounds, his mind raced with this new information. Leadership was always a lonely path, the weight of every decision, the responsibility for every life—a burden he accepted, but one that became heavier with each whisper of dissent.

Nate had learned many years ago that the wagon train was a microcosm of society, with all its politics and power plays.

A short while later, the wagons rolled forward. Nate was still caught up in his thoughts. He knew he had to address the undercurrents of discontent before they erupted into something that could not be controlled. He needed to reaffirm his leadership, quell the doubts Jacob was sowing, and remind everyone why they had chosen him to lead in the first place. The journey ahead was fraught with enough dangers; the last thing they needed was to be fighting amongst themselves.

Nate sat rigidly on the driver's bench of his wagon, guiding the oxen along the winding trail with a distracted hand.

Beside him, Sarah seemed to notice his tension. “Is everything all right, Nate?” she asked softly, her voice blending with the wagon's gentle creaks and the cattle's distant lowing.

Nate exhaled deeply, his hands tensing on the reins.

“It's Jacob," Nate finally said, his voice low.

He didn't want to admit it, to give her something else to worry about, but another part did not want to keep it from her. As he glanced at Sarah, he saw the concern etched across her face.

“What has he done?” she asked.

“Samuel told me he’s been stirring doubts among the folks, spreading unease about my decisions,” Nate explained.

“I am sorry, Nate,” she said.

“You have nothin’ to be sorry for,” Nate reminded her.

Sarah pursed her lips, her brow furrowed. “What are you going to do?”

Nate sighed, his gaze drifting to the horizon where the land met the sky. “I’ll have to talk to him. It’s critical everyone understands that questioning leadership out here isn’t just about discontent—it’s dangerous. Doubts can split the group, leading to hesitation when decisiveness is needed most.”

Sarah nodded, her hand reaching out as if to offer a physical anchor. "Would you like me to talk to him?" she offered.

He shook his head more sharply than he intended. "No. I appreciate it, but this is on me. He needs to hear it from me."

Sarah pulled back slightly, respecting his decision. "I understand. But I am here, Nate, if you need anything."

Her support was a comfort, a small warmth against the chill of his task. Nate managed a grateful smile.

As the wagon train rolled forward, each turn of the wheels carried them deeper into uncertain territory, both literally and metaphorically. Nate felt the weight of his leadership, knowing how he handled Jacob could set the tone for the rest of their journey.

With a deep breath, he looked across the land spread before them, feeling a flicker of gratitude for Sarah's presence beside him. Her understanding and support did not erase the challenge ahead. Still, they made it more bearable.

Chapter Thirteen

"We need some more firewood," Mary said, pressing her lips together.

"I'll go and get some," Sarah volunteered.

Mary frowned.

"It's all right," Sarah said, walking over and picking up the wicker basket, which she balanced on her hip. "I won't be long."

As the afternoon sun began to dip behind the trees, Sarah ventured to the outskirts to gather firewood. She spotted a wooded area in the distance, half a mile or so, and made her way there.

As Sarah walked, her thoughts twisted tighter around the uncomfortable situation with Jacob. It was difficult enough to navigate her new life without Robert, but having Jacob, her brother-in-law, stir up trouble added a layer of tension she felt ill-equipped to handle. She couldn't shake off the nagging feeling of responsibility, knowing that Jacob's behavior was, at least in part, propelled by his feelings toward her—feelings she did not and could not reciprocate.

As Sarah approached the woods, she stopped to pick up a fallen branch, brushing off the dirt. Not long after Robert's death, Jacob had made it clear that he expected her to consider him a replacement to maintain the family alliance. Her refusal had stung his pride, and now his actions suggested he was using his dissatisfaction with Nate to cover his vendetta against her. The thought weighed heavily on her heart; her personal decision should not endanger Nate's leadership or the welfare of the entire wagon train.

Sarah made her way down the narrow, winding path through the trees. As she walked, she piled the wood in her arms, feeling the rough bark against her skin before dropping the collection of twigs and branches into the wicker basket at her feet. Sarah knew she wasn't responsible for Jacob's actions or his character, yet the implication of her involvement hung around her like a shadow. She couldn't help but feel that somehow this was her fault, that her personal complications were spilling over, affecting people she cared about—like Nate.

Nate had been nothing but kind and protective, and the last thing Sarah wanted was to bring him trouble. Nate had said he would talk to Jacob, but maybe Sarah needed to confront Jacob to make it clear that any issue he had was with her and not with Nate's leadership. The thought was daunting; confronting Jacob would require a strength she was still gathering, piece by piece.

Just then, a coyote's distant, eerie howl echoed across the forest, and Sarah froze, heart pounding in her chest. The sound seemed both far away and terrifyingly close. She'd been so lost in her thoughts that she hadn't concentrated on where she was going.

Sarah looked around, trying to recognize anything that could guide her back to camp. But the trees looked all too similar, the paths made by the deer and other wildlife indistinguishable. The soft rustling of leaves and the occasional snap of a twig underfoot sounded unnaturally loud in the growing silence of dusk. Panic began to set in as Sarah realized she had wandered too far from the safety of the camp. The light was fading fast, and the forest felt like it was closing in on her.

Her breath quickened, and she clutched the firewood tightly against her as if it could offer some protection. Sarah tried to retrace her steps, but everything looked different now, altered by the shadows and her growing fear. Another howl pierced the twilight, closer this time, and her pulse raced. She knew coyotes were often more bark than bite, but fear wasn't rational, and she was painfully aware of her vulnerability.

"Think, Sarah, think," she muttered to herself, trying to calm her racing mind. She attempted to remember the way back, the twists and turns she'd taken. But nothing came to mind.

With the darkness thickening, Sarah knew she couldn't wander aimlessly. She needed a plan. Her first instinct was to call for help, but she hesitated, not wanting to draw the attention of any predators. Despite the fear gnawing at her insides, Sarah had learned one of two things since being on the Trail. She imagined what Nate would do in a situation such as this one. So, instead, she decided to move in the direction she thought was correct, keeping an eye out for any familiar signs or the glow of the campfires.

She walked as quietly as she could, her ears straining for any sounds other than the wildlife—a shout from the camp, the laughter of children, anything that indicated human presence. The wicker basket in her arms was now a cumbersome load, and the baby was fluttering against her ribs, aware of Sarah's distress.

As the sky turned from twilight blue to the deep black of night, Sarah's sense of isolation deepened. Each minute felt like an hour, and every leaf rustle made her jump.

As despair began to gnaw at her resolve, a flicker of light caught her eye through the trees.

"Sarah?" Nate called.

"Nate!" she called back, her body flooding with relief as she turned toward his voice.

A few moments later, she saw him, and she raced forward. Without thinking, she dropped the basket of firewood and threw herself into his arms. He held her tightly for a long moment before stepping back, his arms on her elbows.

"What were you thinkin' comin' out here on your own?" he asked, his voice full of concern.

"I am sorry," Sarah said. "I was lost in my thoughts, and before I knew it, I was lost in the woods."

Nate sighed. "Well, the whole camp is out lookin' for you," he said. "We'd better get back and let them know you are all right."

The knots in Sarah's stomach tightened as she nodded. She hated to think she'd caused everyone trouble.

Nate picked up the wicker basket and returned to the camp together.

As their camp came into view, Sarah glanced at Nate. The relief of being safe brought a mix of emotions. Gratitude was foremost, weaving through her thoughts with every step they took together away from the forest. Relief was another. Nate had come to her rescue yet again.

As they entered the camp, a chorus of relieved exclamations greeted them. Mary hurried over her expression with a mix of relief and reproach. "Oh, Sarah," she scolded. "I should've never let ye go off on your own."

"I am fine," Sarah said, reassuringly patting the older woman's arm. "Nate found me."

"Aye," Mary said, smiling fondly at him. "That he did."

Sarah looked around at the relieved faces: Emma, Clara, Elijah, and Sam. The only one who didn't look relieved was

Jacob. His mouth was set in a scowl, his eyes fixed on Nate with undisguised animosity.

"Our hero," Jacob sneered, stepping forward so that he was uncomfortably close to Nate.

"Not now, Jacob," Nate warned.

"What?" Jacob said, his eyes widening innocently. "Don't tell me you aren't enjoying this."

"Enjoying it?" Nate repeated. "No, Jacob."

Jacob smiled humorlessly, tilting his head to the side. Nate gave him one last hand look before he turned away, but Jacob caught him by the arm.

"Take your hand off me, Jacob," Nate warned, his eyes flashing dangerously.

"Look at you," Jacob said, his eyes glinting back at Nate's. "Walkin' back into camp like some hero when you're the one who let her wander off in the first place."

The accusation hung heavy in the air. Nate clenched his jaw, his hands balled into fists at his sides. Around them, the camp grew quieter, the tension palpable.

Sarah, stepping slightly forward, tried to intercept. "Jacob, please, it was my fault—I wandered off, not—"

But Jacob was not listening, his eyes still fixed on Nate. "And what about my wagon?"

"What about it?" Nate challenged.

"It's your fault it's sitting at the bottom of a river," Jacob accused, his voice rising. "You call yourself a leader, but you're all hat and no cattle—"

"That's enough, Jacob," Nate said sharply, cutting him off. His patience snapped. "If you have a problem with the way I am leading this wagon train, you are more than welcome to leave."

"I ain't leavin'," Jacob said. "I paid my way."

Nate exhaled slowly. "Well, then I suggest you fall back in line."

"Or what?" Jacob said, his shoulders bristling.

The camp was utterly silent now, all eyes fixed on the unfolding scene. Sarah felt a chill that had nothing to do with the night air.

Nate held Jacob's gaze for a moment longer before turning sharply and walking away, his shoulders tense.

Jacob smirked, shaking his head. "Like I said, all hat and no cattle."

The crowd began to disperse, murmuring among themselves; Sarah looked across at Jacob.

"Jacob," she said, trying to keep her voice steady despite her pulse quickening. "What are you doing?"

Jacob looked at her, the lines of his face hardened by resentment. "I don't trust him, and I don't like him."

"Jacob," Sarah reasoned. "What is this really about?"

Jacob's jaw clenched, his eyes gleaming. "You seem quite taken with our mighty Wagon Master," he said, his tone disparaging. "How do you think it looks? Keeping such close company with the man who let your husband die?"

Sarah's face flushed. "Nate couldn't have saved Robert without risking his own life. It was an impossible situation."

Jacob's jaw clenched, and he shook his head stubbornly. “No. He could have done somethin’, anything more than he did.”

Sarah stared at Jacob for a moment. He was using Robert’s death to turn Nate into an enemy.

“You need to stop what you are doing,” Sarah warned.

“Why?” Jacob challenged.

“Because we need Nate to survive out here,” Sarah said. “We need to stick together.”

Jacob smirked, and there was a brief silence as the night deepened around them, the air cool and slightly tense. Then, unexpectedly, Jacob’s demeanor changed. He stepped closer, his eyes softening as they fixed on Sarah.

“Maybe I could go easier on him,” he murmured, his voice coaxing, “if you’d just spend some more time with me.”

His gaze was too intense, too hungry. It made her skin crawl. Sarah recoiled as he reached out to touch her face and stepped back.

Jacob’s hand froze in midair, and his expression hardened instantly, his brief show of tenderness vanishing. “So it’s going to be like that, huh?” he said coldly, his voice now edged with a hint of menace.

“You need to stop this, Jacob,” Sarah said, trying to keep her voice steady.

Jacob stared at her for a long, tense moment, then abruptly turned and strode into the darkening camp, leaving Sarah alone by the fire. As she watched him go, her stomach was in knots. She knew that this was only the beginning. When something got under Jacob’s skin, he was precisely like Robert. He would not stop his crusade against Nate, and

Sarah was sure she'd just made things worse. Still, despite her fear, Sarah was determined to do something. She couldn't let Jacob's threats dictate her actions—or Nate's leadership.

***

Sarah sat in the back of the wagon, the early morning light filtering through the canvas cover. The air was cool and crisp, and she could see her breath as she exhaled. She shivered slightly, reaching for her clothes.

As she dressed, her mind raced with thoughts of Nate and Jacob, and the trouble that seemed to be brewing between them.

She pulled on her woolen undershirt, the fabric warm and comforting against her skin. Her thoughts drifted to Nate, his steady presence and kind eyes. He was a good man, and she hated seeing him caught in the middle of Jacob's anger and resentment. She sighed, pulling on her cotton blouse and tucking it into her skirt. If only there were a way to stop Jacob from making so much trouble for Nate. She tied her apron around her waist, smoothing the fabric with a determined hand.

Sarah slipped on her stockings and laced up her boots, the familiar ritual grounding her at the moment. She knew she had to be strong for herself and the baby growing inside her. She couldn't let Jacob's bitterness and anger dictate her life any longer.

As she climbed down from the wagon, she suddenly heard Jacob's loud voice cutting through the morning air.

"What kind of leader lets a woman carrying a child go off on her own to find firewood?" he ranted.

Frustration welled up inside her, and before she could stop herself, she walked up to the group of men, her eyes flashing with anger. Jacob turned, his blue eyes widening slightly.

“Maybe if you pulled your weight and stopped drinking so much, women wouldn't have to go and fetch firewood,” she announced, her voice clear and strong.

Jacob's face flushed with anger, and there were titters of amusement from the group. He grabbed her roughly by the elbow, his grip tight and painful, and marched her behind a wagon, out of sight of the others.

“Let go of me,” Sarah insisted, trying to wriggle out of his grasp.

“You know, you're embarrassing yourself, falling all over the Wagon Master," he hissed, his breath hot against her face.

“I want you to leave him alone," Sarah shot back, her voice trembling with fear and defiance.

Jacob smirked, the cruel expression sending a chill down her spine. She knew immediately she had said the wrong thing.

Just then, Samuel appeared, his brow furrowed with concern. “Is everything all right?” he asked, his voice gentle but firm.

“Fine,” Jacob snapped, releasing Sarah's elbow and straightening his jacket. He turned on his heel and stalked off, leaving Sarah standing there, her heart pounding in her chest.

Samuel gave her an encouraging smile. “Better get some breakfast,” he said.

She nodded as Samuel turned and left. She exhaled shakily, wishing she hadn't let her frustrations get the better of her. She was certain she had only made things worse with Jacob.

Chapter Fourteen

The relentless sun bore down on the wagon train, its fiery grip tightening as the day wore on. Nate could feel the heat penetrating the fabric of his shirt, sticking it to his skin as he guided the oxen through the arid landscape. The air was thick and still, suffocating in its intensity. He was constantly scanning the horizon, hoping for any sign of a break in the weather, but the sky remained a mocking, cloudless blue.

Nate's mind kept drifting back to Sarah, who was asleep in the back of the wagon. He had noticed her quietness this morning, an unusual subduedness that didn't sit right with him. When the last stop was made for water, her face seemed paler than usual, her smile forced. When they got back on the road, Sarah had retreated into the back, hoping the shade of the canvas would offer her some respite from the heat.

As the heat grew even more oppressive, Nate felt a spike of worry.

"Sarah?" he called. "How you doin' back there?"

But there was no reply.

"Sarah?" Nate called. "Can you hear me?"

Her silence was more oppressive than the heat, and Nate pulled back on the reins, stopping the oxen. He shifted on his seat, pulling back the canvas flap to check on her.

Inside, the wagon was like an oven. Sarah was lying down, her face flushed and her breathing shallow. Sweat beaded on her forehead, and her hands lay limply by her sides.

Without wasting a moment, Nate hurried out of the wagon. He jumped down, running down the train to fetch Emma.

"Emma, come quick! It's Sarah—something's not right."

Emma followed Nate quickly back to the wagon.

"She's overheated," Emma declared with a furrowed brow. "We need to cool her down now. Get some water, and soak any cloth you can find."

Nate nodded and dashed to fetch what was needed. Returning with a bucket of water and several cloths, he watched as Emma wrung out the cloths and placed them over Sarah's forehead, neck, and wrists.

"Keep changing them out, keep them cool," Emma instructed as she prepared a saltwater solution. "She needs to sip this slowly—it'll help replenish the salts she's lost from sweating."

Nate took the bowl from Emma, his hands steady as he helped Sarah to sit up slightly. She was as limp as a ragdoll in his arms. Gently, he brought the bowl to her lips.

"You need to drink, Sarah, " he encouraged, trying to mask his fear with a calm he didn't feel.

As Sarah sipped the salty water, Nate's mind raced. The heat wave was proving more dangerous than he had anticipated, and Sarah's condition was a stark reminder of the fragility of life on the Trail. He felt a fierce protectiveness over her, a desire to ensure no harm came her way.

"We need to get her out of this wagon," Emma said, her voice serious but steady. "Somewhere cooler."

Nate's mind raced. "There's a patch of cottonwoods not far from here, near the river."

Emma nodded. "That will have to do."

Nate scrambled back to his seat at the front of the wagon and grabbed the reins. The oxen pulled forward begrudgingly as Nate steered them toward the trees about two miles north.

A short while later, he brought the wagon to a halt again. He jumped down and hurried around the side.

With Emma's help, they managed to get Sarah out of the wagon. Nate carried her in his arms to the trees while Emma laid a blanket on a patch of grass in the shade. Sarah's eyes were closed, her dark lashes brushing against her cheeks. She was still breathing too shallowly.

"Put her here," Emma instructed.

Nate slowly put Sarah down on the blanket.

"Fetch the cloths and some more water," Emma instructed.

Nate hesitated, not wanting to pull himself away from Sarah.

"Hurry!"

Nate turned and ran back to the wagon.

"Nathaniel?" Mary said from the wagon as she and the others began to arrive. "What's goin' on?"

"Sarah is not well," Nate explained as he grabbed the clothes and water.

Without giving more explanation, Nate hurried back to Emma.

"Thanks," she said as she took the cloths from him, and Nate put the water pail down on the ground beside her.

As Nate watched Emma work, he could not ignore the gnawing sensation in the pit of his stomach. He'd seen people die on the Trail; it wasn't uncommon, but this was different. This was Sarah.

As the minutes ticked by, it felt like hours to Nate. When Sarah's condition finally began to show signs of improvement, Nate could barely conceal his relief.

"I don't think we should go anywhere until the heat breaks," Emma said, looking up at Nate. "In her condition, Sarah gets hotter than everyone else, and she could easily dehydrate."

"Okay," Nate nodded. "We'll stay until the heat lets up."

Emma turned back to Emma as Nate walked back toward the wagons.

"We'll camp here," he said, walking over to Elijah, who was still in the saddle. "It's too risky to continue in this heat. Spread the word."

Elijah tipped his hat as he turned and rode down the line of wagons to inform everyone of Nate's decision.

For the rest of the morning, Nate remained by Sarah's side. Emma continued to replace the cloths with cooler, wetter ones. Nate sighed in relief when a gentle breeze blew from the north across the water.

"How is she?" Nate asked for the millionth time.

"Better," Emma said. "Much better."

"Good," Nate sighed. "That's good."

After a moment, he turned to the wagons arranged in a large circle on a flat expanse near the river. Their white covers reflected the bright sunlight in a manner that was blinding.

The oxen, their sides still heaving with exertion, were unhitched and now stood grazing on the riverbank where the water ran calm and clear.

The children, their energy undiminished by the heat, splashed in the shallows of the river, their laughter rising above the low murmur of the adults' voices. Mary, Sam, and others were erecting what shelter they could get from the sun—stretching canvas between wagons, creating makeshift awnings under which they could prepare the midday meal.

Clara and some other women collected firewood, albeit with languid, heat-slowed movements, from the nearby stands of willows, their branches pliant and suitable for fuel.

The air was filled with the sounds of the camp coming to life: the clank of pots and pans, the chop of axes, the gentle lowing of oxen, and the constant, soothing murmur of the river. Smoke from the cooking fires began to curl lazily into the sky, carrying the smell of bacon and beans.

Nate looked around for Jacob, but he was nowhere to be seen. In fact, he hadn't seen him since their confrontation the night before.

"Nate?" Emma said suddenly. "She's awake."

Nate turned to see Sarah's eyes open and rushed to her side.

"How are you feeling?" he asked.

"Better," Sarah said, her voice faint. "The baby?"

"Baby is fine," Emma said encouragingly.

Sarah nodded as she closed her eyes again, her hands traveling down to her stomach.

"We should let her rest," Emma said softly.

Nate hesitated.

"She's out of the woods, Nate," Emma said, smiling. "You can relax."

Nate nodded. "Thank you, Emma."

Emma pressed her lips together in a tight smile. "I'll come and check on her in a little while."

Despite Emma's reassurances, Nate did not leave Sarah's side.

A short while later, Mary walked over carrying a plate of food.

"Here," she said.

Nate took it from her. "Thanks."

Nate sat on the soft ground, and Mary sat beside him, her knees creaking.

"Emma said Sarah's out of the woods?" Mary confirmed.

Nate nodded, his plate of foot resting untouched in his lap.

"You all right, lad?" Mary asked, her voice gentle.

"I've never been so frightened in my life," Nate confessed, running a hand through his hair, his face showing the strain of the morning. "Seeing her like that... It scared me, Mary. It scares me how much it scared me."

Mary looked at him, her eyes soft. "Aye," she said.

Nate exhaled slowly; the fear of losing someone again, the fear of that profound, aching loss, was at the forefront of his mind. "I swore I'd never get close to anyone again, not after..." His voice trailed off. "Not after my parents."

“Aye, I know,” Mary replied gently. “But sometimes, we don’t get a choice, do we? It sneaks up on us. One day, we’re fine; the next, we can’t imagine our lives without that person.”

Was that what this was? Could he not imagine his life without Sarah? Nate looked over his shoulder at her. She was still lying peacefully, her chest moving up and down. “What am I supposed to do, Mary?” he asked, almost rhetorically.

Mary placed a hand on his shoulder, her touch grounding. “Whatever comes, you’ll face it like ye face everything else.”

Nate nodded, the weight of her words sinking deep. “Do I have a choice?”

“Ye always have a choice,” Mary said. “The tricky part is makin’ the right one.”

Nate said nothing as he stared at the river where some of the women were washing clothes, their skirts gathered up against the wet. He had always prided himself on his strength and his ability to endure and lead without letting his personal feelings get in the way. Yet, here he was, feeling vulnerable, almost exposed, by the growing depths of his feelings for Sarah.

Nate knew that to love someone in such an uncertain and often cruel world was to open oneself up to the possibility of profound pain. The very idea terrified him.

Admitting how he felt about Sarah, allowing himself to truly feel those emotions, felt like standing on the edge of a precipice. To love her openly would be to change everything about his life as he knew it. His role as a Wagon Master required a level of detachment, a capacity to make hard decisions without personal feelings clouding his judgment. How could he maintain that detachment if his heart was irrevocably tied to someone else’s well-being?

As his gaze moved away from the water and around the camp, he sighed softly, the knots in his stomach tightening. These people, their lives depended on his decisions. A solitary purpose had always fortified his resolve: safely getting everyone to their destination. Yet now, his motivations were tangled up with his desires for a future that included Sarah. It wasn't just about protecting the group; it was about protecting her.

If Mary was right, Nate had a choice: to continue forward in the life he knew and loved or to turn his whole world upside down and hope for the best.

Chapter Fifteen

The oppressive heat seemed to swell even thicker as the late afternoon wore on, as if the air refused to move. Nate sat beside Sarah, his concern visible as he watched her closely. Sarah was feeling better, her condition slowly improving after the morning's ordeal. However, her head and shoulders ached, and she was very aware of the layers of sweat that clung to her body. She knew it was silly, given everything, but she hoped that she did not smell too terrible.

Suddenly, a low rumble of thunder rolled across the plains, a sound so deep and resonant that it seemed to vibrate through the ground beneath them. Nate glanced up sharply, his eyes scanning the sky, which was now darkening with the promise of a storm.

"Sounds like we might get some relief soon," he remarked, a note of hope threading through his voice.

Sarah nodded weakly as she shifted slightly, her hand instinctively resting on her belly. To her relief, she felt a gentle kick, a reassuring sign that the baby was active and unharmed by the day's harsh conditions. A soft smile touched her lips, and she turned to Nate.

"The baby just kicked. I think it's telling us it's all right."

Nate's face broke into a relieved grin, the tension easing slightly from his shoulders at her words. "Of course, the baby's all right," he said, his voice softening. "He or she is a fighter, just like their ma."

Sarah smiled again as the conversation lapsed into a comfortable silence, filled only by the distant rumblings of the approaching storm.

After a few moments, Sarah turned her head to look at Nate again, her expression tinged with guilt.

"I feel bad that everyone had to stop because of me," she confessed, her eyes troubled.

Nate shook his head firmly, his gaze earnest. "Stoppin' was the right thing to do. Ain't no sense in treatin' a scorcher like it's a spring breeze."

Sarah chewed the inside of her cheek. With Jacob and some of the others questioning Nate's decisions, she did not want to do anything to do anything to escalate the situation.

Just then, the first raindrops began to fall, light at first, then growing heavier.

"Come on," Nate said. "Let's get under cover."

Sarah looked up, sighing contently as the rain splashed on her face. "Just one more minute."

Nate chuckled, shaking his head. "Come on," he said, pulling her to her feet. "The last thing you need to do is catch a chill."

Nate clutched Sarah's hand as he led her back to the wagons. Everyone had already taken up shelter under their canvas roofs. Nate helped Sarah up and into the back of his wagon. As she climbed inside, he came in behind her. They sat side by side on the floor, wedged between the crates and supplies.

As the storm intensified outside, the wagon became a small haven, cocooning Sarah and Nate from the elements. The rain beat a steady rhythm on the canvas above them, and occasionally, the sudden flare of lightning illuminated the interior, followed by the rolling growl of thunder. Sarah flinched slightly with each flash; the storm's ferocity was awe-inspiring but also unnerving.

“Not a fan of lightnin’ then?” Nate asked.

“Not really,” Sarah admitted.

Nate leaned a little closer, his voice low and comforting against the sound of the storm. “You know, many Native American tribes have stories about lightning.”

Sarah turned toward him. "Really? What kind of stories?"

“Well, the Navajo believe that lightning is the spark of life, created by the holy ones. It’s seen as a symbol of speed, power, and illumination. They even make lightning-shaped arrows for ceremonies that are thought to protect and bless the people.”

Sarah listened, the sound of Nate's voice blending with the rain, making the storm outside seem less threatening. The idea of lightning as something sacred and protective was a stark contrast to her perception of it as merely dangerous.

“There’s also a story from the Lakota people," Nate continued. “They believe that lightning is the fire of the sky spirits, flashing in moments of powerful spiritual revelations. According to legend, these spirits use lightning to communicate, to show their approval or displeasure.”

Sarah smiled, her earlier anxiety ebbing away. “I like that idea. It makes the storm seem more like a conversation, less like... just noise.”

Nate smiled, and Sarah could not help but marvel at his ability to turn her fears and worries around. It was as if he could shine his light over all her shadows.

They heard the oxen bellowing, and Nate’s shoulders tensed.

"I should go and check they are all right," he said. "If they manage to break out of the corral, we'll be in trouble."

"You're going out in this?" Sarah said, her voice full of concern.

"I'll be fine," he said, smiling at her.

Sarah frowned as Nate pushed open the canvas flap and disappeared outside. She sat back.

A short while later, she heard the wagon creak.

"Nate?" she said.

The canvas flap opened again, but it was not Nate. It was Jacob.

"Jacob," Sarah said, her brow furrowing. "What are you doing?"

Jacob was soaking wet, his dark hair plastered to the sides of his face as water dripped off the end of his nose.

"I came to see if you were all right," Jacob said, his words slurring a little. "You and the baby."

"We're fine," Sarah said.

Jacob nodded, but he did not leave. "I wanted to come and check on you earlier," he said, his jaw hardening. "But Saint Nathaniel wouldn't leave your side."

Sarah sighed. "Don't call him that."

Jacob said nothing as he stepped into the wagon. "Don't you care that I worry about you too?"

Sarah sighed. "Can we not do this tonight, Jacob? I am tired."

"But not too tired to listen to Nate's foolish stories," Jacob spat.

Sarah frowned. "Were you listening outside the wagon?"

Jacob said nothing as he climbed inside, and Sarah retreated further back.

Sarah and Jacob faced each other, tension coiling tight between them. There was nowhere to go, the storm still raging outside, and yet, given a chance, Sarah would rather rush out into the thunder and lightning than be trapped in this wagon with Jacob.

"Sarah, you need to stop all this foolishness," Jacob said, edging closer still. "It's time you considered doing the right thing—marrying me. It's what's appropriate, given everything. We are family."

Sarah felt a familiar flare of frustration at his words. Why couldn't he just leave her alone? Robert was gone, yet he was still clinging to her as if she somehow belonged to him. She'd been owned for so many years, treated as nothing more than a possession, and she was tired of it. She just wanted to be free.

Sarah folded her arms, her posture stiffening as she met his gaze squarely. "Jacob, I've told you before, and I'll say it as many times as needed. I will not marry you. My decision is final."

Jacob's face hardened, his frustration morphing into anger again. "What do you think the others are saying, huh? You and Nate are always together—it's not proper."

Sarah's cheeks flushed with anger. "That's none of your business, Jacob."

"It is," Jacob insisted.

"It's not," Sarah argued. "And no one would be saying anythin' if it weren't for you stirring up trouble. Besides, I don't have to justify my actions to you or anyone else. Leave my wagon. Now."

But Jacob didn't move. Instead, he stepped closer, his tone venomous. "You think you're better off with him?"

"Better than I would be with a drunk who should've stayed in Independence," Sarah challenged.

Jacob's eyes narrowed. "So you admit it then?"

Sarah said nothing for a moment. "Nate and I are friends. He's looking out for me and my baby."

"I'd do the same," Jacob said, his face softening again. "If only you'd give me the chance."

Sarah stared at him; her thoughts drifted back to the earlier days. Jacob had always been there, a constant presence in her and Robert's life. She remembered how Jacob sometimes looked at her with a longing that made her uncomfortable. His eyes seemed to follow her whenever she moved around their house or in the town, his gaze lingering a little too long or too often. But despite those looks that suggested affection or perhaps desire, Jacob never did anything to help her when she needed it most. When Robert's temper flared and his hands or words struck her, Jacob would turn away, his eyes dropping to the floor or finding something suddenly interesting in the opposite direction. It was as if he couldn't bear to witness her suffering, yet he also couldn't muster the courage or care enough to intervene.

A bitter resentment swelled within her. How could Jacob claim to care for her now when he had stood by and done nothing while she was treated like less than nothing? His passivity had been a silent betrayal, one that had allowed Robert to continue his abuse unchecked.

Sarah's eyes blazed with defiance. "You call yourself family, Jacob? Where were you when Robert was hurting me? You watched and did nothing. If you were a real man, if you truly cared, you would have stood up for me!"

Jacob's face paled at her words, but Sarah was done holding back. She had been kept silent for too long.

"I wanted to," Jacob said, his voice wavering now. "But Robert..."

Jacob's voice trailed off, and Sarah shook her head.

"You're a coward and a bully," she said. "Just like your brother."

Jacob's face flushed.

"And wouldn't marry you if you were the last man on this earth."

Jacob's face twisted with rage at her words, and Sarah knew she'd gone too far. Then, before she had time to react, Jacob reached out and grabbed her arm, his grip tight and painful. "You ungrateful—"

Sarah cried out, not just in pain but in fear. "Let me go!"

Just then, Nate reappeared. Without hesitating, he grabbed Jacob, pulling him away from Sarah. The two men tumbled out of the wagon, rolling into the mud outside as the rain had softened the ground into sludge.

"Nate!" Sarah cried as she scurried to the door of the wagon.

The men grappled fiercely on the ground, each driven by a storm of emotions—Nate's protective fury clashing against Jacob's bitter resentment.

"Stop!" Sarah cried.

But they seemed deaf to her pleas. Suddenly, Elijah was there. He managed to pull them apart.

Breathing heavily, mud-splattered and seething, Jacob pointed at Nate, his voice thick with contempt. "You think you're her savior? Preying on a vulnerable widow!"

Nate clenched his jaw, his voice cold with anger. "I've offered her nothing but my protection and respect, something you know nothing about."

Jacob scoffed, sneering. "You're a snake," he spat. "You just wait; your day will come."

"Is that a threat?" Nate said, his eyes flashing.

"It's a promise," Jacob said.

Nate stood firm, wiping the mud from his hands onto his pants, and met Jacob's gaze. "I'm not afraid of you, Jacob," he replied, his voice steady. "Threaten me all you want."

Jacob sneered, his eyes narrowing as he took a step back. "Watch your back," he muttered before turning sharply and stalking away into the diminishing rain, leaving a trail of heavy footprints in the mud.

Sarah watched him go, her body tense, a chill running down her spine. She felt a mixture of relief and looming dread. As he disappeared from view, Sarah turned to Nate. He walked over to her, his expression softening as he approached.

"Are you all right?" he asked, his concern evident.

Sarah nodded, trying to muster a smile, but her eyes were troubled. "Yes, I'm fine. But Nate, what if he—"

“Whatever he tries, we'll handle it,” Nate interrupted gently.

Sarah pressed her lips together tightly. The promise of more trouble hung over them like the clouds that had just emptied themselves upon the earth.

Chapter Sixteen

The dawn broke gray and heavy, the storm's aftermath revealing their campsite in disarray. The once orderly circle of wagons was now bordered by puddles of muddy water, with various belongings scattered by the gusts of wind. The ground itself was a quagmire, thick with mud that sucked at the feet of anyone who dared to traverse it.

As the camp stirred to life, the extent of the night's havoc became evident. Tents and awnings hastily erected for shelter now lay in twisted heaps, some torn from their moorings by the wind. Cooking pots and utensils were strewn about, abandoned in the rush to seek shelter from the pelting rain.

Nate emerged from his wagon, his face set in a grim line as he surveyed the damage. He knew they couldn't move until the ground had dried sufficiently to prevent the wagons from becoming bogged down. This delay was frustrating, yet another challenge in their already arduous journey.

"All right, let's get to work," he called out, his voice carrying across the camp. "We need to clean up and re-secure everything. We're not going anywhere until this mud dries."

Always ready to lend a hand, Sam was already pulling a large canvas tarp back over a supply wagon.

"You heard the man!" he shouted cheerfully to a couple of younger men nearby, trying to inject some energy into the beleaguered group.

Mary, her skirts hitched up as she waded through the mud, was organizing a group of women to salvage what food supplies they could. The storm had soaked much of their flour and meal, and what was salvageable must be dried out quickly.

"Come on, lasses, let's see what we can save here," she instructed.

Meanwhile, Thomas, the blacksmith, examined the wagons, checking for any damage to the wheels and axles that the storm might have exacerbated.

"Nate, this one's going to need some work," he called over, pointing to a wagon whose wheel had partly sunk into the mud, stressing the wood and threatening to crack it.

Nate joined him, kneeling to inspect the damage. "Good eye, Thomas. Let's prop it up and see if we can reinforce it somehow."

As the camp worked together, the sounds of their efforts filled the air—a mixture of commands, the squelch of mud, the clank of metal, and the occasional laugh as someone slipped and steadied themselves. The scene was one of controlled chaos, but underneath it all lay a thread of resilience. Each person, from Nate to the smallest child helping to collect scattered items, contributed to a tapestry of collective endeavor.

Yet, as glad and relieved as Nate was to see everyone pulling together, he could not shake what had happened last night or what Jacob had accused him of.

As Nate bent to lift a waterlogged trunk back onto the wagon bed, his muscles straining against the weight, his mind replayed the confrontation with Jacob. The harsh words echoed in his head: *"You're preying on a vulnerable widow!"* Those words stung, festering deep in his thoughts.

He straightened up, pausing to wipe the sweat and grime from his brow with the back of his hand, his eyes scanning the camp. The people around him were busy with the clean-up, yet he couldn't help but wonder what they truly thought of him. Did they see him as Jacob portrayed? A manipulator taking advantage of Sarah's vulnerability? The thought twisted uncomfortably in his gut.

Nate had always prided himself on his leadership, being a moral compass for the group, guiding them not just across the physical terrain but through the ethical complexities of their communal life. His intentions with Sarah had been pure; at least, he had convinced himself of that. He cared for her deeply but had never intended for his feelings to complicate his role as Wagon Master or to cast a shadow on his character. But Jacob's accusations had sown seeds of doubt, not just in Nate's mind but potentially in the minds of others. Was his growing closeness with Sarah obscuring his judgment? Was it compromising the respect necessary to lead effectively?

He watched as Mary instructed two younger women on how to best dry out some of the dampened clothing, her authoritative yet nurturing manner reminding him of the delicate balance of leadership. He respected Mary greatly; she managed to maintain her role without letting personal feelings get in the way. Could he say the same for himself anymore?

The road to hell is paved with good intentions. Nate knew all too well that good intentions could lead to unintended consequences. Was his affection for Sarah becoming a liability? Was it leading him down a path that might endanger their small community's cohesion and mutual respect?

As he tossed another damaged piece of wood to the side, Nate realized that Jacob's challenge might force him to make a choice he wasn't ready to make—between his duties as a Wagon Master and his feelings for Sarah.

Nate sighed, glancing toward the wagon where Sarah was resting. He knew nothing about love or romantic relationships. They were as foreign to him as a fish on a saddle. But he knew what it was to be a Wagon Master, and he knew the Trail. Leading these people, that was who he was.

As the late afternoon sun cast long shadows across the partially dried campsite, Nate found himself wandering with a restlessness that matched his troubled thoughts. The clean-up from the storm's havoc was nearly complete, yet a different kind of turmoil was stirring within him, and it centered around Sarah.

He spotted Mary, who was efficiently reorganizing supplies outside her wagon. Her capable hands and firm set of her jaw as she worked reminded Nate of her steadfast nature, something he felt he was currently lacking. Drawing a deep breath, he approached her.

“Mary, can I have a word?” Nate asked. His voice was heavy, burdened.

Mary looked up from her tasks, her expression softening as she saw his troubled face. “Aye, of course, Nathaniel,” she said. “What's on yer mind?”

Nate hesitated, his boots scuffing the dirt. “I've been thinking... about the setup. I think it might be best if Sarah rides with you from now on,” he said, not meeting Mary's eyes.

Mary paused, her brows knitting together in concern. “Oh? And why's that, Nathaniel? This isn’t about Jacob's nonsense, is it?”

Nate shifted uncomfortably. “I need to focus on the journey, Mary, on the group. I've been... too distracted by Sarah. Pulled in too deep by her story. We're behind schedule, and the Trail's only getting tougher.”

Mary set down the supplies, wiping her hands on her apron as she stepped closer. "Nathaniel, don't let Jacob get to ye. You're letting him win by pushing Sarah away."

Nate looked away, his jaw set. "It's not just about Jacob," he said, shaking his head. "It's about being a good Wagon Master. I can't afford to be distracted, not when everyone's depending on me to get them to California safely."

Mary sighed deeply, a mix of frustration and disappointment lining her face. "Nate, ye're making a mistake. It's plain to see ye care for her, and she for ye. Life on the Trail is hard and cruel; don't push away a good thing when ye have it."

Nate felt a sting at her words, knowing she spoke the truth, yet his resolve remained. "I appreciate your concern, Mary, but my mind's made up. It's what's best for everyone."

"Yer offered her yer protection," Mary reminded him.

"I know," Nate said. "And I am not goin' back on my word, but I can still keep her safe at a distance."

Mary shook her head, her expression disappointed. "I hope you don't regret this, Nate. I truly do."

She turned back to her work, signaling the end of the conversation.

As Nate walked away, the weight of his decision pressed down on him. Mary's disappointment was a mirror of his own. He knew he was sacrificing his personal happiness for what he believed was the greater good, yet the doubt lingered like a shadow at his back. As he watched the sunset, coloring the sky in hues of orange and pink, Nate felt a profound sense of isolation. His duty as a Wagon Master had never felt so burdensome nor so lonely.

***

The wagon train rolled forward under a clear blue sky, the crisp morning air filled with the distant sounds of birds and the steady creak of wagon wheels on the rough trail. It was the kind of day that usually lifted Nate's spirits—a reminder of why he had chosen this life, with its freedom and its connection to the wild landscapes of the West. But today, a palpable sense of loss overshadowed his usual appreciation for the open road.

Nate sat at the front of his wagon, hands automatically managing the reins. The seat beside him, usually occupied by Sarah, was painfully empty. He hadn't had the courage to tell her directly that she would be riding with Mary from now on; instead, he had arranged it quietly. He couldn't face Sarah, couldn't bear to see the look of disappointment—or worse, hurt—in her eyes. It made him feel like a coward.

As the landscape rolled by, Nate's mind replayed the moments he and Sarah had shared in this very seat. Her laughter, how she'd point out a bird or a particularly beautiful tree, the serious conversations, the comfortable silences. Pushing her away was one of the hardest things he had ever done, and the reason behind it—to remain focused and impartial as a Wagon Master—felt increasingly hollow as the miles stretched on.

Nate's gaze drifted over the line of wagons trailing behind him. He could just make out the one where Sarah now rode with Mary. Jacob had refused to ride with Mary any longer, choosing instead to ride with some of the men he'd made friends with on the Trail.

Nate watched Sarah for a moment and then looked away. The rational part of his mind knew he had made this decision for the sake of the group, to maintain his role effectively without personal feelings complicating his judgments. But another part, a deeper, more instinctive part, was filled with regret and self-reproach.

A shout from one of the drivers at the back of the train pulled him from his thoughts, snapping him back to the present, back to his responsibilities. With a deep sigh, he refocused on the road ahead. This was his life, his duty. He had responsibilities to everyone on this train, not just to Sarah, not just to his own conflicted feelings.

The midday sun was high in the sky as the wagon train made its routine stop for lunch. The women, including Mary and Sarah, busied themselves preparing the meal, pulling out sacks of dried beans, hardtack, and salt pork.

As the food was prepared over a hastily assembled fire, a pleasant aroma began to fill the air, mingling with the sounds of the stream and the occasional lowing of the oxen.

A short while later, the lunch bell rang.

"Come and eat, everyone," Mary called. "Let's fill up while we can."

Despite the inviting smell of food, Nate found that he had little appetite. Excusing himself with a brief nod to Mary, he wandered over to the area where the oxen were being rested and watered. He felt a presence behind him as he checked each ox for signs of wear or injury.

Turning, he saw Sarah approaching. Her expression was a mix of concern and something else he couldn't quite place. "Nate, can we talk?" she asked quietly, her voice tinged with uncertainty.

Nate's stomach tightened. He nodded stiffly, not trusting himself to speak just yet.

"Is everything all right?" Sarah asked, her eyes searching his face, looking for an answer. "Did I do something?"

Nate swallowed hard, avoiding her gaze. He hated that she was blaming herself, that he'd made her feel like she'd done something wrong.

"You haven't done anything wrong, Sarah," he said, not meeting her eye. "It's just... I need to focus on leading this train. I can't afford any more distractions."

"I'm sorry if I've been a distraction," she said.

Her apology stung him, and the sincerity in her tone made him feel even smaller.

"Don't apologize, Sarah. Please," Nate said quickly, finally meeting her eyes. "I'm glad we're friends. But I can't do this—whatever this is—anymore."

"Nate—"

"I am sorry, Sarah," he said. "But I just can't."

"Is this about what Jacob said?" she asked, stepping toward him.

"It's not about Jacob," he lied, partly to her and partly to himself. "It's about doing what's best for the group. We have a long road ahead, Sarah."

"You can't tell me this has nothing to do with Jacob," Sarah said, her voice rising in anger.

Nate said nothing, and after a moment, Sarah shook her head, her anger fading back to hurt. "And a long road means there's no room for kindness or whatever else might be between us?" Her voice cracked with emotion.

Nate said nothing for a long moment; he did not know what to say.

"You should go and get something to eat," he said, his words sounding weak.

She stared at him for a moment longer before she turned away from him, her shoulders dropping.

Nate watched her go, a hollow pit forming in his stomach. He knew he had hurt her, perhaps irrevocably, but he believed it was a necessary pain—at least, that's what he kept telling himself. As he turned back to the oxen, his hands resumed their work, but his actions were mechanical. His thoughts were with Sarah, with his words and the look of disappointment and pain in her eyes—a look he knew would haunt him for many miles to come.

Chapter Seventeen

The campfire crackled and popped, throwing sparks into the night sky as Sarah sat wrapped in a thick blanket against the chill. It seemed impossible that they were engulfed in a heat wave only a day or two ago. Still, Sarah was learning that about being out in the wild—nature was in charge, and its elements were its own.

Across from where Sarah sat, Mary stirred the embers with a stick, adding a log to keep the fire going. The rest of the camp was settling down for the evening, with quiet conversations and the occasional laughter creating a backdrop of comforting, yet poignant, normalcy.

Sarah's eyes unintentionally met Jacob's across the fire. His gaze was steady, almost smug, as if he took pleasure in the distance now evident between her and Nate. He seemed to think his machinations would drive her into his arms, but Sarah felt only a deepening resolve to keep her distance. She quickly looked away, focusing instead on the warm, inviting flames that seemed to offer a kind of sanctuary.

She turned to Mary, whose knowing eyes had been watching her closely. "Did Nate eat tonight?" Sarah said quietly, her voice barely above the crackle of the fire.

"Aye," Mary said. "I took him a plate."

Sarah nodded, a hollow in the pit of her stomach. She'd hardly seen Nate at all these past few days. He'd kept himself busy, away from her. His decision to distance himself stung more than Sarah thought possible.

Mary laid a comforting hand on Sarah's arm as if she could hear her thoughts. "Nate's been on this trail for a long time, lass," she said. "He's seen a lot and lost a lot, too. It makes a man cautious, scared even of anything that looks a little different."

Sarah sighed, watching the flames dance and flicker. "I miss him, Mary."

"Aye," Mary said, nodding sadly.

Sarah did miss Nate. Her growing belly felt surprisingly empty, a Nate-shaped hollow she did not know how to fill. Yet, what was she to do? For so long, she'd allowed herself to be steered by the decisions of others. Perhaps it was time she started acting like the captain of her own ship.

"Maybe this is for the best," Sarah said. "This is the first time I've ever truly been on my own; with no father or husband, maybe it's time I learn who I am."

Mary squeezed her arm gently. "There's wisdom in that," she said. "But remember, finding out who you are doesn't mean you have to do it alone. We're all a bit lost out here, making it up as we go along. That's the beauty and the curse of the Trail."

Sarah smiled sadly. "I need to be sure I can stand on my own two feet when this baby comes."

"Well, you've got an entire train of folks who'll look after you."

The fire began to dwindle to glowing embers. Sarah could not help but wonder if Mary's words were true. Would they all stand by her after what Jacob was saying about her? With all the rumors he was spreading about her and Nate.

"Well," Mary said after a few moments. "We should get to bed."

As Sarah settled into her bedroll for the night, the campfire remnants still glowing softly outside, her thoughts turned inward, weaving through the tangled emotions of the past few days. Now, in the quiet solitude of the night, her mind focused on the future—one that included her unborn child.

She placed her hands gently on her belly, feeling the subtle movements within. Each flutter was a reminder of the new life depending on her, a life she was determined to nurture in freedom and strength, far removed from the shadows of her past with Robert. She wanted her child to know a different kind of existence, one defined by love, resilience, and the joy of discovery.

With Robert gone, a path lay open, rugged and uncharted, but hers to shape. She envisioned herself not just as a survivor of her past circumstances but as a pillar of strength for her child. She thought about the skills she would need to hone, the knowledge she would need to acquire, and the independence she would need to cultivate. Her resolve to become a woman capable of raising a child alone filled her with a newfound sense of purpose.

Yet, amidst this determined vision lingered an ache, a hollow pang of longing for Nate—the companion who had shared her laughter and listened to her fears. His presence had become a comfort she cherished, and his absence now left a void that echoed with the remnants of their shared moments.

Sarah knew this yearning for Nate was a part of her journey—not a path to be followed but a feeling to be acknowledged and understood. She realized she could not let this longing undermine her primary focus—to strengthen herself for her child. Instead, she channeled this emotional energy into her growth and independence.

She imagined teaching her child about the stars they traveled under, the stories of the land, and the many lessons of resilience and courage that life on the trail had taught her.

She pictured herself as a caretaker and a guide, instilling in her child the values of curiosity, strength, and self-reliance.

This focus on her future role as a mother gave Sarah peace. It didn't fully erase the complexity of her feelings for Nate, but it helped prioritize her immediate responsibilities. In becoming the mother she aspired to be, Sarah found profound empowerment—a sense of identity that was hers alone to define and cherish.

As sleep finally began to claim her, Sarah felt more anchored, her heart buoyed by the thought of the life she would build. It was a life that would be shaped not just by the circumstances of her journey but by her deliberate choices along the way, each step guided by a love profound enough to transform her and her child's future.

***

The morning sun crested the horizon, casting long, warm rays over the camp as it slowly came to life. Sarah emerged from her wagon, her demeanor one of quiet determination. Today, like every day for the past few days, she was set on learning and growing, on forging a new path for herself and her unborn child.

Her first stop was Emma's wagon. The woman had become not just a mentor but a friend. Under Emma's guidance, Sarah was learning how to maintain and improve her health on the Trail—essential knowledge for her and her baby's well-being.

"Morning, Sarah," Emma greeted her with a warm smile. "Ready for today's lesson?"

"Absolutely," Sarah responded, her eyes bright with eagerness. They sat on a pair of stools beside the wagon, and Emma began explaining the importance of nutrition, even with their limited supplies.

"You need to make sure you're getting enough iron and protein, especially now," Emma advised, handing Sarah a small bag of dried beans. "These are good for iron. Try to eat some every day."

Sarah nodded, absorbing every word. They discussed meal variations that could maximize her nutritional intake and herbs that were good for pregnancy—some of which could be found along the Trail.

After their talk, Sarah joined a group of women at the riverbank to wash clothes. Robert had always insisted such tasks were beneath him, leaving Sarah isolated and dependent. Now, as she scrubbed fabric alongside Mary and a few others, she felt a camaraderie she'd never known before. They shared stories and tips, and Sarah felt a part of something genuine and supportive—a community.

Later, as the afternoon heat began to wane, Sarah took to long, reflective walks. These were times for her to think and strengthen her body and spirit. She followed trails along the river, practicing breathing exercises Emma had taught her, exercises meant to fortify her for childbirth. With each step, she felt stronger and more capable.

But physical and mental health weren't her only focuses. Sarah also started learning about basic first aid from Emma and understanding how to treat common ailments on the Trail. This knowledge gave her a sense of security, an entirely new feeling of preparedness.

In the evenings, Sarah would often sit by the fire, participating in communal activities. But she always found a moment to slip away, to gaze at the stars and reflect on her day. Though Nate was often just at the edges of these gatherings, a silent, supportive figure, Sarah kept her distance. She appreciated his presence—it was a comfort, knowing he was there—but she was learning to stand on her own.

As the days passed, Sarah's confidence grew. She was not the same woman who had started this journey; she was becoming someone new, someone who could raise a child on her terms, in her own strength. And while Nate lingered in the fringes of her mind, a part of her past and perhaps a part of her future, she knew that this journey she was on—this journey of becoming—was hers alone to define.

It had been nearly a week since Nate and Sarah had last spoken. She was seated on the wagon with Emma, a small journal open in her lap. Emma gave it to her, and Sarah started writing down her thoughts to process her journey and experiences. She'd never known that writing things down could be so cathartic, but as she scribbled away, she felt a sense of relief. They'd been on the wagon trail for almost two months, and Sarah still couldn't believe how much had happened since they left Kansas.

After a moment, Sarah looked up and found Emma watching her, a smile on her lips.

"Sorry," Sarah said. "I am not being very good company."

"You apologize a lot, you know," Emma said.

"Sorry," Sarah said again.

Emma chuckled, and Sarah smiled, shaking her head. "It's a hard habit to break," she admitted.

The two friends fell silent for a moment.

"Emma," Sarah said. "I've always wondered, how did you come to be on the Trail? It seems like you were meant to do this, to help people."

The truth was that Sarah was curious and envious of Emma. She was so independent and strong.

Emma smiled. “My pa was a doctor,” she explained. “He was a good man who believed in the healing arts and helping others. He taught me everything he knew—not just about medicine, but about having the courage to follow your heart and mind.”

Sarah listened intently. “What happened to him?” she asked. “Your pa?”

“He got sick,” Emma confessed, a hint of sadness in her voice. “And he never got better.”

“I’m sorry,” Sarah said softly.

Emma pressed her lips together for a moment and then sighed.

“When he passed, my aunt, with whom I lived, pressed me to marry. She believed a woman’s place was in the home, not practicing medicine.” Emma’s tone held a note of defiance as she spoke. “She told me that being a nurse or a doctor wasn’t suitable for a lady. But I couldn’t give up on my dream, not for any man or societal expectation.”

“So, what did you do?” Sarah asked, already admiring Emma’s resolve.

“I left,” Emma said. “I joined a wagon train headed for California. I knew the miners and the families there would need a nurse, maybe even a doctor. And I thought, what better place to start anew, where the rules of the east don’t apply quite so strictly?”

Sarah’s eyes widened with admiration. “That’s incredibly brave, Emma. To leave everything familiar behind for the unknown.”

Emma smiled, a twinkle in her kind brown eyes. "Perhaps it was brave, or maybe it was just necessary. But I've never regretted it. As hard as it's been, this journey has shown me that my skills are needed and that I can make a difference. And that's all my father ever wanted for me."

Emma's story inspired Sarah, and her admiration for her deepened.

"Your story makes me think that maybe I'm exactly where I need to be, too," Sarah admitted. "Maybe this is my chance to discover who I really am, just like you did."

Emma nodded, placing a comforting hand on Sarah's arm. "I believe so, Sarah. And remember, no matter where this trail leads you, what matters is that you walk it in your own way, true to yourself. That's the key to everything."

Sarah smiled as the two women fell silent. She felt a renewed sense of purpose and connection, not just to Emma but to her own journey on the Trail. With friends like Emma, she felt more confident that she, too, could carve out a path defined by her desires and abilities.

***

Sarah sat by the dwindling fire. The camp was quiet now, with everyone else having retired to their bedrolls for the night. She felt a sense of peace in the solitude, the cool night air wrapping around her. She opened her journal and began to write.

In the shadows of our home so cold,

Where love was traded, bought, and sold,

A heart once tender, now turned stone,

In silence, I endured alone.

His words, like daggers, sharp and fierce,
Cut through my soul, my spirit pierced.
The nights were long, the days a blur,
A life of fear, a living slur.

Bruises hidden, scars unseen,
A prisoner in a cruel routine.

I learned to tread on eggshells thin,
To hide the pain, to keep it in.
The dreams I had were swept away,
In darkness, night replaced the day.

Now as I sit beneath the stars,
Their light a balm to all my scars,
I write these words, a silent cry,
For all the years that passed me by.

Sarah paused, reading over the words she had written. As a girl, she remembered how she used to write poetry, pouring her heart onto the pages in the quiet of her room. It had been a way to find comfort and solace, a refuge from the world. But after she married Robert, that part of herself had been buried under years of fear and pain. He had taken so much from her. Yet, in his death, she was slowly finding herself again. She was returning to the things that had once brought her peace, rediscovering the strength and creativity she had thought lost forever.

Sarah sighed, closing her journal, but just then, she heard a twig snap behind her. She turned quickly, her heart racing, and saw Jacob approaching. She promptly closed her journal and tucked it away as he drew near.

"What are you writing?" he asked, his voice rough and unsteady.

"Nothing," Sarah lied.

They fell into an uncomfortable silence, Jacob's eyes locked on hers. Then, unexpectedly, his face crumbled, and he began to cry. Sarah was utterly taken aback, unsure of what to do.

"I did it," Jacob confessed through his tears. "I stole from Mr. Fields' wagon. It's my fault Robert is dead."

Sarah's mind raced, trying to process his words. This confession was completely unexpected.

"If I hadn't taken those things, Robert never would have gotten into that fight and fallen into the river..."

Jacob's voice trailed off as he shook his head. Sarah remained silent, struggling to find something to say, but no words came.

"It was an accident," she finally managed, her voice gentle but firm. "No one's to blame."

Jacob looked at her, his blue eyes filled with guilt and hope. “Do you really mean that?” he asked, his voice trembling. “You don’t blame me?”

“No,” Sarah said.

Jacob’s shoulders relaxed, and Sarah suddenly realized this might be a moment she could use to her advantage.

“It was no one’s fault,” she repeated. “Not yours, and not Nate’s.”

Jacob's expression darkened at the mention of Nate. “Can't we have one conversation without bringing him up?” he snapped.

“Jacob,” Sarah said, trying to keep her voice calm. “You need to stop blaming Nate for what happened to Robert. It wasn't his fault, either.”

Jacob's face twisted in anger. "You're glad he's dead, aren't you?” he spat, his voice full of bitterness. “You're happy to be free of Robert.”

Sarah felt a pang of guilt and fear. “That's not true,” she said quietly.

“Liar,” Jacob spat. “Did you ever shed a single tear?”

Sarah said nothing as Jacob continued to glower at her. The truth was that Sarah was a liar; she wasn’t sorry Robert was gone.

“I am going to bed,” Sarah said, getting up. “It’s late—”

Jacob took a step forward, blocking her path, and Sarah tensed.

“Did you and the Wagon Master conspire together?” he asked, his voice low and his eyes glinting dangerously.

"Don't be ridiculous," Sarah said.

Jacob raised an eyebrow, but before he could say anything else, Sarah caught a movement out of the corner of her eye and turned to see Mary.

"Sarah?" she said. "Ye should get yerself to bed, it's late."

Sarah nodded, and after a moment, Jacob stepped out of the way. Sarah hurried to her wagon without looking back. Only when she was safely in the back of the agon did she allow herself to breathe.

Jacob's behavior was becoming more erratic and unpredictable, and she was scared. She hated not knowing what he would do next.

Chapter Eighteen

Nate stood at the edge of the camp, his gaze fixed on Sarah and Emma's distant figures as they wandered through a patch of wild herbs. Sarah's laughter, carried on the gentle breeze, reached Nate's ears, stirring mixed emotions deep within him.

He had kept his distance, as he'd insisted was necessary, but his resolve hadn't stopped him from watching over her, observing her transformation from afar. Each day, she seemed to grow more confident and self-assured, as if each step on the Trail was a step away from her past shadows and into a new light. It was exactly what he had hoped for her, yet it filled him with a bittersweet longing. He missed her—her presence, her laughter, her thoughtful conversations. Watching her now, liberated and laughing, he couldn't deny the ache in his heart.

Mary approached him quietly, following his gaze to where Sarah and Emma were now crouching to examine some plants.

"She's doing well, isn't she?" Mary remarked with a hint of pride in her voice.

Nate nodded, keeping his eyes on the distant figures. "Yes, she is. It's all worked out for the best," he replied, his voice carrying a forced note of conviction.

Mary turned to look at him, her expression thoughtful and probing. "Aye, has it, though?" she challenged gently.

Nate's jaw tightened slightly. "Leave it, Mary. Things are as they are meant to be," he said, a hint of frustration creeping into his tone. "Jacob has backed down, Sarah is doing well... It's better this way."

But Mary wasn't convinced. "Nate, ye can fool yourself, but not me. Ye hardly smile anymore, ye buried yerself in yer work. Is that really how things are meant tae be?"

Nate's frustration flared. "Just leave it," he insisted more sharply. "It's done. I made my decision."

Mary sighed, her eyes softening with sympathy, but she nodded, respecting his boundary even if she disagreed. "Aye, Nate. I'll leave it. But just remember, sometimes the hardest paths we take are the ones we choose ourselves, not the ones chosen for us."

With that, Mary turned to go, leaving Nate to his thoughts.

"Mary?" Nate said.

She turned back to him.

"Happy birthday," he said.

Mary pressed her lips together in a tight smile before she left.

Nate watched her go, then turned his gaze back to Sarah and Emma, who were now returning to the camp, their arms filled with gathered herbs. As he watched Sarah talking animatedly with Emma, a part of him wondered if he had indeed chosen the right path, not just for her but for himself as well.

Nate stood alone for a moment longer, the weight of his choices heavy on his shoulders. Then, with a deep breath, he turned and headed back to his duties, the unresolved feelings and his silent longing for Sarah settling back into the corners of his heart.

The evening air was filled with the scent of pine and the warmth of a large campfire as the wagon train settled into a festive atmosphere to celebrate Mary's birthday. The Scottish matriarch had always insisted on a celebration no matter where they were, and this year was no exception. Lanterns hung from the wagons cast a soft glow, and the sound of fiddle music mixed with laughter. A large pot of stew simmered over the fire, and Mary oversaw baking a simple but hearty cake in a Dutch oven.

Despite his frustrations with Mary, Nate had thrown himself into helping set up for the celebration, grateful for the distraction from his tumultuous feelings. He and Emma were busy setting out old crates around the fireplace.

"How old is Mary, exactly?" Emma asked, looking up at Nate.

"No one knows," Nate replied. "She insists on celebrating every year but won't actually tell anyone her age."

Emma's eyebrows shot up as she smiled.

Nate turned to see Sarah standing a few feet away. In the light from the campfire, her smooth skin glowed. He watched her for a long moment and then turned away to find Emma watching him.

"She's doin' really well," Emma said.

"So everyone keeps sayin'," Nate replied shortly.

"She misses you," Emma said plainly.

Nate said nothing, his heart in his throat. She missed him? He missed her too, more than he could put into words.

As the evening progressed, Nate found himself inadvertently drawn to Sarah, Emma's words echoing in his mind. He'd been able to keep himself busy enough to distract himself, but that night, nothing he did could take his mind off her.

After dinner, Nate looked around for Sarah and saw that she was helping some children decorate small oatcakes with dried fruits. Watching her with the children, seeing her smile and eyes light up with genuine happiness, stirred something deep within him. Before he realized it, he was walking over to her.

"Need a hand?" Nate asked, his voice casual but his heart pounding louder than he cared to admit.

Sarah looked up, surprised.

A moment of awkwardness passed between them, a silent acknowledgment of the weeks of distance.

"Sure," she said with a small smile, handing him a bowl of dried berries. "We're just adding the final touches."

Working side by side, Nate was reminded of the countless times they had shared simple tasks like this and how much he had always enjoyed her company. Their ease gradually returned as they talked about everything and nothing, from the Trail to the festivities.

The fiddle music swelled, and some of the group began to dance. Mary, ever the heart of any party, appeared.

"Dancin' time," she said brightly.

"Mary," Nate protested.

"No arguin'," she said sharply. "No one sits out at my birthday."

Nate looked at Sarah, who raised her eyebrows as if to suggest that fighting her was pointless.

Mary dragged them to the dance floor and, caught up in the moment and the infectious laughter around them, Sarah and Nate found themselves together. As Nate touched Sarah's lower back, his heart began to race. They were a bit clumsy at first, but as the music swelled, Nate relaxed. However, just as he was starting to enjoy himself, Jacob appeared.

"Mind if I cut in?" he said, his words slurring.

Without waiting, he pushed himself between Nate and Sarah. Nate was aware of the entire camp's eyes on him, and he did not want to spoil Mary's party, so he did not put up a fight. Jacob was drunk, and the last thing they needed was another scene. Instead, Nate turned around and walked to the fire, sitting on a turned-over crate. He watched Jacob and Sarah dance, his stomach in knots. He could tell how uncomfortable she was, and it made him physically sick. What was wrong with Jacob? Why couldn't he just leave her alone?

Nate stayed seated on the crate as the song ended, and Sam began to play another, the fiddle secured loosely under his chin.

"I don't want another dance, Jacob," Sarah insisted over the music.

"Don't be such a wet blanket," Jacob argued, pulling her against his body tightly.

Without hesitating, Nate got up and walked over to them.

"She's made herself clear, Jacob," Nate said.

Jacob exhaled heavily. "This is none of your business," he said between gritted teeth.

Suddenly, Emma appeared, looking between them with a crease between her brows. "Mary says it's time for cake."

Nate glared at Jacob as Emma took Sarah by the hand and led her toward the table where Mary and the others were gathered. After a moment, Jacob turned and stalked off toward the wagons.

After cake and singing, the party began to disperse. Despite the desire to celebrate late into the night, they had to be on the road again first thing in the morning.

"I'll help clear up," Mary volunteered.

"No, go to bed," Nate said, smiling at her. "You are the birthday girl, after all."

Mary reached up and cupped his face in her hand. "Girl," she said wistfully. "Aye, I'll tell you what, I still feel like a lass inside."

Nate smiled at her as she patted his cheek and then turned to go.

Nate helped Emma, Sam, and the others clean up, but he and Sarah were soon the only ones left.

"I thought that you'd gone to bed," he said.

"We didn't get our dance," Sarah reminded him.

"There is no music," Nate said.

"I don't mind," Sarah said, smiling.

Nate hesitated.

"I've missed you, Nate," Sarah said sincerely.

"I've missed you too," Nate confessed after a moment.

Sarah put out her hand, and Nate took it. She pulled him closer, and he slipped his hands around her waist. As Nate looked down into her eyes, the camp around them faded into the background. Nate looked down at Sarah, her face illuminated by the firelight, and realized just how much he had missed this—missed her.

Without thinking, he leaned in, and their lips met in a kiss that felt inevitable and transformative. It was a confession of everything unsaid, a surrender to the emotions they had both tried to deny.

“What is this?” Jacob’s angry voice cut through the moment, harsh and jarring. Nate and Sarah sprang apart, the magic of the moment dissolving instantly.

Jacob stood there, his expression twisted with anger and jealousy, his eyes locked on Nate with undisguised hatred. “You think you can just take what you want? Even when it ain’t yours to take?”

The accusation hung in the air, heavy and uncomfortable. Nate felt a rush of anger and protectiveness surge through him.

“Jacob, it’s not like that,” Sarah started to say, her voice firm despite her shaking hands.

But Jacob was beyond listening, his presence so full of hostility and fury, fueled even further by his drunkenness. “So this is what's been going on," he spat, his eyes blazing with anger as he stared at Nate. “You've had your eyes on her since the start, haven't you? You probably let Robert die on purpose so you could have your way and claim her!”

The accusation was so absurd, so vile, that Nate felt a mixture of shock and fury wash over him. He stepped forward, his posture rigid with indignation. “You're out of your mind, Jacob,” Nate retorted sharply. “To even suggest I had anything to do with Robert’s death is crazy. You know how dangerous this trail is, how unpredictable. What happened to Robert was an accident, not a scheme.”

"Jacob, please, stop this," Sarah said, her face pale and eyes wide with shock. "You're making no sense. Nate has been nothing but honorable."

But Jacob was beyond reason, his voice rising as he pointed an accusatory finger at Nate. "Oh, I'll stop when everyone knows the truth about what kind of man Nate really is. How he's been plotting and waiting, pretending to be the leader we can trust. I'll tell everyone—see if they'll still follow you then!"

Nate's jaw clenched, and he took a deep breath, struggling to maintain his composure in the face of Jacob's wild allegations.

"Go ahead and tell them, Jacob," Nate said, his voice steady despite the turmoil inside him. "Tell them whatever twisted version of the truth you've convinced yourself of. But know this—lying about me won't help you win her back. It won't change the fact that Sarah is her own person, not a prize to be claimed."

Jacob scoffed, his face contorted in a sneer. "We'll see about that. We'll see who they believe."

With that, Jacob turned and stormed off into the night, leaving a trail of tension behind him. Nate watched him go, his stomach in knots.

Nate sighed, running a hand through his hair in frustration. He turned to Sarah, her troubled expression mirroring his own.

"I talked to Jacob the other night," Sarah said quietly. "He confessed to stealing from Mr. Fields' wagon."

Nate raised an eyebrow in surprise.

"He confessed to me that he thinks it's his fault Robert is dead," Sarah said. "I tried to convince him it was no one's fault, but as soon as I brought you up, he shut down completely."

Nate sighed, running a hand through his hair in frustration. "It makes sense," he said, his voice heavy with resignation. "If Jacob feels guilty, it might be easier for him to push the blame on me. It would make him feel better, but it's dangerous. He could turn everyone against us."

Sarah nodded, her eyes reflecting the flickering light of the campfire. "I don't know this Jacob," she admitted. "Ever since Robert died, he's changed. He used to be quiet in an unsettling way, but now he's found his voice, and it's almost like he can't be stopped."

Nate looked at her. "Him catching us together tonight didn't help matters," he sighed.

Sarah pressed her lips together.

"What are we going to do?" she asked, her voice trembling slightly.

"I don't know," Nate admitted, a knot of worry tightening in his chest.

They fell silent, and all Nate could think was that after everything they'd done, the weeks of keeping away from Sarah, it had been undone in the space of a single kiss.

Chapter Nineteen

Sarah lay awake in her wagon as the birds began to chirp outside, signaling the arrival of morning. The events of the previous night replayed in her mind. The kiss with Nate had been unexpected but wonderful—a culmination of weeks of growing tension and unspoken feelings that had finally found expression. It had been unlike anything she had ever experienced—a moment of profound connection and raw emotion that had seemed to stop time itself.

The warmth of Nate's lips on hers had sent a jolt of electricity through her, awakening feelings she hadn't realized she harbored so deeply. In that brief, perfect moment, she felt a sense of belonging and understanding she had longed for all her life. It was as if all the pieces had fallen into place, and for that infinitesimal point in time, everything made sense.

But the harsh intrusion of Jacob's voice had shattered that moment, dragging her back to a reality she wasn't ready to face. His accusations, so venomous and bitter, had poisoned the air around them, leaving her heart pounding and her mind reeling. The memory of the kiss was now tainted with the fear of what Jacob might do next. His anger and resentment were unpredictable forces, and Sarah lay there, wrapped in her blankets, worrying about the repercussions that might follow.

As the camp slowly woke up around her, the sounds of morning routines filtering through the canvas of her wagon, Sarah felt a profound sense of loss. She wanted to cling to the memory of the kiss, to hold on to the feelings it had evoked within her, but fear clouded her thoughts. What if Jacob's words turned the others against Nate? What if his lies damaged the delicate balance they had all been working so hard to maintain?

At breakfast, Sarah was quiet. Nate was nowhere to be seen; thankfully, neither was Jacob.

“Are you all right?” Mary asked, her eyes full of concern.

“Not really,” Sarah confessed.

“What happened?” she asked.

Sarah exhaled deeply as she recounted the events of last night after everyone had gone to bed. When she told Mary about the kiss, her eyebrows shot up so fast that they almost disappeared into her hairline.

“Dinnae ye worry about Jacob,” she said firmly, placing a comforting hand on Sarah’s shoulders. "We all ken Nathaniel. We ken his character. Jacob’s been troubled since his brother passed. His words carry more grief than truth.”

Sarah nodded, but Mary’s words did little to silence the gnawing in the pit of her stomach. Jacob had been troubled long before Robert died but was coming unhinged.

“I think I should talk to him again,” Sarah said. “Try to see if I can’t convince him to stop this ridiculous crusade against Nate.”

The look in Mary’s eye reflected the doubt Sarah felt. She’s tried on so many occasions to speak with Jacob, but her words only seemed to fuel the fire that burned within him, which he was determined to use to destroy Nate.

“Maybe just let him be for a day or so,” Mary suggested. “Let him cool down.”

Sarah said nothing. The truth was she had no idea what she would say to Jacob if she went to speak with him. He wanted only one thing from her: for Sarah to give herself to him and be his wife. But she couldn’t do that, not now. She was finally learning who she was, to be strong and independent. She would not become his possession. She couldn't.

Sarah and Nate had decided the night before that they should keep their distance for a few days in the hopes of not inspiring any more anger in Jacob, but it frustrated Sarah that she couldn't be with the only person she really wanted to be around. Still, she did not want to get Nate into any more trouble.

Sarah was quiet as the wagon rolled forward that morning. Every now and again, Mary cast a worried glance her way.

"Stress ain't good for the bairn," Mary reminded her.

"I know," Sarah agreed as she ran her hands over her growing stomach.

They fell silent again as the wagon creaked and the stone crunched beneath its powerful wheels.

At noon, they stopped for lunch; however, Sarah opted to stay in the wagon. She was feeling queasy.

"I'll send Emma with some peppermint tea," Mary promised.

Sarah smiled gratefully as Mary turned and left. She climbed down and sat on the ground, pressing her back against the hard wood of the wheel. Sarah closed her eyes and began to drift off to sleep. A few minutes later, she heard someone approaching and opened her eyes again, expecting to find Emma, but it was Jacob.

"Jacob," Sarah said, straightening up.

Jacob looked down at her with a mixture of contempt and longing.

"Too ashamed to show your face?" he asked cruelly.

“No,” Sarah said. “I am not ashamed, Jacob.”

“Maybe you should be,” he said.

Sarah sighed. She was so tired, too tired for another fight with Jacob. Why couldn’t he just leave her be?

“Where’s your beau?” Jacob asked, looking around.

“He’s not my beau,” Sarah insisted as she struggled to get to her feet.

Sarah leaned on the wagon for a moment before she turned to go, but as she did, Jacob grabbed her wrist, twisting the skin painfully.

“I’ve told the others,” he hissed, his voice laced with a vindictive satisfaction. “About you and the Wagon Master’s little dalliance last night.”

Sarah felt a stab of anxiety as Jacob tightened his grip on her wrist, and she winced in pain. “Told them what exactly?”

“That he’s been taking advantage of the situation,” Jacob said, his blue eyes flashing. “That he’s been using his position to...” Jacob’s voice trailed off, but his implication hung heavily between them.

Anger coursed through Sarah’s body as she stared at Jacob. “That’s a lie, and you know it,” she countered, her voice rising. “Nate has done nothing but support me—us—throughout this journey.”

Jacob sneered, stepping closer still. “Oh, I think he’s been doing a bit more than just supporting you, hasn’t he? Everyone knows now. And he’s going to get what’s coming to him. No one wants a leader who can’t keep his personal feelings separate from his duties or someone who might throw a man to his death in order to steal his wife.”

The threat in his words was palpable, and Sarah felt a surge of concern wash through her, mingling with the anger. "You're trying to ruin a good man's reputation out of spite because I rejected you. Nate has been nothing but honorable."

Jacob's face twisted into a mask of disdain. "Honorable? Don't fool yourself, Sarah. I'm just making sure everyone sees the truth. He won't be leading us much longer if I have anything to say about it."

The raw malice in Jacob's statement made Sarah's heart race. She knew she had to remain strong, not just for her own sake but also for Nate's. "You can say whatever you want, Jacob, but the people here know Nate. They trust him. Your lies won't change that."

Jacob scoffed, his gaze darkening. "We'll see about that. Just remember, I offered you a way out. You chose this instead."

Just then, footsteps approached, and Emma appeared around the corner of the wagon, a cup of peppermint tea in her hands. Her arrival startled Jacob, causing him to release Sarah's wrist and step back. He smiled smugly at Emma for a moment and then turned to go.

As he disappeared from view, Sarah took a deep breath, trying to quell the tremor of fear, but suddenly, her knees buckled, and her body swayed unsteadily.

"Sarah!" Emma exclaimed, her eyes wide with concern. The cup slipped from her grasp, clattering to the ground. The tea spilled into the dirt, forming dark, wet patches as Emma rushed forward, catching Sarah just before she collapsed.

Sarah clung tightly to Emma as the world moved in and out of focus.

“Sit,” Emma said, her voice soft but urgent.

Sarah said nothing as Emma helped her sit on the hard ground.

Emma sat down beside her, her brow furrowed with worry. “Are you all right?”

“Not really,” Sarah admitted as she rubbed her wrist, the skin red and sore from Jacob's grasp, her heart still pounding in her chest.

“What was that about?" she asked, her tone gentle yet insistent.

Sarah sighed, shaking her head. “It was about... Nate. Last night, he... we...” She paused, struggling to find the words.

Emma nodded, understanding dawning on her. “You mean you two shared a moment, and Jacob saw?”

Sarah nodded, tears pricking at the corners of her eyes. “Yes, and now he’s told everyone, and he’s threatening to turn the entire train against Nate. He's spreading rumors, saying things that aren't true. I'm so worried, Emma. What if he succeeds?"

Emma placed a comforting arm around Sarah’s shoulders. “I noticed things were a bit frosty around the fire this morning,” she admitted. “But Sarah, you mustn’t worry too much, especially in your condition. It’s bad for the baby.”

Sarah felt the warmth of Emma’s side against hers, a small comfort in the storm that seemed to be brewing around them. “I know, I’m trying not to, but it’s hard. Nate doesn’t deserve this. He’s just tryin’ to protect me and the baby.”

Emma reached out and squeezed her hand reassuringly, and Sarah exhaled deeply.

"Jacob can stir as much as he likes, but he won't find it easy to turn folks against a man they trust," she said.

Sarah nodded but could not ignore the gnawing pit in her stomach.

"Now, I am going to get you some more tea," Emma said, getting up. "You stay here and rest."

Sarah said nothing as Emma got up and left.

Sarah sat quietly in the solitude of her thoughts; a deep sense of guilt and turmoil churned within her.

She couldn't shake the feeling that she was to blame for the unrest that had befallen the group. If only she had been more cautious, more reserved in her moments with Nate, perhaps Jacob would have had nothing to fuel his bitter rumors. Now, Nate's honor, his position as a leader, was being called into question, and it was all because of her, because she longed for the affection she had been so cruelly denied in her marriage.

As she picked at dry skin at the edges of her fingernails, Sarah's mind wandered back to her life with Robert, to the dark, hidden corners of her existence that no one in the camp knew about. Robert had controlled every aspect of her life, his harsh words and harsher hands shaping her days into a continuous struggle. No one else but Nate knew the depth of her suffering, understood why she so desperately sought connection, why the idea of love held such a powerful, almost desperate allure.

She thought about how, in Nate, she had found a kindred spirit, someone who had seen her not as a burden or a duty but as a person worthy of kindness and respect. Their connection had been a balm to her scarred heart, a glimpse of what life could be when shared with someone who truly cared. And now, because of her, his reputation was at risk.

Sarah knew the rumors would not just affect how others viewed Nate but could influence their entire journey. The thought of causing harm to the group, to the man who had shown her such genuine kindness, was almost too much to bear.

Chapter Twenty

The fire crackled and popped, sending sparks dancing into the darkness, yet its usual warmth seemed absent tonight, replaced by a palpable tension that Nate could feel pressing in from all sides.

Across the fire, Nate could see Jacob and a small group of men, their faces flickering in the orange glow. Every so often, they would throw glances his way, their expressions hardened, whispers barely audible over the crackling of the wood. The atmosphere was thick with unease, and Nate felt every disapproving gaze like a physical weight.

Beside him, Mary shifted, her face lined with concern. "It's nae good, this," she muttered in her thick Scottish brogue, her eyes darting across the fire. "I ken ye've done no wrong, Nathaniel, but these whispers are like dry tinder just waiting for a spark."

Nate nodded grimly, his hands tight around his mug. "I know, Mary. It's getting out of hand. I can handle disputes and disagreements, but this feels different. Jacob's stirring up more than just idle talk."

Mary sighed, her gaze steady and serious. "Ye cannae let this fester, lad. Ye need to speak your peace and clear the air before it turns ugly. This lot," she gestured subtly toward the group across the fire, "they're getting fed a story that ain't true, and it's souring their view of ye."

Nate's jaw set firmly. He knew Mary was right; he had faced arguments and challenges before, but nothing that threatened the group's cohesion quite like this.

"But what if confronting it head-on just makes things worse?" Nate asked, the doubt clear in his voice. "What if it ends up dividing everyone even more?"

Mary shook her head, her eyes reflecting the firelight. "Sometimes, the hard thing and the right thing are the same. Ye've got to trust that the truth will out. And ye need to give them a chance to see the man I know ye are, not the one Jacob's painting ye to be."

Nate looked into the fire, watching the flames lick at the logs, turning them into char. He took a deep breath, feeling the resolve build within him. He wouldn't go to them now, not after they had been drinking, but he needed to sort this out once and for all.

"Tomorrow," he said. "I'll talk to them tomorrow."

Mary nodded, placing a reassuring hand on his shoulder. "Aye, that's the spirit."

The night wore on, the fire slowly dying to embers, but the weight of Mary's words stayed with him. Tomorrow would be a decisive day, one way or another.

Nate tossed and turned all night. The image of Jacob's sneering face haunted his dreams. Whenever he closed his eyes, the sharp sting of accusation and the murmurs of doubt among the men replayed like a refrain. It was still dark when he finally gave up trying to sleep. Rising from his bedroll, he left the wagon and went to the river.

The cool water lapped at his legs as Nate waded into the river. When he was waist-deep, he dived under the river's chill, washing away the remnants of his restless night. He turned over on his back, floating for a moment as he looked up at the sky. The stars were quickly fading now as dawn crept across the sky. He closed his eyes, focusing on the quietness of the moment and clearing his mind for the confrontation he knew he couldn't avoid.

The sun was just beginning to rise over the distant hills when Nate returned to camp, feeling more awake and determined.

As he approached the circle of wagons, he ran into Emma. "Mornin', Emma," he greeted her, trying to keep his voice even despite the turmoil inside.

Emma looked up, her expression immediately softening when she saw him. "Morning."

"How's Sarah doing?" Nate asked.

He had not spoken to Sarah since the night they kissed. He'd wanted to, but they'd both agreed to keep their distance so as not to give Jacob any more reason to spread more gossip. Still, he'd thought about her every second and missed her.

Emma sighed, shaking her head. "Not well," she admitted. "She's not eating much. All this trouble with Jacob is making her unwell. She's stressed, and you know stress isn't good for the baby."

Nate felt the knots in his stomach tighten uncomfortably. "I know," he agreed. "I am goin' to talk to Jacob now, straighten things out."

"Good," Emma said.

Nate nodded as he walked toward the fire, where the group gathered for breakfast. The air was filled with the smell of cooking bacon and the rich, earthy aroma of coffee brewing over the fire. People were sitting on logs or standing in small groups, plates in hand.

He spotted Mary across the fire, stirring a pot of oats. She gave him a reassuring smile as she caught his eye. Turning, he saw Jacob and his group of supporters sitting together, their laughter a bit too loud, their glances in his direction a bit too pointed.

Nate took a deep breath and walked over to them, his boots crunching on the gravel.

As he approached, the men stopped eating.

"Mornin'," he said, keeping his voice level.

"What do you want?" Jacob asked, not looking up from his plate of food.

"To talk," Nate said.

Jacob said nothing for a moment. Seated beside him were Curtis Weller, a stocky man with a permanent scowl etched into his face, and Pete Marston, who had a nervous twitch in his left eye and a quick temper to match. Nate did not know either of them very well.

"I haven't got anythin' to say to the likes of you," Jacob said as he shoveled a spoon of beans into his mouth.

The two men chuckled dryly as Nate stiffened.

"I'm here to clear the air," Nate said. "We need to work together if we're going to make it to California. This division isn't helping anyone."

Jacob sneered as he turned to face Nate. "Work together? With a man who preys on vulnerable widows?" His voice was loud enough to draw the attention of nearby pioneers, some pausing to listen.

"Yeah, we've all seen how you've been hovering around Mrs. Turner," Curtis said.

Pete nodded vigorously, his eyes darting around the group. "And who's to say you won't grow bored of her and start eyeing someone else's wife?"

Nate clenched his fists at his sides, struggling to keep his composure under the barrage of accusations.

"You fought with Jacob's brother, and he ended up at the bottom of the river," Pete reasoned. "Seems a bit of a coincidence to me."

Curtis nodded in support.

"Jacob admitted that he stole from Mr. Fields' wagon," Nate insisted. "Is he not to be blamed for his part?"

Pete and Curtis frowned as they turned to Jacob.

"I never said that," Jacob lied. "I'd offer for you to search my wagon, but thanks to you, it's at the bottom of a river, just like Robert."

Nate gritted his teeth.

"We need a leader we can trust," Curtis said. "And we just don't trust you."

Nate exhaled heavily. "I have not, nor would I ever, take advantage of anyone in this camp," he stated firmly, his gaze locking on each man in turn. "My relationship with Mrs. Turner has been nothing but respectful. Jacob is twistin' things because of his own grievances."

Jacob scoffed as he stood up, his plate clattering to the ground. He stepped forward, so close to Nate that they were almost nose to nose. "You callin' what I witnessed the other night respectful? My brother's barely cold in his grave, and you have your dirty hands all over his wife."

Nate inhaled sharply. "Be careful, Jacob."

"Or what?" Jacob challenged. "You think this is just about me? Open your eyes. People are talkin'. And I won't stop making sure they know the kind of man they're following."

The intensity in Jacob's eyes and the harshness of his words made Nate's blood boil. He had to use every ounce of self-control not to punch him in the jaw. Around them, the murmurs of the gathering crowd grew louder, a mix of agreement and shock weaving through the air.

"Stop this, Jacob," Nate said, his voice low and dangerous. "You're dividing the camp over nothing—over your own jealousy and spite."

Jacob laughed, a harsh, mocking sound that echoed slightly in the morning air. "I'm protecting the camp from you. Maybe it's time we found a new Wagon Master—one who doesn't mix duty with... personal pleasures. What do you think, boys?"

"Yeah," Curtis and Pete said in unison as they got up and stood behind Jacob to show his support.

"Jacob," Nate said, trying to keep his voice even. "If you continue on this road—"

"Then what?" Jacob challenged. "You gonna kick me off the wagon train?"

Nate said nothing.

"Because I think Curtis, Pete, and some others might have somethin' to say about that," Jacob said, a smug smirk twisting his features.

Curtis and Pete crossed their arms, their expressions hardening as they nodded in agreement, backing up Jacob's words with silent, ominous gestures. The small crowd that had gathered around the confrontation seemed to tighten, and they were charged with tension.

"You keep away from Sarah," Jacob continued, his voice rising aggressively. "Or I'll do more than talk."

Nate's mind raced as he turned, scanning the faces around the campfire to gauge how deep Jacob's influence ran. The crowd nodded and murmured agreement, but many faces were filled with concern and uncertainty.

He turned back to Jacob, who was smiling smugly.

"Now, why don't you go and check the wagons or somethin'," he said, his eye glinting. "Your face is puttin' me off my breakfast."

There was a smattering of laughter from Curtis, Pete, and some of the others.

Nate did not move for a moment. Part of him knew that continuing the argument would only escalate tensions, and without knowing how many were swayed by Jacob's words, he couldn't risk an outright conflict that might split the group or turn violent. He needed to step back and plan how to handle this with a cooler head and perhaps more private conversations with the families and individuals who might still trust in his leadership.

With a heavy heart and a last look around at the group—some faces sympathetic, others amused by Jacob's crude dismissal—Nate turned on his heel and walked away. Each step felt heavier than the last, a mixture of defeat and determination settling within him. This wasn't the end of the matter; it was a strategic retreat.

He needed to regroup, to talk to Sarah, Mary, and others who might help him navigate this delicate situation. His leadership, his place in the wagon train, and perhaps even more personal stakes with Sarah depended on what he did next.

***

Nate paced back and forth in the dim light of the secluded clearing. He had called this meeting secretly, away from prying eyes and ears. The air was thick with tension, the weight of his worries pressing down on him. He glanced around at the faces of those gathered: Mary, Emma, Samuel, Elijah, and Thomas. Each one of them had been chosen for their trustworthiness and loyalty. Nate had not asked Sarah to come; he did not want to worry her anymore.

Nate took a deep breath, steadying himself. "I've just had a conversation with Jacob. As you all know, he's been stirring up trouble and is unhappy with my leadership. He's making suggestions about my intentions with Mrs. Turner."

Emma's eyes widened in concern. "What kind of suggestions?"

Nate sighed, running a hand through his dark hair. "He's implying that I had something to do with Mr. Turner's death, that I wanted him out of the way so I could be with Sarah. He's feeding these ideas to some of the other men, trying to turn them against me."

Samuel, the old veteran, frowned deeply. "That's a dangerous game he's playing. If people start believing him, it could cause real trouble."

Nate nodded. "Exactly," he agreed. "I'm not sure what Jacob will try next, but I want to avoid any civil war breaking out in the camp."

"What can we do?" Elijah asked.

"I need your support to quell any unrest. We need to keep the peace, no matter what."

Thomas stepped forward. "You've got my support," he said, his voice gruff. "I've seen how hard you work to keep everyone safe. I won't let this man ruin that."

"Aye," Mary said, nodding. "Ye ken ye have my support, lad. We'll stand by ye and make sure this camp stays together."

"I'll do whatever I can to help," Emma said, her voice firm. "Sarah and the baby need stability, and we all must stick together."

Nate felt a wave of relief wash over him. "Thank you, all of you. We need to be vigilant and keep an eye on Jacob and anyone he's been talking to. If we see any signs of trouble, we need to address it quickly and calmly. We can't let this escalate."

Samuel nodded. "We'll keep watch. And if Jacob steps out of line, we'll deal with it."

Nate looked around at his friends, feeling a renewed sense of determination.

"Aye," Mary said. "We're a strong lot and won't let one man's bitterness tear us apart."

The group dispersed, each returning to their tents with a sense of purpose. Nate watched them go, his heart heavy but hopeful.

Chapter Twenty-One

Sarah sat atop the wagon, her body feeling every jolt and bump of the uneven trail beneath them. Despite the rhythmic sway of the wagon, her stomach churned uncomfortably, a persistent knot of anxiety tightening with every mile they covered. Beside her, Emma seemed unusually quiet, her usual chatter replaced by a thoughtful silence that only added to Sarah's sense of unease.

Glancing at Emma, Sarah could sense her concern. The lines on Emma's face seemed deeper that morning; her brows furrowed in what appeared to be a deep worry.

“Emma,” Sarah began, her voice shaking slightly. “You seem quieter than usual today. Is everything all right?”

Emma sighed deeply, turning to meet Sarah's gaze. “I didn't want to worry you more,” she finally said, her voice tinged with reluctance. “But there’s been more trouble with Jacob and Nate.”

Sarah's heart sank, and the knot in her stomach tightened further. “What happened?” she asked, bracing herself for the answer. Her hands gripped the edge of the wagon seat a little tighter.

“Nate tried to talk with Jacob at breakfast this morning,” Emma explained. “Things got heated.”

“What did they say?” Sarah asked.

Emma sighed, shaking her head. “I couldn’t hear exactly what they were saying,” she admitted. “But it’s pretty obvious that Jacob and some of the men don't trust Nate, and they don’t want him to lead us anymore.”

“What?” Sarah breathed, her eyes widening in disbelief.

The news hit Sarah like a physical blow, intensifying her headache as the implications spun through her mind. The thought of Nate facing such hostility and potentially being ousted from his role filled her with a profound sense of helplessness and fear.

"It's getting serious, Sarah. They're questioning his decisions and intentions. It's not just about you and him anymore—it's about his leadership and his character. Jacob is stirring things up bad."

Sarah's eyes filled with tears, the landscape around her blurring as the wagon trundled along. She felt overwhelmed by guilt and worry—not just for herself but for Nate, who had only ever shown her kindness and respect. The thought that she might be the cause of his downfall was unbearable.

"Emma, what are we going to do?" Sarah asked, her voice trembling. I can't stand the thought of Nate suffering because of me—because of us."

Emma reached out, placing a hand on Sarah's arm. "It'll be okay," she said. "We'll figure this out."

Sarah nodded, but the truth was that she didn't know how they were going to figure this mess out.

As the wagon train came to a halt for lunch, the usual bustle of activity didn't inspire Sarah's appetite. Her stomach was still tied up in knots, and the thought of sitting around the campfire under the watchful eyes of Jacob and his cohorts made her feel even queasier.

"I'm not hungry, Emma," Sarah murmured as she stayed perched on the wagon seat, her gaze distant.

Emma, who was unpacking some provisions nearby, looked up with a concerned frown. "You need to eat," she said firmly, "for you and the baby."

Sarah knew Emma was right, so she nodded despite the tightness in her stomach. "All right, but I...I don't think I can face everyone there. Not today."

"I'll bring you a plate," Emma promised.

A short while later, Mary, not Emma, arrived with a plate of food. "Here ye go, lass," she said. "Eat up; it'll help give ye strength."

Sarah took the plate from her as Mary settled beside her on the wagon step.

Sarah picked at the food, and after a few moments, she looked across at Mary. "How bad are things? Honestly?"

Mary sighed deeply, her eyes scanning the camp, where scattered groups of people sat, the mood notably subdued. "I'm worried," she admitted. "It's nae good, this division. It's stirring up fears and doubts among the folk. Jacob's words are like wee seeds of dissent, and they're taking root faster than we'd like."

Despite the warmth of the midday sun, a chill ran down Sarah's spine. "What's Nate going to do?" she asked, her voice low.

Mary shook her head slowly, her lips pressed into a thin line. "I dinnae know. He's caught in a tough spot. But a Wagon Master's leadership cannae be questioned, not out here. It's too dangerous. On the Trail, everyone needs to listen to him and trust him. If they don't..." She paused, her gaze serious, "Well, things could fall apart pretty quick."

The gravity of Mary's words hung in the air, heavy and ominous. Sarah's hands tightened around the plate, the reality of their situation settling in. The delicate balance of trust and leadership that had once held their group together was now at risk of unraveling, and the consequences could be disastrous.

"Then we need to do something," Sarah said, her resolve hardening. "We can't just sit back and watch everything fall apart."

Mary nodded, a determined glint in her eye. "Aye, you're right. We'll think of something. We always do, don't we?" She patted Sarah's hand reassuringly.

The sun was dropping in the west as the wagon creaked and groaned along the dusty trail. Sarah sat with her journal in her lap; however, the words refused to come. Her pen hovered above the page, ink ready to spill, but her mind was a tumultuous sea of worry and uncertainty.

Mary's words from lunch echoed in her mind. "We'll think of something," she'd said. But as the afternoon wore on, Sarah found it increasingly difficult to see a solution. She and Nate could maintain their distance and act as if their shared moment had never happened, but would that be enough? Jacob's bitterness and anger seemed boundless, and his influence was growing. It was not just about her and Nate anymore; the entire wagon train's harmony and safety were at stake.

Sarah's hand trembled slightly as she placed the pen back in her journal, closing it without a single word written. The idea lurking in the darkest corner of her mind began to take a clearer, more definite shape. There was, perhaps, one thing she could do to protect Nate and stop the spread of Jacob's poisonous words.

Marry Jacob.

The thought made her stomach turn, but as she played out the scenarios in her mind, each pathway seemed to return to this drastic option. Marrying Jacob could satisfy his vindictive pride, secure his silence about Nate, and perhaps shift his focus away from sabotaging the Wagon Master. It was a sacrifice—one immense and soul-crushing—but wasn't it her responsibility to consider it if it meant protecting everyone else?

The wagon lurched as it hit a huge rut in the road, jolting her from her thoughts. She glanced around, seeing the prairie stretch endlessly around her, feeling more trapped than ever. How could marrying Jacob, a man she despised, be the solution? Yet, how could she risk the potential fallout of refusing to appease him?

The weight of her predicament settled heavily on her shoulders as she considered her next steps. Jacob and Robert were brothers, but they weren't the same man. At least, she believed Jacob was in love with her, which was more than she could say for Robert. Yet he wasn't a good man, not like Nate.

As the sun began to dip low in the sky, casting long shadows over the land, Sarah felt the chill of the evening begin to set in. Wrapping her shawl tighter around her shoulders, she sighed softly. Having only just escaped being trapped in one marriage, would she be able to survive another?

***

As the evening settled over the wagon train, a sense of unease lingered, much like the faint wisps of campfire smoke that drifted lazily above the group. Sarah, already on edge from her contemplations throughout the day, sat near the outskirts of the camp, her eyes scanning the familiar faces illuminated by the flickering firelight. Everyone seemed to be doing their usual routines, yet the normalcy of the scene did nothing to soothe her nerves.

Sarah got up from where she was sitting, feeling restless and troubled. Perhaps a walk would help to clear her mind. As she strolled along the edge of the camp, she moved close to a cluster of trees when suddenly she heard voices and stopped, holding her breath. The voices were unmistakably those of Jacob and his close allies, Curtis and Pete. Worry gnawing at her insides, she moved closer, staying hidden in the shadows, listening.

"...we need to do something about him for good," Jacob's voice was tense, laden with a venom that made Sarah's stomach clench.

"Yeah," Curtis agreed.

"What are you thinking?" Pete asked, a note of eagerness in his tone.

"We need to make it look like an accident," Jacob said. "A little accident happens; he doesn't come back."

Sarah's hands were trembling.

"We can say he fell, hit his head on a rock," Curtis said. "Got swept away by the river."

"Maybe had a nice little run-in with a native," Pete added.

Sarah's heart raced as the real weight of their malice—this was no mere rivalry or bitterness; it was deadly intent. She felt panic rise within her, the urgent need to protect Nate.

She backed away from the trees slowly, careful not to make a sound that would reveal her presence. Once she was far enough away, she turned and hurried back to the camp.

***

A coyote howled in the distance as Sarah approached Jacob's wagon. The clinking of a bottle cut through the otherwise quiet night. He was sitting alone, silhouetted against the dim lantern light, his posture slack with drink.

Taking a deep breath, Sarah called out softly, “Jacob?”

He looked up, squinting into the darkness before recognizing her. “Sarah? What are you doing here?” His voice was slurred, heavy with alcohol.

Sarah exhaled shakily, gathering all her courage as she took another step forward. “I have a proposition for you,” she said, her voice trembling despite her efforts to sound confident.

Jacob raised his eyebrows in surprise, then clumsily jumped down from the wagon, stumbling slightly as he approached her. He grinned, a predatory glint in his blue eyes that reminded her of Robert. “A proposition, eh? This should be good.”

Sarah steeled herself as he closed the distance between them, the smell of whiskey heavy on his breath. “I'll marry you, Jacob," she blurted out, her heart pounding, “but only if you agree to one condition.”

Jacob stopped short, his grin widening. “Oh? And what's that?”

“You leave Nate alone. You stop this crusade against him. No harm comes to him from you or anyone else,” Sarah said firmly, trying to mask her desperation.

Jacob's expression shifted to one of calculation. After a moment, he nodded slowly, clearly pleased with the turn of events. “All right, Sarah. I'll leave your precious Nate alone. You've got my word.” He stepped closer, his intentions clear, as he reached out to touch her face.

Sarah recoiled instinctively, but Jacob grabbed her chin, his touch rough. "If we're getting married, I want a real wife, Sarah. Understand?" His voice was low and menacing.

She forced herself not to pull away as he ran his thumb over her bottom lip, her skin crawling under his touch. It took her every ounce of strength not to flee from him right then.

Jacob, seemingly satisfied with her submission, let her go and stepped back, chuckling to himself. "We're gonna be family now, Sarah. Best get used to it."

He turned back toward his wagon, his laughter echoing in the night air, leaving Sarah standing alone, shaken and nauseated by the encounter.

As she watched his retreating back, the reality of what she had just agreed to began to sink in. Marrying Jacob—this man who repulsed her to her very core—was the price she had to pay to protect Nate.

After a moment, Sarah turned to go, her heart in her stomach. She walked back through the camp, which was quiet now that everyone had gone to bed. When she reached Emma's wagon, a figure stepped out of the shadows, and Sarah jumped, startled. It was Nate.

"Nate," she breathed.

Their eyes locked in the dim moonlight. Sarah's heart was in her throat as she thought of the sacrifice she'd just made for him, because she loved him so much.

"We need to talk," he said.

Chapter Twenty-Two

The night was cool, a slight breeze rustling through the leaves, carrying the weight of his heavy thoughts. Sarah stood before him, her posture tense as if carrying the world's weight on her shoulders.

“Sarah,” Nate began, his voice low.

“Nate,” she replied, her voice equally soft, a tremor of unease running through it. “I know about your conversation with Jacob and how he’s challenging your leadership.”

Nate sighed, shaking his head. “I don’t know what to do,” he admitted, the burden of his responsibilities heavier than ever. “It’s not just about me; it’s about everyone here. I can’t let him divide us.

He paused, holding her gaze. “But despite all this... I can’t stop thinking about you, about that kiss.” His voice faltered slightly, betraying his turmoil. “I know I should keep my distance for the good of the train, but I can’t stop caring about you—or the baby.”

Sarah turned to face him, her expression somber in the moonlight. “Nate—”

“I know it’s foolish,” he said, stepping forward and reaching for her hand. “But I am too involved now—”

“I’m going to marry Jacob,” Sarah blurted.

The words hit Nate like a physical blow, his heart stopping for a split second as he processed what she’d just said. “Marry Jacob?” he echoed, incredulity lacing his tone. “Why would you do that, Sarah? You’ve just broken free from one man like him. Marrying Jacob would be like chaining yourself to the same life again.”

Sarah's eyes held a deep sadness as she met his gaze. "It just makes sense," she insisted, though her voice lacked conviction. "He's Robert's brother. He's related to the baby. It's the most respectful thing to do."

"It makes no sense," Nate argued. "Don't do this, Sarah."

Sarah exhaled shakily. "How many times have you told me how much you love it out here, being a Wagon Master? This is your life, Nate."

Nate shook his head, disbelief and hurt swirling through him. "So you're doin' this for me? *Are* you doing this for me?" he asked, desperate for another answer, for something that made sense. "Because things aren't that bad—"

"No, Nate," Sarah said, her voice firm, though her eyes did not meet his. "It's for the best. For everyone."

Nate felt a sharp sting in his chest, the pain of rejection mixed with confusion. He dropped her hand as he took a step back. He'd thought there was something real between them, something meaningful beyond mere circumstance or duty. He wanted to voice these thoughts, to tell her how much she meant to him, but the words caught in his throat, unspoken.

They stood in silence, the only sound the gentle rustle of the wind through the grass. Nate struggled to compose himself, to respect her decision even if he couldn't understand it. Finally, he nodded, his frame stiff as he tried to mask the turmoil inside.

"If that's what you think is best," he said quietly, his voice rough with suppressed emotion. "I'll respect your decision."

"Nate—"

"Goodnight, Sarah," he said.

With one last look, a mix of sorrow and unresolved love in his eyes, Nate turned and walked back to his wagon, leaving Sarah in the moonlight. As he walked away, his mind raced with thoughts of what could have been and what now seemed an impossible dream.

***

Nate was already sitting by the dwindling fire when the first light of dawn began to paint the horizon in pale orange and dusty pink hues. He hadn't slept, not really, his thoughts a tangled mess that refused to unknot themselves. He looked every bit as disheveled as he felt, his clothes rumpled from a night spent tossing on his bedroll.

Mary approached, a steaming cup of coffee in her hand, and sat beside him with a concerned glance. "Laddie, did ye sleep in yesterday's clothes? Ye look all turned about," she joked lightly, trying to coax a smile from him.

Nate managed a weary shake of his head, but no smile came. His eyes stayed fixed on the dying embers, watching as the last sparks faded into ash.

"What's eating at ye?" Mary pressed, her tone shifting to worry as she handed him the coffee.

Nate took the cup, his hands wrapping around it for warmth more than anything. "Sarah's going to marry Jacob," he said flatly, the words tasting bitter as they left his mouth.

Mary's reaction was immediate; her brows shot up in shock, and she almost dropped her cup. "She's what? Marry that weasel? Oh, that lass needs a good talking to, and I'm just the one to do it," she declared.

Nate held up a hand, halting her brewing storm. "No, Mary. Let it be," he said quietly, his voice carrying a weight that made her pause.

Mary frowned, sitting back as she studied his resigned expression. "Nathaniel, ye cannae be serious. Ye're just going to let her marry that snake? After everything?"

"I've been up all night thinking on it," Nate admitted, his gaze distant. "Maybe it's for the best. Jacob's determined to tear the train apart. This way, maybe he'll stop his fighting."

Mary's face hardened, her disappointment clear. "Ye can't let him win like this. It's not right, and deep down, ye know it."

"It's Sarah's choice," Nate countered, a hollow ache spreading through his chest. "And I won't take that away from her. She thinks this is the best way to protect the train and all of us."

Mary's anger flared, her cheeks coloring with frustration and disbelief. "And what about what ye want? What about fighting for her, for what the two of ye could have together? I thought ye had more courage, laddie. I thought ye wouldn't just roll over for the likes of him."

Nate looked away, unable to meet her fiery gaze. "Sometimes courage means doing what's best for others, not just what you want for yourself."

With a huff, Mary stood, her disappointment palpable. "I never thought I'd see the day Nathaniel Jameson would give up without a fight. I'm disappointed in ye, truly."

With that, Mary turned and walked away, grumbling under her breath.

As Nate sat, the sun rising higher and the camp beginning to stir around him, He wrestled with his own doubts.

Nate understood Sarah's reasoning to a degree. They both shared a profound sense of responsibility for the group, an unspoken commitment to see everyone safely to their destination. Protecting the group was paramount, and Sarah's choice, as painful as it was, came from that same place of selfless duty. But knowing this didn't make it any easier to accept.

The idea of Sarah marrying Jacob made his stomach ache. It was a gnawing, relentless pain that refused to let him rest. Whenever he saw her, the thought of Jacob being the one to hold her and share a life with her, twisted something deep inside him. It felt wrong, a cruel twist of fate that he was powerless to change.

Yet, amidst the pain and the conflict, Nate couldn't help but admire Sarah's bravery. Her decision wasn't made lightly. It was an act of profound courage and sacrifice, putting the group's well-being above her own happiness. That selflessness and strength made him love her even more, even if he hated the circumstances that had brought them to this point.

He thought back to their conversations, the quiet moments they had shared, and the deep connection that had grown between them. Sarah's resilience and determination had always drawn him to her, but this decision showed a new depth to her character. She was willing to endure personal hardship to protect those she cared about, a rare and admirable quality that made his feelings for her even stronger.

But loving her in this situation felt like a double-edged sword. Every time he thought about what she was sacrificing, what she was enduring for the sake of the group, the ache in his heart became even more acute. He wanted to protect her, to be the one to shield her from pain, but he was the one causing her to make this unbearable choice.

Nate clenched his fists, frustration bubbling up inside him. He hated feeling so helpless, hated that there was nothing he could do to change the situation without putting everyone else at risk. The balance between personal desire and duty to the group was delicate; right now, it felt like a battle he was losing.

Finally, he sighed, a deep, weary exhalation of a man caught between duty and desire, his decision unclear as the day began in earnest.

As the morning sun rose brightly above the peaks of the blue hills, the wagon train bustled with the activity of breaking camp. The pioneers, who were now well-versed in the routine, moved with a purposeful efficiency.

Nate was adjusting the harness on the oxen, focusing on the task with a determination that belied the turmoil churning within him.

Around him, Mary was folding tents with her usual brisk efficiency, directing some of the younger children with a firm yet kind hand. Elijah, the scout, was checking his horse, ensuring the animal was ready for the day's journey ahead. Old veteran Samuel was securing loads on his wagon with his weathered face and steady hands. While. Thomas, the blacksmith, was doing a final check on the wagon wheels, his large hands skillfully adjusting anything that seemed amiss.

Nate tried to lose himself in the work, focusing on his role as Wagon Master, but a pit of dread sat heavy in his stomach. The sound of raised voices suddenly cut through the morning calm, pulling his attention away from the oxen. It was Emma and Jacob, their argument escalating just a few wagons down.

"Sarah's riding with me on Pete's wagon," Jacob insisted loudly.

"No, Jacob," Emma countered with equal intensity. "She'll ride with me. I've been keeping an eye on her, especially with the baby. It's best she stays where she is."

Nate's hands clenched around the harness straps as he listened. With a heavy sigh, he made his way toward the quarrel, his presence commanding enough to make the surrounding pioneers pause in their tasks.

"What's goin' on?" Nate asked.

"Jacob is insisting Sarah ride with him," Emma said. "But I need to keep a close eye on her and the baby—"

"You need to mind your own business is what," Jacob snapped.

"Jacob," Nate said, trying to keep his voice level. "I think it's best if you leave Sarah to ride with Emma."

Jacob rounded on him, his blue eyes gleaming triumphantly. "Oh, you think it's best?" he said, his voice smug. "Well, Sarah and I are gettin' married, so I think it's up to me to decide what's best for her."

"You're what?" Emma said, her eyes widening in disbelief.

"We're gettin' hitched, " Jacob repeated as he stared at Nate, hoping for some kind of reaction.

"I know," Nate responded evenly, though every fiber of his being rebelled at the thought.

The wind seemed momentarily knocked out of Jacob's sails at Nate's calm acknowledgment, but he quickly recovered, his expression hardening.

"She rides on my wagon," Jacob insisted again, looking at Nate as if daring him to challenge his decision.

Nate's jaw tightened. The thought of Sarah in the close confines of a wagon with Jacob all day, every day, made him deeply uncomfortable. He knew Jacob's temper and rough manner, not to mention the drinking. It was no place for Sarah, much less for her and the baby.

Before Nate could respond, Sarah appeared, her face drawn but composed. "It's fine, Emma," she said quietly, her voice carrying a resignation that made Nate's heart ache. "I'll ride with Jacob. We need to keep moving."

"Sarah—" Emma said.

"You heard her," Jacob hissed. "Now leave us be."

Emma frowned, glaring at Jacob in disgust. Sarah tried to catch Nate's eye, seeking some kind of connection or reassurance, but Nate couldn't bear to hold her gaze. The pain was too sharp, too raw. With a curt nod, he turned away, focusing on the tasks at hand.

"Let's get on the road," he said gruffly.

As the wagon train started moving, Nate kept his eyes fixed on the path ahead, the weight of his decision—to let Sarah go to Jacob—sitting like a stone in his stomach. He had to trust that she knew what she was doing, that her sacrifice was for the best, but every instinct screamed otherwise.

Chapter Twenty-Three

Sarah found herself squeezed on the narrow seat between Jacob and Pete in the wagon's dusty cradle. Despite the boundless prairie stretching horizon to horizon, the air around her felt stiflingly tight, like the walls of the world were pressing in on her. She shifted, trying to ease the discomfort of the wooden seat beneath her, but there was no relief. The sun beat down mercilessly, and the heat was oppressive.

Jacob, with a bottle dangling loosely from his hand, laughed heartily at something Pete had said. His laughter, though jovial to an outsider, sounded grating to Sarah. Jacob's hand would occasionally land heavily on her thigh as if compelled by some thoughtless habit. Each touch sent a shiver of repulsion, skittering across her skin, her body tensing involuntarily.

She dared not look at him for fear her eyes would betray the scream trapped inside her chest. Instead, she focused on the endless plains, trying to imagine herself alone in that vast space, unencumbered and free, not trapped here beside a man who saw her as nothing more than a trophy.

Sarah shifted subtly, trying to edge away from Jacob without making it obvious, but the wagon's confined seating left her little room to maneuver.

Jacob took another swig from his flask, wiping his mouth with the back of his hand before chuckling lowly to Pete.

"Did ya see Nate's face this morning?" Jacob sneered, a smirk spreading across his features. "Like he'd swallowed a bug. Couldn't even muster up a word when I told him Sarah's riding with us."

Pete laughed, his eyes crinkling with amusement. "Yeah, he looked all kinds of defeated. Thought he was so high and mighty, our grand Wagon Master, but look at him now."

"Exactly!" Jacob exclaimed, his voice growing louder with his burgeoning bravado. "He thinks he's leading us? He couldn't even lead a horse to water."

Pete nodded, grinning as he glanced at Sarah, who was doing her best to appear absorbed in the passing scenery. "You've got him under your thumb now, Jacob. He'll think twice before crossing you again."

Jacob's laugh was harsh, filled with a vindictive pleasure. "He's nothing now. Just watch; I'll have this whole train dancing to my tune soon enough."

The conversation continued in this vein, each man feeding into the other's contempt for Nate, their voices blending mockery and misplaced triumph. Sarah sat quietly, each word a dagger, but she kept her gaze fixed on the horizon, the rolling hills a blank canvas against the turmoil inside her.

The only thing she could do was to keep reminding herself why she was enduring this—Nate. Knowing what Jacob and his friends had planned for him was a heavy burden she bore alone. If she had not agreed to this, to marry Jacob, who knew what lengths they might have gone to? A confrontation, even a violent clash, could have torn the wagon train apart, putting everyone at risk.

Still, the reality of her situation was harsh. With each passing mile, each unwanted touch from Jacob, the weight of her decision pressed down on her. She was trapped, not just on this wagon beside a man she despised but in a web of her own making. Her choices, once made to protect Nate, now felt like chains binding her to a life she never wanted.

The day wore on, the sun tracing its relentless path across the sky, and Sarah felt the distance growing not only between her and Nate, but between her and the woman that she was becoming. With each rotation of the wagon's wheels, she moved further from her past and deeper into a future she had never wished for. But it was a path she had chosen, a path paved with good intentions, however fraught with regret and sorrow it might be.

The wagon train came to a halt for the midday rest. Sarah scanned the camp for a glimpse of Nate, but he was conspicuously absent.

As she reluctantly picked at her food, Emma approached, her face lined with concern. "Sarah, can I have a moment with you? I'd like to check on you and the baby," she said softly, eyeing Jacob and Pete warily.

Jacob rolled his eyes, irritation flashing across his face. "We're eating," he said dismissively. "Go away."

Sarah suddenly felt a surge of protectiveness over her only ally. "Don't be rude, Jacob," she snapped. "Emma is only trying to help."

Jacob's eyes flashed in anger.

"Don't you care about the baby?" Sarah said, her voice softening. "About my health?"

Grudgingly, Jacob waved a dismissive hand. "Fine, go then. But don't take all day," he muttered, returning to his meal with a scowl.

Grateful for the escape, Sarah quickly followed Emma to her wagon, a safe haven from the oppressive atmosphere at the lunch spot. Once inside, Emma gently examined Sarah, her hands skilled and reassuring as she checked the baby's health.

As she worked, Emma's expression turned serious. "Sarah, are you sure about marrying Jacob? After everything you've told me about him and Robert, why would you do this?" Her voice was soft but insistent, filled with worry and confusion.

Sarah sighed, the weight of her secret pressing down on her. She looked at Emma, her trusted friend, and contemplated whether to reveal the truth.

"You can tell me anything," Emma pressed. "You know that."

Sarah nodded, her bottom lip quivering. "I heard something," she said hesitantly, her voice barely above a whisper.

"What?" Emma asked, her voice low.

"The other night, I overheard Jacob and some of the men talking," Sarah continued. "They... they were planning to kill Nate. Make it look like an accident."

Emma gasped, her hands pausing on Sarah's belly. "Oh, Sarah... that's horrible. But, marrying Jacob—do you think that will stop them?"

Sarah met Emma's gaze, her eyes filled with uncertainty and fear. "I don't know, but I have to try. It seems like the only way to protect Nate, to keep him safe. He's done so much for us, for the wagon train. I can't just stand by and let something happen to him."

Emma nodded slowly, processing the heavy revelation. "This is a big burden for you to carry, Sarah. But you're not alone in this, remember that. We'll find another way, we must. Marrying Jacob can't be the solution."

Sarah felt a flicker of hope at Emma's words, her resolve strengthening. "Thank you, Emma. I needed to hear that."

As they left the wagon to return to the group, Sarah felt slightly lighter, bolstered by Emma's support.

***

The cool night air brushed against Sarah's face as she quietly slipped out from the confines of the wagon where Jacob lay, his snoring a harsh counterpoint to the gentle rustling of the night breeze. Clutching her shawl around her shoulders, she needed to stretch her legs, cramped and sore from the day's long ride and the tension that never quite left her body. The camp was quiet; most of its inhabitants already settled down for the night, lost in their own dreams or worries.

As she walked, her thoughts were on Nate, and then, as if she'd magically conjured him up, she caught sight of a solitary figure standing a short distance away, silhouetted against the pale glow of the moon. Nate's posture relaxed yet somehow laden with a heaviness she could feel even from afar. He stood with his back to her, his shoulders broad and strong yet bearing an invisible weight. For a moment, Sarah allowed herself to admire him, the line of his back, the way he seemed so firmly a part of this wild landscape.

The longing to go to him, to wrap her arms around him and forget everything else, was overwhelming. But she couldn't do that. So instead, she turned away from him, but as she did, her boot caught on a twig, snapping it sharply underfoot. The sound shattered the silence, and Nate turned quickly.

"Sarah?" he said, his voice tinged with concern, cutting through the stillness. "You shouldn't be wandering around at night on your own."

She turned to him, managing a small, sad smile. "I just needed a walk," she confessed.

Nate glanced around, then back at her. "Where's Jacob?" he asked, his voice hard.

"Asleep… Drunk," she replied, her voice low.

A shadow passed over Nate's face, but he said nothing.

"I didn't see you much today," Sarah said.

"I was busy," Nate replied shortly.

Sarah stepped closer, her heart aching to bridge the distance between them. "Nate?" she ventured, her voice barely above a whisper.

But he shook his head, stepping back slightly. "I can't do this, Sarah. Seeing you with him…" His words trailed off, laden with pain and resignation.

Sarah's heart sank, her arms falling limply to her sides. "I am sorry," she said, the words sounding hollow despite how much she meant them.

Nate's shoulders stiffened.

"Maybe you're right. Maybe it's for the best," he said, his tone flat. "I never wanted a wife and child anyway. I'm better off alone."

The pain was sharp, and her throat was tight with unshed tears. Sarah opened her mouth to say something but could not find the words.

"I should get back," Nate said.

Without another word, Nate turned away, and it felt as if the ground had been pulled out from beneath her. His words echoed in her mind, a cold, sharp blade cutting through her heart. The finality in his tone was like a death knell, resonating with a deep, painful truth she hadn't wanted to face.

She had always seen Nate as a pillar of strength and integrity, a man who had been there for her when she needed him most. He had saved her, protected her, and shown her a glimpse of a future she had thought was out of reach. But now, his words shattered that image, revealing a different reality. Maybe he was never the man she thought he was. Maybe he was just another person who couldn't commit, who was afraid to truly care.

Her heart ached with a profound sense of betrayal. She had let herself believe in him, in them. The hurt was almost unbearable, a sharp, relentless pain that left her feeling hollow and abandoned.

A wave of bitterness washed over her. How could he turn his back on her so easily, leaving her to face an uncertain future alone? She had hoped he would fight for her, for their love, but instead, he had chosen the easy way out, retreating into his solitude and fear.

Sarah felt a tightening in her chest, the weight of his rejection pressing down on her. She had to remind herself to breathe, to hold onto the strength she had found within herself. She had faced so much already, and she would face this too. But the pain of his words, the sense of being unwanted and unworthy, was a burden she hadn't anticipated.

After a long moment, Sarah turned slowly and returned to the wagon, each step heavier than the last.

Chapter Twenty-Four

Nate sat outside his wagon, an old rag in hand as he methodically polished his boots, the leather slowly regaining its sheen under his careful ministrations. It was a mundane task, yet it offered a brief respite from his thoughts, a momentary focus amid the chaos of his mind that threatened to unravel the life he'd built for himself.

As Nate worked, his gaze drifted across the campfire, where the usual evening gathering had formed. The laughter and chatter were distant to his ears, overshadowed by the sight of Jacob, bottle in hand, raucously laughing with some of the men. Beside him, Sarah sat, her posture rigid, her face a mask of forced neutrality. Every so often, she would offer a small nod or a tight-lipped smile, but her eyes were distant, her spirit seemingly miles away from the jovial scene around her.

It was torture for Nate to have to watch them together. He remembered the words he had spoken to her that night under the moonlight, meant to push her away and make her think he didn't care. He had thought it was for the best, to make her marriage to Jacob easier, perhaps to make his own heartache more bearable. But he regretted those words now, regretted the pain he had seen flicker across her face, the way her shoulders had slumped as if he had physically wounded her.

Nate was lost in thought when Mary approached quietly and sat beside him. They hadn't spoken much in the past week, not since their tense conversation about Sarah's decision to marry Jacob.

Mary glanced over at where Sarah sat, and she sighed softly before turning to Nate. The deep wrinkles around her eyes and mouth were more pronounced in the dancing light of the campfire. "She's lookin' a lot like she did when we set off on this trail, doesn't she? Dwindled to a wee spark."

Nate's gaze followed Mary's, observing Sarah from across the fire again. He turned back to Mary. "Do you think it's my fault?" he asked, his voice laden with guilt.

Mary was silent for a long moment, but it spoke volumes.

Nate exhaled deeply, the weight of his decisions pressing down on him. "I don't know if I'm doing the right thing," he murmured, more to himself than to Mary.

Mary leaned in slightly, her voice soft but firm. "Sometimes the right thing doesn't clear the storm. It just gets ye through it."

Her words resonated with him, stirring something deep within. "I just..."

Nate's voice trailed off as he shook his head. Was he making the wrong choice?

Mary watched him for a moment, then spoke again. "The only way ye can protect the lass is to get her away from him before he consumes her entirely."

Nate looked up, meeting her eyes, the gravity of her words sinking in. "I know, Mary. It's just—"

"No justs, Nathaniel," she said, cutting him off. "Ye've seen what he's like. That man's darkness, it'll smother all the light in her. If ye care for her, if ye truly do, then ye'll fight to pull her back from that brink."

Nate sighed, running his hand through his short, dark hair. "She made this choice," he said. "She is choosin' to marry Jacob."

"Aye," Mary agreed. "But did ye ever stop to ask yourself why?"

Nate frowned. "She told me why because it's the right thing to do, the respectable thing. She's tryin' to keep the peace for the group... the greater good."

Mary scoffed. "And ye believe that?"

Nate said nothing. The truth was that Sarah's decision to marry Jacob had hurt him, and he retreated too quickly. Afraid of being hurt more.

"No," Nate admitted.

"Then ye need to talk to her," Mary insisted. "Fight for her."

"And what about Jacob, the others who follow him?"

"We've faced bigger challenges than that man," Mary said.

Nate said nothing for a moment. "He won't give her up without a fight."

"Aye," Mary agreed.

Nate stared into the flickering flames again, his thoughts turbulent as he considered the implications of standing up to Jacob.

"I am just worried about what a fight would mean for everyone else in the wagon train," he said. "We're supposed to be a community, but this could tear us apart."

Mary nodded, understanding the weight of his concerns. "Aye, it might come to that. But some things are worth fighting for, Nate. Sarah's safety, her well-being and the bairn's—ye canna let fear of disruption stop ye from doing what's right. And ye won't be alone in this."

Nate looked at her, the fear of potential consequences clear in his eyes. “But what if people get hurt?”

Mary reached over, placing a steady hand on his shoulder. “Nate, ye’ve led these people through thick and thin. They trust ye more than ye know. If it comes to a head with Jacob, they’ll see the truth of it. They’ll stand by ye.”

Nate exhaled deeply. He wanted to believe her, but he was doubtful.

“Ye need to act,” Mary pressed. “Leavin’ her with Jacob and lettin’ her marry him just to keep the peace is not looking out for her best interests. It’s puttin’ a bandage over a wound that’s festerin’. Ye know it, I know it.”

Nate absorbed her words, the truth in them resonant and clear.

“Real courage is about standin’ up against the darker battles that threaten what’s good in our lives. And Sarah, she’s good, through and through.”

Nate said nothing as Mary put a hand on his arm again. “Think about it, lad.”

Without another word, Mary stood to leave; Nate sat by the fire for a while longer, his mind racing. He knew Mary was right. He’d made a vow a long time ago to protect Sarah and the baby, and he was nothing if not a man of his word. Tomorrow, he would talk to Sarah, really talk, and whatever came of it, he would make sure she knew he was truly there for her.

***

Nate gripped the reins tightly as the wagon train made its way along the precarious trail. He kept a vigilant eye on the path ahead. The recent rains had left the ground treacherous, with deep muddy patches and large holes that could easily trap a wagon wheel.

"Watch the road closely! Mind the holes!" he called back over his shoulder, his firm and clear voice carrying back along the line of wagons.

The words had just left his mouth when a sudden commotion erupted from somewhere in the middle of the train. The jarring noise of a wagon jerking violently pulled Nate's attention away from the path ahead. He shouted for the train to halt and jumped down, his boots landing in the mud, as he sprinted back toward the source of the disturbance.

As he approached, his heart sank. Sarah lay crumpled on the side of the road in the grass, her face contorted in pain. Emma was already by her side, her skilled hands moving quickly to assess Sarah's condition and, more critically, the baby's state.

Fueled by fear and anger, Nate's gaze quickly found Pete, who had been driving the wagon from which Sarah had fallen. In two long strides, he reached Pete and grabbed him by the collar of his shirt, pulling him close.

"Didn't you hear me?" he snarled. "To mind the holes?"

"I-I-I," Pete spluttered, his rodent-like face turning puce.

Suddenly, Nate felt a calming hand on his back—Elijah. "Easy, Nate," he urged softly.

Realizing that all eyes were on him, Nate released his grip on Pete. The man fell back, coughing and wheezing. Nate gave him one last hard glance before he turned back to Sarah.

"How is she?" he asked.

Emma looked up at him. “She’s all right,” she said, her voice steady despite the chaos. “Just a bit shaken, but the baby seems fine.”

Before Nate could say anything, Jacob emerged from the back of the wagon, disheveled and reeking of alcohol. He staggered slightly as he took in the scene.

“What’s going on here?” He blinked blearily, trying to focus. “Why are we stopped?”

Jacob’s drunken state only fueled Nate’s anger.

“You’re supposed to be lookin’ after her,” Nate hissed, his eyes glinting dangerously.

Jacob’s expression hardened. “It ain’t my fault she went and fell off the wagon.”

Nate took a step forward, his hands balled into fists at his side. He held Jacob’s gaze, his anger rising like bile in his throat.

“Nathaniel,” Mary said. “We should assess the damage to the wagon.”

It took every bit of self-control Nate possessed to turn away from Jacob. He met Mary’s eye and gave a curt nod.

“I am goin’ back to bed,” Jacob grumbled.

A short while later, Nate wiped the sweat from his brow as he supervised the repairs on the broken wagon wheel, the sun beating down relentlessly. Thomas and Elijah were deep in their work, their skilled hands making quick work of the task. The rest of the train had sought out patches of shade and now sat waiting. There was no sign of Jacob or Pete.

As he handed Thomas a tool, Nate's gaze drifted across the camp to where Sarah sat in the shade of a tree with Emma at her side.

"You've got this?" Nate asked.

Thomas nodded, and Nate turned to go. He walked over to Sarah, and they looked up as he approached.

"May I have a word?" Nate asked.

Emma got up. "I'll fetch you some water."

Nate waited until Emma was out of earshot.

"Are you all right?" he asked.

"I think so," Sarah said, her face pale. "A little sore."

Nate's heart was in his throat as he met her eyes. He took a deep breath. "I need to talk to you. It's important."

Just then, Nate heard gravel crunch underfoot. He turned to see Jacob, who was squinting at them suspiciously.

"Wagon's fixed," he said, crossing his arms.

Nate nodded as he looked back at Sarah again, but he knew Jacob would not leave them alone.

"Right," Nate said. "Well, we should get back on the road. Are you sure you are well enough to travel?"

"She's fine," Jacob said, answering for her.

"I wasn't askin' you," he challenged.

Jacob took a step forward.

"I am fine, Nate," Sarah said. "I promise."

Nate looked at her, his eyes full of tenderness, wishing he could just take her in his arms and hold her.

Just then, Emma appeared and helped Sarah to her feet. Jacob turned and followed them back to the wagon. As Nate watched them go, the knots in his stomach tightened. Would he ever get a chance to speak with Sarah? What with Jacob always lurking in the shadows?

Nate sighed deeply as he turned and headed back to his wagon. He wasn't going to give up. But he needed a plan to get Jacob out of the way for just long enough that he could talk to Sarah without being interrupted.

"Nate?"

He turned to see Emma approaching.

"What is it?" he asked. "Is it Sarah? The baby?"

"They're fine," Emma said. "Well, as fine as they can be given the circumstances."

Nate grimaced.

"There is something I need to tell you," Emma said, lowering her voice.

Nate said nothing as he waited for her to continue. She glanced nervously over her shoulder, worried someone else might overhear them.

"I know the real reason Sarah agreed to marry Jacob."

Chapter Twenty-Five

As the evening settled over the camp, a tense atmosphere enveloped Sarah, Jacob, and Pete in their wagon. Sarah was thinking about Nate. He'd tried to talk to her earlier. What had he wanted to say?

"He had no right to grab Pete like that," Jacob slurred, his voice thick with resentment. "He should've taken us on a different road. It's his fault for leading us through that mess."

"There wasn't another road," Sarah said. "The road is the road."

Jacob turned to her, his expression darkening dangerously. "What did you just say?" he demanded, his voice low and menacing.

Sarah met his gaze. "It wasn't Nate's fault. We all saw the road—there was no other way."

Jacob's face twisted into an even more menacing scowl. "Don't you defend that man in front of me," he snapped, his tone venomous. "He's responsible for Robert's death. Everything wrong here is because of him."

"It was an accident," Sarah retorted.

Jacob's anger flared out of control as he grabbed Sarah's wrist violently, his grip tight and painful. "I never asked for your opinion," he hissed, his breath foul with alcohol. "Keep your mouth shut."

Sarah winced, the pain in her wrist sharp as she tried to pull away. "Jacob, you're hurting me," she pleaded, her voice strained with both fear and pain.

"Maybe you should let her go," Pete said, his voice wavering. "She is pregnant, after all..."

Pete's voice trailed off, and he swallowed nervously, his Adam's apple bobbing.

Jacob shot a furious glare at Pete. "Mind your own business," he snapped, but his grip on Sarah's wrist did not loosen.

Jacob turned his attention back to Sarah, his anger not abated. "You probably fell out of the wagon on purpose, just to make me look bad," Jacob accused, his logic twisted by drunkenness. "Hoped your hero Nate would come runnin' to your rescue, that it?"

Sarah's heart raced, panic setting in as she realized her precarious situation. Jacob's grip was a painful reminder of the control he believed he had over her, mirroring her helplessness. The night around them seemed to close in, the sounds of the camp distant as she faced the immediate threat alone.

"Jacob," Sarah said, trying to keep her voice level. "Please."

She held his gaze, and after a moment, he let go of her wrist.

"Let's go get somethin' to eat," he said.

Sarah hardly touched her supper, the food turning to sawdust in her mouth. Every now and again, the baby turned over; the feeling had brought Sarah so much comfort only a couple of weeks ago but now made a lump rise in her throat. She'd convinced herself that Jacob was better than Robert, that his love for her would make him kinder somehow. But she'd quickly come to realize how foolish she'd been. He was worse than Robert in some ways. His mood swings were unpredictable, veering from anger to an unsettling, sentimental soppiness.

Sitting close beside Sarah, Jacob's arm slung heavily around her shoulders, he leaned uncomfortably close. "I felt so bad seeing you on the ground today, Sarah," he slurred, his breath heavy with the smell of whiskey. "It just broke my heart, you know?"

Sarah tensed under his touch, her stomach churning as he continued, oblivious to her discomfort.

"We're gonna have a good life together, you and me. And the little one," Jacob mumbled, trying to sound affectionate but only managing to deepen the dread pooling inside her. His vision of their future, spoken with such a drunken, misguided earnestness, made her feel even more trapped and desperate for a way out.

"And when we are all settled in California, we can have more babies," Jacob said. "*Our* babies."

Sarah's stomach churned at his words. The way he said "our" babies sent a cold shiver down her spine. The very idea of having more children with Jacob, of being bound to him forever, filled her with a deep sense of dread.

As she sat there, the fire casting flickering shadows around them, Sarah's mind raced with thoughts and emotions. She had come to see just how complicated Jacob's feelings for Robert truly were. As the younger brother, Jacob always looked up to him and did his bidding. But beneath that admiration had been a seething cauldron of envy, jealousy, and anger.

With Robert gone, Jacob saw an opportunity to step out of his brother's shadow to take what he believed was rightfully his. But his way of doing it was twisted and wrong. He wasn't just trying to build a life; he was trying to reshape the past and create a future that would erase his feelings of inadequacy and failure. His desire to have their babies was part of his need to assert his dominance, to claim something that had always been out of his reach. It wasn't about love or family but power and control. And that terrified her.

She looked a cross at Jacob, seeing the mix of longing and determination in his eyes. He was desperate to prove himself, to create a life that would validate his existence. But in doing so, he was willing to trample over her feelings, desires, and dreams.

As they finished their meal, Sarah felt almost relieved when Samuel and Elijah approached their wagon, though she knew Jacob's mood could turn on a dime. The two men looked hesitant but determined as they stopped by Jacob, their hats in their hands.

"Jacob, we need help securing the livestock. Coyotes have been heard nearby," Samuel explained, his tone respectful but firm.

Jacob scowled, annoyed at being asked to do anything after his meal. "Can't you see I'm busy here?" he growled, gesturing sloppily toward Sarah.

Elijah, quick on his feet, chimed in. "We sure could use a strong man like you, Jacob. No one knows how to handle a rifle under the moon like you do," he said, with a tone that played to Jacob's ego.

Visibly preening under the praise, Jacob's expression softened. "Well, when you put it that way... All right, I'll help out," he conceded, pushing himself up with a grunt. Turning to Sarah, his voice was dismissive. "Go to bed; I'll be there soon."

Sarah nodded silently, watching as Jacob stumbled off with Samuel and Elijah. When Jacob's back was turned, she felt a breath she hadn't realized she'd been holding escape her lips.

After a few moments, Sarah pushed herself to her feet. She walked slowly toward the wagon, her hands wrapped tightly around her growing stomach. As she neared her bedroll, preparing to settle down for the night, approaching footsteps halted her. She guessed it was Jacob returning, but her heart skipped when she saw Nate's tall figure emerging from the shadows. The lamplight cast a soft glow on his face, highlighting the stern set of his jaw and the deep furrows of worry etched across his brow.

"Nate," she said softly.

"Why are you really marrying Jacob?" he asked, his green eyes searching hers, intense and probing. "You don't have to do this."

Sarah wrapped her arms around herself again, suddenly vulnerable under his gaze. "It's the most respectable thing to do," she repeated, though her voice wavered, betraying her uncertainty.

Nate's expression hardened, and he took a step closer. "Hang respectability," he said firmly, his voice tinged with frustration. "I can see what he's doing to you, Sarah. It's just like what Robert did, isn't it? Controlling, isolating..."

Sarah's eyes filled with tears, her heart pounding in her chest. She looked down at the ground, unable to hold his gaze. Nate gently lifted her chin with his hand, forcing her to look at him.

"I know the real reason you agreed to marry him," he continued, his voice softer.

Sarah's breath caught in her throat, her eyes wide with surprise and a flicker of fear.

"I know about their plans... Jacob and the others were scheming to kill me, make it look like an accident," Nate confessed, watching her closely for her reaction. "But I can't let you sacrifice yourself for me, Sarah. Not like this."

Sarah's defenses broke down, her voice trembling as she responded. "Nate, you've saved me countless times since we've been on this trail. And not just in the physical sense," she admitted, her eyes glistening with unshed tears. "You made me feel as if I were worth saving. How is it fair that I can't do the same for you?"

Nate's face softened. He reached out, his hands gently grasping her shoulders. "Because marrying Jacob is not saving me," he said. "It's destroying you. And I can't stand by and watch that happen. I care too much about you to let you walk into a fire for me."

Sarah's heart thudded painfully as she met Nate's earnest gaze. In that moment, she couldn't help but reflect on Nate's previous attempts to push her away. At the time, his words had stung deeply, leaving her feeling rejected and confused. She had wondered if she had misjudged him, if the man she thought she knew was different from reality.

But now, she saw things more clearly. Nate's actions hadn't been about her; they had been about him. He had been trying to protect himself, to shield his heart from the potential pain of loss. She understood that now. He had been hurt before, and his way of coping had been to build walls around himself, to push people away before they could get too close. Despite his efforts, though, he had never truly been able to distance himself from her. Time and again, he had come to her aid, saved her from danger, and stood by her side through thick and thin. His attempts to keep her at arm's length had ultimately failed because his true nature shone through every time.

Nate was a man of integrity, compassion, and deep, unwavering love. He had shown her strength when she had none, offered her comfort in moments of despair, and given her hope when she had felt hopeless. He was everything she had believed him to be from the beginning and more.

As Sarah continued to look into Nate's eyes, the intensity of his concern and the sincerity in his voice made her resolve waver. Yet she was scared. Could there really be another way to protect him without losing herself in the process?

"Nate—"

Just then, Nate leaned in, closing the final space as their lips met in a kiss that was both comforting and promising. The kiss was soft and careful but also spoke of protection, shared burdens, and a future they dared to shape together despite the lingering shadows.

After a moment, Nate pulled away.

"I won't let you do this," he said firmly. "We'll find another way together."

"How?" she whispered, her voice barely audible. "How will we get me out of this marriage to Jacob?"

"I have an idea."

Chapter Twenty-Six

Nate took a deep breath, the weight of her question settling heavily on his shoulders. He'd been turning over their situation in his mind, wrestling with the complexities of their predicament.

“I've been thinking about it,” he began, his voice low and earnest, “and there's no clean way out. If we confront this head-on here, it could lead to a fight; there is no doubt that Jacob will retaliate. I'm not worried for myself but for you, the baby, and everyone else in camp.”

He paused, searching her eyes. “Can you keep this up until we reach the next supply stop? It's not far, just a few days' travel. There, we can make sure Jacob and anyone loyal to him are left behind. It's the only way to ensure no one gets hurt.”

Sarah's expression hardened with determination, a silent strength radiating from her. “I can do it,” she said, her voice steady despite the fear Nate knew she felt. “I can keep it going.”

Nate reached out, gently cupping her cheek, his thumb brushing softly against her skin. “I know you can. You are the strongest person I’ve ever met.”

Sarah closed her eyes for a moment.

“Sarah,” Nate said.

She opened her eyes again.

“I'm in love with you.”

Her brown eyes widened with a flash of surprise, and something deeper flickered within them. But before either could speak further, the sound of footsteps and the murmur of Jacob's voice fractured the moment. Nate's heart sank as the real world rushed back in. He stepped back, his figure retreating into the shadows just as Jacob staggered into the clearing, his eyes searching.

"Sarah? There you are!" Jacob called out, loud and oblivious to the tension he had interrupted.

Sarah turned toward Jacob, her face composed into a mask of neutrality as Nate disappeared completely into the night. Hidden in darkness, Nate watched for a moment longer, his heart aching to stay by her side, yet knowing he must wait for the right moment to act.

As he returned to his own campsite, Nate's mind was a whirl of plans and possibilities. Nate had no idea if their plan would work, but one thing was clear: he would do whatever it took to protect Sarah and the baby.

***

A few restless days had passed since Nate confessed his love to Sarah, each passing moment marked by the tension of their secret plan and the poignant undercurrent of their newly acknowledged feelings. Despite the strain of watching Sarah maintain her façade with Jacob, Nate found hope in their shared glances and the fleeting touches they exchanged whenever they could steal a moment away from prying eyes.

Standing at the outskirts of the camp, pretending to check the riggings on one of the wagons, Nate allowed himself a glance toward Sarah. She was helping to distribute the evening meal, her movements slow and clumsy as she maneuvered around her swollen belly. Jacob was talking too loudly to Curtis, not paying Sarah any mind. Just then, Nate caught her eye, and a silent communication passed between them—a reassurance, a promise. His heart quickened, and he felt the corners of his mouth lift in a small, involuntary smile.

"Sarah?" Jacob barked. "Where's my supper?"

Nate turned back to his task, his hands working automatically.

"Nathaniel," Mary said.

He turned to find the older woman walking toward him with a plate.

"You missed dinner," she said.

"Sorry," Nate apologized. "I was distracted—"

"Aye," Mary said, raising an eyebrow. "But I dinnae think it was those riggins that made you forget your empty belly."

Nate frowned. He hadn't told anyone about his plan or conversation with Sarah the other night. However, he should have guessed Mary would figure something was up; nothing ever went unnoticed by her.

"Dinnae fash," Mary said, smiling. "Jacob pays more attention to his whiskey bottle than anything else, thank heavens. But what are ye planning, laddie?"

Nate exhaled slowly. "To leave Jacob and his friends at the next stop. To continue the journey without them."

Mary nodded. "Aye, although you won't get rid of him easily."

"No," Nate agreed. "But it's the safest route. We're close to the next stop. I just need to keep my distance a while longer. But it's hard, now that..."

"Now what?" Mary prodded gently, leaning in slightly, her eyes soft yet curious.

Nate paused, the words catching in his throat before tumbling out. "Now that I've told Sarah I'm in love with her."

Mary's face broke into a warm, understanding smile. "Ah, Nate, I'm proud of ye," she said, her voice rich with affection. "It's about time ye admitted how ye feel. It's no small thing to acknowledge yer heart, especially in times like these."

He didn't regret telling Sarah that he loved her. If anything, the admission had liberated something within him, a part of his soul that he'd restrained for too long under the guise of duty and self-preservation. Acknowledging his love for Sarah had shifted something fundamental in his perspective. Yet the truth was that he'd got so caught up in Sarah, in his feelings for her, that he hadn't stopped to consider what would happen when all this trouble with Jacob was over.

"It's scary," Nate admitted. "All this unchartered territory."

"Aye," Mary agreed, her gaze steady and reassuring. "But you are no stranger to unchartered territory."

Nate scratched the stubble on his chin thoughtfully. "I've charted a lot of rugged terrain in my days," he said, his voice reflecting his uncertainty. "But navigating love? That's territory I'm not sure I know how to handle. Can I really have this life and Sarah? She's known so much hardship. I don't even know if she would want to stay on the Trail and raise a baby out here. It's not exactly a good place for children."

Mary listened intently, her expression softening with empathy as Nate voiced his doubts.

"My husband and I chose the Trail over startin' our own family. It was our choice, and I never regretted it until after he passed. Then I found myself all alone," she admitted, a hint of sadness threading through her words. “It's not an easy life, but it was ours, and it was full until it wasn’t.”

Nate nodded slowly, absorbing her words. “When I told Sarah I was in love with her, I didn’t stop to think about it, but now I don't know how I can give up all this. The open skies, the feeling of the whole world stretching out before me. I love her, Mary, but this is the only life I’ve known for so long.”

Mary smiled gently at him, placing a reassuring hand on his arm. “Laddie, ye don’t have to decide everything at once. Try takin’ on one challenge at a time,” she advised. “And talk to Sarah. Together, ye can figure out what’s best for both of ye. Maybe there’s a way to blend both worlds, or maybe ye'll find a new path altogether."

It was true; he didn’t need all the answers right now. What he needed was to open up to Sarah, share his fears and dreams, and see how they might build a future together that respected both their needs.

“Ye’ll find your way, lad. Ye always do.”

Later, as the camp settled down for the night and the sounds of conversation and laughter faded into the soft crackling of the campfire, Nate walked a little ways off from the others. He stood looking up at the stars, contemplating the vast, uncharted paths of his future.

The quiet of the night was usually soothing to Nate, but that evening, he felt burdened. He had confronted his feelings for Sarah, been honest about how he felt, and was proud of himself for finally being able to let someone in. Yet, he didn’t know anything other than being a Wagon Master. What would he do if he wasn’t one anymore?

What made it worse was that Nate wished he could just talk to Sarah and ask her what she thought their future might look like. But he couldn't, at least not yet.

***

The following day, Nate stood at the edge of the wagon train, peering out over the vast expanse of the Great Plains. The air was unusually still, and the sounds of rustling grass and chirping birds were ominously absent. The sky, usually a clear, boundless blue, was now tinged with a yellowish hue, a stark warning of the changing weather conditions.

He felt a sense of unease; the stillness was like the deep breath before a plunge. As he scanned the horizon, he noticed a faint haze beginning to form in the distance, the landscape slowly blurring under a growing veil of dust. The atmosphere felt charged, heavy with the scent of dry earth, a telltale sign that a dust storm was brewing.

Turning back to the camp, Nate saw Elijah checking the harnesses on his horses, ensuring everything was secure. Deciding to voice his concerns, Nate approached him, his boots kicking up small puffs of dust that lingered in the air, reluctant to settle back to the ground.

"Elijah," Nate called out, his voice carrying a slight edge of urgency. Elijah turned, his face marked with lines of experience, eyes squinting slightly against the strange light.

"Nate, what's up?" Elijah responded, wiping his hands on his trousers.

"Look at the sky, the stillness. Somethin's brewing," Nate said, nodding toward the horizon where the haze had thickened, slowly advancing toward them.

Elijah followed Nate's gaze, his expression turning contemplative. "Yeah, you might be right. This quiet is unnerving. Haven't seen birds in a bit, either. We better prepare the wagons and tighten everything down."

Nate nodded in agreement, his mind racing through the necessary preparations. "We should cover the supplies, make sure nothing's exposed, and tell everyone to wrap their faces and protect their lungs. The last thing we need is folks choking on dust."

Elijah clapped Nate on the shoulder, a grim smile on his face. "I'll round up some men and start securing the camp. You warn the families, get them ready."

As Nate moved through the camp, alerting the families and helping to secure personal belongings, the wind began to pick up, a sudden gust that hinted at the storm's imminent arrival. The sky darkened further, the yellow deepening to an almost sinister ochre.

Nate found Emma in her wagon. "Emma, a dust storm's blowin' in. Will you stay with Sarah?"

"'Course," Emma said.

Nate nodded in gratitude as he turned to go. People were rushing around, their clothes covering their mouths and noses. Some were shepherding children under the cover of their wagons, and others were draping blankets over the openings of their wagons. The animals, sensing the change, were growing restless.

"Thomas, Sam," Nate called over the wind. "Will you try to calm them?"

By the time the first real blast of wind hit, laden with fine grit, the camp was as prepared as possible. Nate stood with Elijah, both men facing the oncoming storm, their faces wrapped in cloth to protect against the biting sand.

Suddenly, Pete appeared, a frown on his rattish face.

"What is it?" Nate asked.

"It's Jacob," Pete said.

Nate frowned, squinting against the wind and dust.

"He's not here," Pete said.

"Well, where is he?" Nate said.

"He went off huntin'," Pete explained. "Said he was tired of all this women's food and needed some real meat."

Nate sighed heavily. *Trust Jacob to go off and get caught in a dust storm.*

"Well, with any luck, he'll find a place to take shelter," Elijah said.

"You ain't gonna do anythin'?" Pete asked.

"No man with any sense will go out in this," Elijah shouted over the howling wind, his voice barely audible. "I hope the meat was worth it."

Pete looked at Nate, but Nate said nothing. Elijah was right. The second you stepped out of camp, you'd be entirely blind, unable to see anything but dust or hear anything other than the wind. Jacob was on his own, and a small part of Nate, a part he did not wish to admit to himself, hoped that Jacob wouldn't make it back to camp.

Chapter Twenty-Seven

The dust storm raged with relentless ferocity, the wagons creaking and groaning under the strain. Inside the covered wagon, Sarah huddled next to Emma. Both women's faces were wrapped in damp cloths, trying in vain to filter the pervasive, fine dust that had invaded every nook and cranny. Despite their efforts, the air was thick with grit, making each breath a laborious effort.

Sarah coughed harshly, the dust irritating her throat and lungs, making breathing increasingly difficult. Emma adjusted Sarah's cloth, trying to provide better coverage.

“Breathe slowly,” Emma instructed gently, her voice muffled but firm. “And try to stay calm.”

Through the dim light filtering through the covered wagon, Sarah's eyes met Emma's, filled with worry and discomfort. “Have you ever seen a storm this bad before?" Sarah asked, her voice raspy as she struggled to keep the panic from her tone.

Emma shook her head, her eyes scanning the small space they occupied. “I've seen dust storms, but nothing like this,” she admitted.

The wagon shifted slightly, and a groan of wood accompanying the movement added to the eerie atmosphere. Sarah's thoughts turned to Jacob, who had gone off hunting when the storm hit.

Just before he’d gone hunting, they’d been sitting around the fire. Jacob had been grumbling about the cooking, about wanting some real meat for a change.

“I’m sick of these rations,” he had complained. “We need some real meat.”

"We're doing the best we can with what we have," Sarah had replied calmly, trying to keep the peace. "It's not easy out here."

Jacob had shut her down with a dismissive wave of his hand. "I'm sick of the Trail, sick of living like this."

Sarah had noticed the clouds gathering on the horizon and the wind picking up. There was tension in the air, a sense of impending change. "I think a storm might be coming," she had said, her voice tinged with concern.

"Oh, so you're an expert now, are you? A storm expert?" Jacob had mocked her, his tone dripping with sarcasm.

Sarah had felt a pang of frustration. "I'm just saying we should be careful. It looks like it could get bad."

But Jacob had ignored her warnings and gone hunting anyway, determined to do things his way.

Now, a part of her, the darker part, couldn't help but feel a twinge of vindication at the thought of him caught in the storm's wrath.

"Emma, do you think Jacob found shelter?" Sarah asked.

Emma paused, her expression contemplative. "Part of me hopes not," she admitted, her voice low. "It's terrible to think that way, but..."

Emma shrugged, and Sarah nodded, understanding and sharing the sentiment.

"I know," she whispered, guilt mingling with a reluctant agreement. "Sometimes I wonder if the Trail might claim both brothers for its own. Would it be so wrong to wish that?"

The question hung in the air, heavy with the implications of her own hardships and losses at the hands of the two men. Emma reached out, her hand finding Sarah's in the dimness.

“The Trail takes a lot from us all,” she said softly. “But it also shows us our strengths. And sometimes, maybe it does claim its own kind of justice.”

As the storm continued to howl outside, Sarah felt a tiny, fierce spark of hope flicker within her. The idea that perhaps nature itself could reset the balance that the likes of Jacob had so disrupted was a comforting thought amid the chaos. Yet despite this spark of hope, Sarah could not ignore the pit in her stomach. After everything she’d experienced, she knew life was rarely fair.

The relentless wind finally ceased its howling, though for how long it had been raging, Sarah could not say. The silence that followed felt almost surreal, the sudden stillness heavy with the echoes of the storm. She and Emma blinked against the dust that hung in the air inside the wagon.

Suddenly, Nate appeared at the opening of the wagon, peering inside with concern etched into his strong features. His dark hair was brown with dust that also clung to his lashes and eyebrows.

“The worst of it is over,” he announced, his voice a welcome sound in the aftermath of the storm's fury.

“Good,” Emma said in relief.

“How are you holding up?” he asked, his eyes finding Sarah's.

“Fine,” she replied, though her voice was breathy and strained from the dust and stress.

Nate turned to Emma, his tone gentle. "Would you mind checking on the others? Make sure everyone is all right?"

Emma nodded and quickly left.

Once Emma had stepped out, Sarah's gaze met Nate's, heavy with questions. "Is there any sign of Jacob?" she asked, her voice low.

Nate shook his head grimly. "No sign yet," he said, his expression somber.

For a second, neither spoke, but they were thinking the same thing—wondering silently about Jacob's fate amidst the storm's chaos.

"Can I get out?" Sarah asked.

Nate nodded as he put out his hand.

Sarah stepped out of the wagon, her movements cautious as she assessed the aftermath. The air outside was thick with lingering dust. Visibility was still reduced to a few feet ahead. Nate stood close by her side.

"It might be like this for a few hours, maybe days," he said. "It's hard to tell with these storms."

Sarah said nothing, her throat like sandpaper.

Looking out over the camp, Nate said, "Visibility is still too low to move safely. We'll have to stay put until it clears."

Sarah's heart sank at the thought. They were so close to their next stop, so close to potentially executing their plan to part ways with Jacob and his loyal followers. Any delay felt like a setback, a risk of prolonging the inevitable and possibly complicating their escape.

“I’ll do everything I can to get us moving as soon as it’s safe,” Nate promised, reading her thoughts. “We won’t stay put any longer than absolutely necessary.”

The aftermath of the dust storm left the camp looking like a scene from a forgotten battle. Wagons stood skewed and off-kilter, some with canvas coverings ripped or hanging loosely where the wind had been most merciless. The ground was a patchwork of trampled earth and deep ruts where the wagons had struggled against the storm. Even the hardiest among them looked visibly shaken as they moved about, assessing the damage and beginning the slow recovery process.

Sarah, her face still covered with a thin layer of dust, moved among the other settlers, offering help wherever she could. Her movements were mechanical but determined as she helped overturn a supply box. Every so often, her eyes would drift to the horizon, searching for any sign of Jacob, but the landscape remained eerily still, the horizon blurring into the dusty haze that hung heavy in the air.

As she lifted a wooden crate back onto a wagon, her back protested, a sharp reminder of the physical toll the past hours had taken. Despite this, she pushed on, her mind needing the distraction, her hands needing to be busy to stave off the worry that gnawed at her insides.

“Sarah, lass, ye need to take a wee rest now,” Mary said, her wrinkled face lined with fatigue, dust matted into her graying hair. “Ye've done more than enough here.”

Sarah shook her head, setting down the crate with a thud. “I need to keep busy, Mary. If I stop, I'll just start thinking about... everything.” Her voice trailed off as she glanced again toward the distant, empty trails leading into the camp.

Mary reached out, her hand firm but gentle on Sarah's arm. “I know ye want to help, and that’s noble, but ye mustn't forget ye're carrying a wee one there. Ye need to look after yerself first, and the bairn," she reminded her, her tone softening.

Sarah's resistance faltered, Mary's concern cutting through her resolve. She nodded slowly, the adrenaline that had fueled her actions ebbing away, leaving her suddenly exhausted. "Maybe you're right," she admitted, allowing Mary to lead her to a nearby seat under the shade of a still-standing wagon.

As Sarah sat, her body grateful for the rest, she watched as the camp slowly came back to life around her. Settlers patched up their wagons, children rounded up scattered livestock, and life, as it always did, found a way to persevere through hardship.

Her mind wandered as she watched the others, considering the possibility of Jacob not returning. It was a thought that brought a complex mix of relief and guilt. As she lost herself in these reflections, the realization of her feelings for Nate crystallized. He had told her he loved her, a confession made under the expansive starlit sky, and although she hadn't voiced her feelings then, the truth was undeniable in her heart. She loved him, too.

Just then, Nate approached, his figure weary but resolute, pulling Sarah from her thoughts. His face showed the strain of leadership and the burden of decisions yet to be made. He stopped before her, his eyes holding a mixture of concern and duty.

"Pete, Clint, and some others are organizing a search party for Jacob," Nate announced, his voice tinged with fatigue. "Elijah and I are going to lead them. We know the landscape best."

Sarah felt a surge of surprise, quickly followed by an understanding acceptance. Despite everything Jacob had done—his threats and the danger he posed—Nate's decision to join the search party was a testament to his character. It was just the kind of man Nate was: honorable to a fault, committed to protecting all members of their community, even those who had become adversaries.

"This is what makes you who you are," Sarah said softly, her voice carrying a mix of admiration and concern. "You'd walk to the ends of the earth to protect the people in this train, even if they are your worst enemy."

Nate gave a tired smile, a soft sigh escaping him. "It's my responsibility," he replied, the weight of his leadership role evident in his demeanor.

Sarah nodded as she chewed her bottom lip. "Be careful out there."

"I always am," Nate said.

As Nate turned to leave, preparing to join the search party, Sarah instinctively reached out and caught his hand. Their eyes locked, and the world around them paused for a brief, charged moment.

"I love you, too," she said, her voice low but imbued with deep conviction.

Nate's eyes widened slightly, the corners of his mouth lifting in a genuine smile. His grip tightened around her hand, silently acknowledging the significance of her words.

"I'll see you soon," he said.

With a final squeeze of her hand, Nate turned and walked away, joining the others as they prepared for the search.

Sarah watched him go, her heart filled with a bittersweet mixture of love and fear.

"How are you feelin'?" Emma asked.

Sarah turned to find her friend at her side.

"Better," Sarah admitted.

"That's good," Emma said.

"How are the others?" Sarah asked.

"Fine," Emma said. "Everyone seemed to pull through without much more than tight chests and scratchy throats."

Sarah nodded, relieved.

"I saw Nate heading off with the others," Emma noted.

Sarah pressed her lips together and then sighed shakily. "Do you think they will find him?"

Emma shrugged. "I don't know," she admitted.

As dusk settled over the camp, a soft, cleansing breeze began to disperse the last remnants of the dust that had hung stubbornly in the air. The atmosphere felt lighter, a tentative sense of normalcy returning after the storm's chaos. Sarah sat with Mary and Emma near a newly kindled campfire and watched the orange flames dance against the growing darkness. The day's events had left everyone drained, and the quiet of the evening was a welcome reprieve.

"It's getting dark," Sarah said, her voice tinged with concern.

"Dinnae fash, lass," Mary said, smiling at her. "Nate and Elijah know these lands like the backs of their hands."

Sarah nodded, trying not to worry, but how could she not?

Just then, Emma's attention shifted toward the outskirts of the camp. "They're back!" she announced, standing up to get a better look.

Sarah quickly rose, her heart pounding as she followed Emma's gaze. The returning group appeared through the fading light. She craned her neck as they approached, but it soon became evident that Jacob was not among them. The men were covered in dust and sweat, their faces etched with the fatigue of the fruitless search.

Nate walked slightly ahead of the others, his shoulders tense as he neared the women.

"Any sign of him?" Mary asked.

Nate shook his head grimly, his eyes briefly closing as he replied, "No, nothing. We searched as far as we could, called out, and checked any possible places he might have sought shelter. But there's no trace of him."

The group fell silent, the gravity of the situation settling over them. Sarah caught Nate's eye across the fire. In that glance, a world of emotions passed between them—relief, guilt, uncertainty. Her mind raced with the implications: *Is it over? Is Jacob truly gone from our lives?*

Nate walked over to where Sarah stood, his expression somber yet visibly relieved to see her safe. "It was gettin' late; we did everything we could," he said softly, his voice almost lost in the crackle of the fire.

Sarah nodded. "What happens now?" she asked, her voice barely a whisper.

"We wait," Nate replied. "If he's out there, he might still find his way back. If not..." He didn't finish the sentence, but he didn't need to. The unspoken words hung heavily in the air.

The possibility of moving on without Jacob was a liberating prospect that left a pang of gnawing guilt in the pit of Sarah's stomach. If Jacob were gone, just like Robert, it meant the potential end of a chapter filled with intimidation and fear. It would also mean the end of the Turner brothers, the men who had dominated and controlled her life for so long. But what if he did return? Would she be able to convince him of her relief? Or would he see right through her, see right through the lie?

Chapter Twenty-Eight

“We can't just leave,” Clint insisted, his voice firm and his brow furrowed with concern. “Jacob could still be out there. He could still be alive.”

Pete nodded in agreement, his arms crossed defensively. “Yeah, we need to keep looking. It ain't right to leave a man behind like this.”

Nate stood with Pete and Clint just outside the circle of wagons, the morning sun casting long shadows across the dusty camp. Tension hummed in the air like a taut wire as the two men faced him, their expressions a mix of frustration and defiance.

Nate exhaled deeply. He understood their concerns and loyalty to their friend, but as the leader, he had to consider the welfare of the entire group.

“It's been two days since the storm passed,” Nate countered, his voice steady despite the rising frustration. “We’ve searched as much as possible. We've called out and checked every possible shelter. At this point, it's likely Jacob is dead.”

Clint's expression darkened at Nate’s words. “Sounds like you're hoping that’s the case,” he snapped, a bitter edge to his tone.

Nate felt a surge of anger at the accusation. Had he not done enough to prove his leadership? Had he not been the one up at dawn leading the search for the past two days? It was then Nate realized he would never be able to prove to these men that he was a good leader, no matter what he did, and that was just how it was. So, instead, he’d stop wasting his breath and do what he did best: lead.

"We can't delay any longer," he said, his voice authoritative, cutting through the morning chill. "Our supplies are dwindling, and we're already behind schedule. We need to reach the next supply stop. We seriously can't delay further."

Nate paused for a moment. "I'm offering two horses to anyone who wishes to stay behind and continue the search. You can take enough supplies for a few days."

Pete and Clint exchanged a look, the weight of the decision pressing down on them. The offer was generous, considering the circumstances, and it put the responsibility of the choice squarely in their hands.

After a moment, Clint shook his head, his voice resigned. "No, we'll go with the train. But if we leave him behind, it's on you, Nate."

Nate nodded, accepting the burden. "I understand," he replied simply.

As they dispersed to prepare for departure, Nate felt the weight of leadership more acutely than ever. He knew not everyone would agree with his decisions, but he also knew that compromise and firmness were necessary to avoid running out of food and fresh water.

Turning back to the wagons, Nate took a deep breath, and as he did, Sarah approached.

"So?" she asked, her brown eyes wide.

"We're leavin'," Nate said.

Sarah nodded, her shoulders visibly relaxing.

"You want to ride with me?" Nate offered.

Sarah nodded, the corners of her mouth turning up.

“Come on,” Nate said, touching her back.

As the wagon train rolled forward, the rhythmic creaking of the wagons and the steady clip-clop of the horses' hooves against the rough trail provided a familiar soundtrack to Nate’s thoughts. With Jacob gone, everything was different.

Having Sarah back beside him on the wagon seat felt right, but Nate could not help but notice her silence, and he wondered what she was thinking.

“You all right?” Nate asked.

Sarah turned to him and nodded, a tight smile on her lips.

They fell silent again, and as the vast and open landscape stretched before them, Nate knew that this was the sense of freedom he had always cherished. Yet, as he glanced at Sarah, her thoughtful gaze on the horizon, he recognized the weight of new responsibilities and the contours of a future vastly different from what he had always imagined.

“Sarah,” Nate said.

She turned to him.

“I know we haven’t really had time to talk, not with everything goin’ on...”

His voice trailed off as he searched for the best way to say his thoughts.

“We’ve still got quite a journey ahead of us before we reach California,” Nate continued. “Chances are the baby will be born before we get there.”

Sarah nodded, her hand moving instinctively to her stomach.

"I've been thinkin' a lot about what happens when we reach the end," Nate said, pausing for a moment.

"It's all right, Nate," Sarah interjected. "I know you never planned for a wife and a baby. You love your freedom, and this... us... it's complicated."

Nate took a deep breath, her words hanging between them like the dust clouds left behind by the wagons.

"Well, that's just it," he admitted, his eyes fixed on the path ahead but his mind on their future. "The Trail is a dangerous place, too dangerous for a baby. I couldn't live with myself if something happened to you or the baby because of a choice I made."

Sarah nodded, absorbing his words, her expression a mix of understanding and concern.

"Sarah—"

But before he could say anything more, a person suddenly appeared on the road ahead. The figure was stumbling forward, dust-caked and disheveled, almost blending into the landscape.

Nate squinted, trying to discern the identity of this unexpected apparition. His hand instinctively moved to the reins to slow the wagon.

As they drew closer, the figure's features became clearer, and a shock of recognition jolted through him.

"It can't be," he muttered under his breath.

Just then, the figure raised his head, and Nate's heart sank. It was Jacob, somehow returned, his appearance as battered and worn as the desert itself.

Sarah gasped softly beside him, her hand reaching out to grasp his arm. “Is it—”

“Jacob,” Nate answered.

Nate brought the wagon to a shuddering stop; the sight of Jacob staggering on the road brought a hush over the nearby parts of the wagon train.

Nate quickly turned to Sarah, his expression firm. "Stay here," he instructed, his tone leaving no room for argument.

He climbed down from the wagon, his boots kicking up dust as he approached Jacob, who seemed on the verge of collapse. The man's clothes were torn and caked with dirt, his face sunburned and lined with exhaustion.

As Nate neared, Jacob's raspy voice broke the silence. “Water...”

Without hesitation, Nate hurried back to the wagon, fetching his canteen.

“Emma!” he called down the line of wagons. “Over here!”

Quickly returning to Jacob with the water, Nate supported him as he gulped down the liquid greedily, some of it spilling down his chin and dampening the dusty collar of his shirt. Emma arrived, and she and Nate helped Jacob get to a nearby tree, providing him shade and a place to sit.

The rest of the camp, alerted by the commotion, began to gather around, their expressions a mix of relief, curiosity, and, in some cases, disbelief. Emma set about treating Jacob, checking his vitals and ensuring he was stable, while the onlookers murmured among themselves.

A while later, Jacob seemed somewhat revived, his breathing steadier.

"What happened, Jacob?" Curtis asked.

"The storm... it snuck up on me," Jacob said. "I couldn't see a thing; it was all dust and wind. I wandered for days, trying to find my way back."

Pete stepped forward, his face etched with mixed emotions. "We looked for you, Jacob," he said. "We called out, searched everywhere we thought you could've gone. But the storm covered everything, making it impossible to track you."

Jacob nodded weakly. "I thought I'd never see anyone again," he admitted, his eyes scanning the faces around him.

As Emma continued her examination, ensuring no serious injuries had gone unnoticed, Nate stood back a little, watching the scene unfold. He caught Sarah's eye across the crowd, her expression mirroring his own conflicted emotions.

"You should ride with me," Emma said. "So I can keep an eye on you."

"Where's Sarah?" Jacob said suddenly.

"I am here," Sarah said, stepping forward.

Jacob's shoulder relaxed as he looked up at her, and Nate could not help but notice his blue eyes were filled with tenderness.

"Will you sit with me?" he asked.

Sarah hesitated a moment and then nodded.

"All right," Nate said. "Let's get back on the road."

They stopped for lunch around midday. Nate had not seen Jacob or Sarah since that morning.

While everyone gathered to eat, Nate stood on the outskirts of the camp, his gaze fixed on the distant hills that rolled under the vast sky. His thoughts were turbulent, wrestling with disappointment and guilt. A part of him, a significant part, had hoped they were finally free of Jacob.

Mary approached him quietly, and Nate turned to her. She held an apple in her hand, which she offered to him as she came to stand beside him.

"Thought ye might need a wee bit of sustenance," she said.

Nate took the apple from her and turned it over his hands. "Thanks," he said, sighing heavily.

"Jacob's sudden reappearance was unexpected," Mary noted.

"You can say that again," Nate agreed, taking a bite of the apple, the crispness of it momentarily distracting him from his heavier thoughts.

Mary placed a reassuring hand on his shoulder, and he turned to her. "Sometimes, a brush with death can humble a man, change him for the better," she said. "Maybe this experience will be good for Jacob."

Nate chewed on her words along with the apple, considering the possibility. He wanted to believe that Jacob could change, that the ordeal might have softened his edges, and that it might have knocked some sense into him.

"I hope you're right," he said, though his tone lacked conviction. "But something tells me Jacob isn't going to turn into a ray of sunshine from now on."

Mary nodded a little sadly. "Aye, people rarely change their stripes so easily," she conceded. "But hope is eternal."

She gave his shoulder one final squeeze and turned to go, leaving Nate alone with his thoughts.

As Nate heard the crunch of gravel under boots, he turned, expecting to see Mary returning with perhaps another comforting word or gesture. Instead, he found himself facing Jacob, whose appearance was still marked by the dust and disarray of his recent ordeal.

"Jacob," Nate said. "How are you feeling?"

The dangerous flash in Jacob's blue eyes was unmistakable, and tension immediately coiled in Nate's stomach.

"Drop the act," Jacob hissed, his voice dripping with venom. "I know what you're up to."

Nate frowned, doing his best to maintain his composure. "You should go and rest," he said.

But Jacob took an unsteady step forward, his balance off but his intent clear. "I know what you're up to," he repeated, his voice low and threatening. "Clint told me she was riding on your wagon that morning."

"I was just looking out for her," he explained calmly. "It's my responsibility to look after everyone in the train."

Jacob's laugh was bitter and hollow. "Liar!" he barked, his face contorted with rage. "You played the hero, searching for me, all the while trying to get Sarah back. Pretending to find me, so when you didn't, you could look respectable."

Nate's patience thinned, but he kept his voice steady. "Jacob, you're dehydrated and not thinking clearly. We did everything we could to find you."

Jacob's anger seemed to swell, his breathing heavy. "I will never let her go," he declared, stepping closer, his intent menacing. “She is mine, and if you try anything, I will kill you.”

Nate met Jacob's gaze squarely, unflinching despite the threat. “Go and rest, Jacob.”

Jacob glowered at him for a moment longer before he turned and staggered away; Nate watched him go, his mind racing. So much for Mary’s eternal hope.

Then, Nate caught a movement out of the corner of his eye and turned to see Elijah riding up, his expression grim.

“What is it?” Nate asked.

“We’ve got a problem,” Elijah said.

Chapter Twenty-Nine

The entire wagon train gathered, and the faces of the passengers reflected the worry and tension that had settled over the group.

Sarah stood beside Jacob, who was glowering at Nate with barely contained fury. He had hardly said two words to her all day, but now and then, she caught him watching her with eyes filled with resentment and anger.

Nate stood before the assembled group, his expression firm yet weary. Elijah stood at his right. As Nate's eyes traveled over the group, he glanced briefly at Sarah, his eyes meeting hers for a heartbeat.

"I've gathered everyone here because we have a decision to make," he began, his voice strong and steady. "Elijah returned from scouting with troubling news. The recent rains have caused a landslide up ahead."

Murmurs of concern rippled through the crowd, and Nate paused to let the news settle.

"In any other circumstance, it would be more prudent to wait for the area to dry out," Nate continued. "But as you all know, the delays from the dust storm have left us with dwindling supplies. We need to decide if we risk crossing the landslide area or holding back and running out of food."

"Why is he bothering to ask us at all?" Jacob muttered, his tone dripping with sarcasm.

Sarah glanced at him, unease creeping into her stomach.

"How bad is it?" Emma asked, directing her question at Elijah.

“It’s possible to cross,” Elijah said. “But it will be tricky.”

There were more murmurs among the group.

“Well, I’d rather risk the crossin’ than run out of food,” Thomas, the blacksmith, said as he stepped forward, his arms crossed over his chest. “I say we take the risk."

Old veteran Samuel nodded his agreement, his grizzled face marked by the lines of his life. “I reckon’ I’ve crossed worse in my day,” he said. “Besides, I trust Nate and Elijah to be able to lead us through this.”

Sarah saw several others nod in agreement.

“We cannae wait any longer,” Mary added. “We’ll all be sufferin’ if we dinnae get to the next supply stop soon.”

“All right,” Nate said. “Then let’s take a vote. Raise your hand if you’re in favor of crossin’.”

Hands went up across the crowd, one by one, including Sarah’s. Jacob’s stayed firmly by his side; his lips pressed into a thin line.

“It’s settled then,” Nate announced, his voice carrying with renewed resolve. “We’ll risk the crossing.”

The crowd began to disperse, whispering among themselves. Jacob grabbed Sarah’s arm as he marched her back to the wagon.

“You're hurting me,” Sarah protested, trying to pull her arm free, but his grip only tightened.

Jacob dragged her around the side of the wagon, out of view from the others, and then turned on her.

“You and that so-called Wagon Master have been trying to make a fool out of me,” he hissed, his face twisted in anger.

"Jacob," Sarah said. "Please—"

"You claim you want to marry me, but it's all lies, isn't it?" Jacob said, pulling her toward him.

Sarah's heart raced, fear mingling with anger. "Jacob, calm down, please," she pleaded, attempting to soothe the rage in his eyes, but her words seemed only to fuel his fury.

He shook his head violently, spittle flying from his lips. "I watched you all those years with Robert," he ranted. "All the time wishing you were mine, secretly hoping that somethin' might happen to my brother."

Sarah's breath caught in her chest.

"Do you know how that feels?" Jacob said, his tone full of guilt, anger, and desperation. "To want your own brother gone so you can have his wife?"

"Jacob—"

"Well, I'll tell you somethin' right now. I won't do it again. You are marrying me, Sarah, and I won't let Nate—or anyone else—get in the way."

"You need to rest," Sarah pleaded. "You're not thinking clearly—you're overwrought. Please, let's just talk about this when you're feeling better."

But Jacob was beyond reason.

"You're mine," he said, pulling her against his body. "Mine and no one else's."

Sarah squirmed and wiggled, fighting to escape him as he tried to bring his mouth to hers.

"Let me go," she gasped.

But it was as if Jacob couldn't hear her, and when she finally freed her hand, she slapped him as hard as she could across the cheek. Jacob let her go, blinking in shock. But before Sarah had a chance to do anything, to say anything, Jacob struck her back. The force of the blow knocked her off balance, and she fell to the ground, landing heavily on her stomach. The air whooshed out of her lungs, and a sharp pain radiated through her abdomen.

Groaning in pain, Sarah clutched her stomach, fear for her unborn baby overshadowing her discomfort. The ground beneath her seemed to spin as she tried to catch her breath, her mind racing with panic.

She looked up at Jacob, who stood dead still, shocked at his own actions. He'd never hit her before. Then, without a word, he turned and walked away briskly, leaving Sarah alone and in pain on the ground.

Sarah lay on the dusty ground for a long while. Closing her eyes, she prayed for some movement telling her the baby was fine. Then she heard gravel underfoot and opened her eyes to see Emma.

"Sarah!" Emma cried, her voice shrill as she hurried over to her and dropped to her knees.

"What happened?" she asked.

"Jacob..." Sarah said.

Emma ran her hand over her stomach, pressing gently. Sarah groaned in pain.

"Is the baby all right?" she asked.

"I think so," Emma said, sitting back. "But you have a cracked rib."

Sarah tried to sit up, but the pain radiated through her entire body, and she lay down again.

"Jacob did this to you?" Emma said, her voice strained.

Sarah nodded

"I am going to fetch Nate," Emma said, her expression hardening as she got to her feet.

"No," Sarah said, grabbing her hand. "Please don't."

Emma frowned, her eyes full of concern. "Sarah—"

"It will just make things worse," Sarah said. "Jacob is unstable; whatever happened during the storm, he's worse now than before."

"But he can't get away with this," Emma insisted.

Sarah winced again. "Nate has enough to worry about with the crossing."

Emma sat back on her heels, frowning. "I don't like this."

Sarah sighed heavily. "Please, Emma," she pressed. "Keep this to yourself?"

"All right," Emma sighed. "Come on, let's get you back to the wagon. You need to rest."

***

Sarah did not leave the wagon again the following day. As the train approached the landslide area, anxiety settled heavily around Sarah, constricting her chest with each jolt and shift of the wagon. She sat huddled in the back, clutching the wooden bench tightly as the wagon creaked ominously, navigating the treacherous, slippery path. The wheels slid occasionally, sending a jolt of fear through her every time the wagon lurched unpredictably on the unstable ground.

Emma had tried to convince Sarah to ride with her, but as much as Sarah wanted to, the events of the day before sat at the forefront of her mind. She worried about what might happen if she pushed Jacob too far, what he might do. So, instead, she stayed with Pete and Jacob.

As the wagon lurched sideways again, Sarah groaned. The strain of the situation was palpable, and within the confines of the wagon, she tried to remain as still as possible, hoping to avoid any unnecessary risks. However, amidst the tense crossing, a sharp, shooting pain suddenly struck her in the stomach. The intensity of the pain took her breath away, and she wasn't sure if it was from the cracked rib from her earlier fall or something far more alarming with the baby.

As she sat crouched on the hard wooden floor, another wave of excruciating pain radiating through her abdomen was unlike anything she had experienced before. She tried to stifle a cry, but the pain was too intense; a scream of agony escaped her lips, piercing the sound of the groaning wagon and the murmur of anxious voices outside.

"Stop your hollerin'," Jacob barked, his harsh voice cutting through her haze of pain as he shouted from the front of the wagon. "We're tryin' to concentrate!" His tone was sharp and devoid of concern, focused only on navigating the perilous path.

But Sarah couldn't stop; the pain was overwhelming, relentless. She screamed again, curling forward as much as she could, her hands clutching her belly. Fear gripped her heart—not just for herself, but for the life of her unborn child. She was terrified this pain meant she was losing another baby, or worse, that something was seriously wrong.

"Please, something's not right," Sarah gasped between bouts of pain, her voice trembling. "I need help. Please, Jacob. I need Emma."

But Jacob, consumed by the task of steering through the landslide, didn't respond to her plea.

As the pain escalated, her mind clung to the hope that the wagon would soon reach stable ground, that she could get to Emma, and that somehow, despite the odds, she and her baby would be safe.

After what felt like a lifetime, the wagon rolled onto solid ground, and they made it through the landslide. Sarah exhaled deeply, the pain lessening some. Emma was the first to arrive, her brow furrowed with concern as she kneeled beside Sarah, who was still moaning in pain.

"I heard you screaming," Emma said, quickly crawling into the wagon beside Sarah. "What is it?"

"I don't know," Sarah admitted. "I thought maybe the baby was coming."

Emma checked her carefully, feeling for the baby's position and listening to the rhythm of Sarah's breathing. "You're not in labor yet," she said, her voice calm and reassuring despite the strain of the crossing. "What you're feeling are practice pains, common in the later months of being with child. The body sometimes needs to practice for what's to come, which can be intense."

"So you are saying that all that hoo-ha was just for nothing?"

Sarah looked over Emma's shoulder to see Jacob hovering at the wagon's entrance.

"I wouldn't expect you to understand," Emma said dismissively. "Now leave us be."

Jacob hesitated a moment and then disappeared, grumbling to himself.

"You've never had practice pains before?" Emma asked. "With your other babies?"

Sarah shook her head. "'Is it normal for it to be this strong?' she asked, her voice trembling.

Emma nodded, offering a reassuring smile. "It's normal. The trick is to keep breathing, and you'll get you through them."

Just then, Nate appeared, peering in through the back of the wagon.

"Sarah," he said, his green eye full of concern and tenderness. "Are you all right?"

"Nate," Sarah said, her voice tense. "You shouldn't be here, if Jacob sees you—"

"I heard you screaming," Nate said. "I couldn't stay away. What's wrong?"

"She's fine," Emma said, smiling. "But I think this baby will be here before too long."

"Really?" Sarah said. "But isn't it too soon?"

"You'll be fine, Sarah," Emma said, smiling. "You're one of the strongest women I've ever met. If anyone can do this, you can."

Sarah tried to smile, but she was scared.

"You need to get some rest," Emma said.

Sarah caught Nate's eye. "I'll be fine. You should get back to the others."

Nate hesitated momentarily and then turned to go, leaving Sarah and Emma alone.

"Lie down," Emma instructed. "I'll stay with you."

"But Jacob—"

"I don't give a flyin' fig what he thinks," Emma said, her jaw locked in determination.

Sarah gave her a tight-lipped smile as she lay down. From outside, she heard Nate command them to push forward, and a moment later, the wagon creaked as the wheels began to roll forward.

Sarah lay quietly, staring up at the white canvas above her, the rhythmic rocking of its wheels providing a constant, albeit uneasy, backdrop to her thoughts. Emma sat beside her, gently rubbing her back as the wagon creaked and groaned over the uneven terrain. Though the contractions had ceased for now, the fear of the baby coming too soon gnawed at her.

"How are you feeling?" Emma asked.

"Fine..." Sarah lied. "I'm scared, if truth be told. I've always known the baby would be born on the Trail, but I never really stopped to think what it would mean."

Emma smiled reassuringly, her eyes soft and kind. "I'll be right there with you, Sarah. I promise. We'll make sure your baby arrives safely into this world."

Sarah took a deep breath, trying to steady herself. The thought of giving birth in such uncertain circumstances was terrifying. The vastness of the wilderness around them, the constant movement, the lack of a stable place to rest—it all added to her anxiety.

“Did I ever tell you about the night my baby brother was born?” Emma asked, a mischievous glint in her eye.

Sarah shook her head, grateful for the distraction. “No, you haven't.”

“It was during a snowstorm,” Emma began, her voice taking on a soft, nostalgic tone. "My father was caught out in the barn, tending to the animals. The storm hit hard and fast, and he couldn't make it back to the house. My mother labored for a whole day and a half, with the wind howling outside and the snow piling up against the windows."

Sarah listened intently, her fears momentarily forgotten as she imagined the scene.

“When it was time for my brother to be born, there was no one else but me,” Emma said. “I was just seven years old.”

“You helped deliver your brother?”

Emma nodded, smiling to herself. “Caught him with my own two hands.”

Sarah stared at her in awe.

“When the storm finally stopped, my father rushed back to the house," Emma continued. "He found my mother exhausted but smiling, holding my brother in her arms.”

Sarah smiled, a warmth spreading through her chest. The story was comforting, a reminder that strength and resilience could carry them through even in the most challenging circumstances.

Emma gave Sarah's hand a reassuring squeeze. “We're all here for you, Sarah. And this little one,” she said, placing a gentle hand on Sarah's belly, "is already surrounded by so much love. You'll do just fine."

As the sun began to dip below the horizon, the wagon train came to a stop. Nate called out for everyone to set up camp, his voice carrying over the sounds of the settling wagons and the low murmur of the travelers.

Emma turned to Sarah. "Are you hungry?"

"Just tired," Sarah replied.

"All right, well, you need to get some rest," Emma said. "I'll come and check on you a little later."

Sarah nodded as Emma crawled out of the wagon, leaving her alone.

Despite her exhaustion, Sarah couldn't get comfortable, and although she longed for sleep, it just wouldn't come. She could hear the others gathered together around the campfire. She hadn't seen Jacob since they crossed the river, but she assumed he was with the others having supper.

Eventually, Sarah sat up, reaching for her satchel for the small leather-bound journal Emma had given her, but it wasn't there. She frowned as she continued to search in the dim light. She overturned the satchel, the contents spilling over the wagon's floor, but nothing. Sarah hoped it had not fallen out during the crossing. The truth was that she had not written much these past days; she'd been too distracted. Perhaps she'd left the journal in Emma's wagon.

Sarah climbed out of the wagon, her eyes scanning the camp for any sign of Emma. As she turned the corner of the wagon, she stopped abruptly, her breath catching in her throat.

Jacob was sitting on the wagon seat, a bottle dangling between his knees. The sight of him drinking alone, his expression dark and brooding, sent a chill down her spine. She had no idea he was there.

"Where are you going?" Jacob's voice was slurred, but his eyes were sharp, locking onto her with an unsettling intensity.

"I was going to speak with Emma," Sarah replied, trying to keep her voice steady. "I've misplaced something."

Jacob's eyes narrowed, his thin lips curled into a sneer, and he held the journal. "Is this what you are lookin' for?"

Sarah's stomach sank. A wave of panic rose within her. "Did you go through my things?" she asked, her voice barely above a whisper.

"I found it near the front of the wagon," Jacob said, ignoring her question.

Sarah said nothing, her heart racing. The journal must have been dislodged during the crossing. "Did you read it?"

Jacob didn't answer. Instead, he took a long swig from the bottle, his eyes never leaving her face.

"Jacob, please," she said, her voice trembling. "Give it back."

"Why are you writing lies about Robert?" Jacob demanded, his tone suddenly harsh.

Sarah's heart sank further. "They're not lies, Jacob. You saw what your brother was like."

Jacob's expression hardened, and he jumped from the wagon seat, the bottle clattering to the ground. "He was a hard man," he agreed. "But this filth—"

"It's all true," Sarah said, her voice gaining strength.

"I was there—"

"You saw what he wanted you to see," Sarah insisted, cutting him off.

Jacob's face twisted in anger, his hands balling into fists. "You're making him out to be a monster," he spat, taking a step toward her.

Sarah stood her ground, her own anger rising to match his. "He *was* a monster. He hurt me, Jacob. In ways you can't even imagine."

Jacob's face contorted with rage, and for a moment, Sarah thought he might strike her. But then he stopped, his shoulders sagging like a great weight had settled on them. "He was my brother," he said, his voice breaking.

Tears welled up in Sarah's eyes, but she held them back. "He was your brother, yes. But that doesn't excuse what he did."

Jacob stared at her for a long moment, the anger slowly draining from his face, replaced by something that looked almost like sorrow. But it was as fleeting as lightning streaking across a black sky, and his expression hardened again.

"It doesn't matter," he spat. "He's gone now."

Sarah said nothing, the air between them thick with pain and tension. Then she put her hand out, her fingers shaking.

"Please give it back," she said.

Jacob hesitated a moment. Then, without another word, he walked over to the small fire.

"Jacob, don't—"

Ignoring her, he threw the small journal into the flames. Sarah rushed forward, but Jacob grabbed her roughly by the arm, her skin twisting cruelly between his thick fingers. She inhaled sharply.

"It's just us now," he said, his voice low as he whispered into her ear.

Then he pulled her toward him, and she could smell the whiskey on his breath. Sarah stood frozen for a moment, her dark eyes fixed on his.

"My brother was a fool," Jacob said softly.

He reached up and touched Sarah's cheek with his thumb, and she recoiled, pushing back against his grip.

"Let me go, Jacob."

He held her gaze, and she saw the desire in his eyes, a dark passenger lurking close to the surface. She wondered if she should shout for help, but he let her go a moment later.

Jacob retrieved the bottle off the ground and, without another word, turned and walked away, leaving Sarah standing there.

As his footsteps retreated, Sarah hurried over to the fire, but it was too late. The journal was now nothing but charred remains. She took a step back, her eyes never leaving the fire. She could see her words and memories rising into the air as ash, dissipating into the night sky.

She knew they would get to Gray's Station soon, and when they did, she would finally be free of Jacob. However, Sarah did not feel liberated by this; instead, she only felt fear. Jacob's behavior was growing increasingly erratic; he was becoming more dangerous. He wouldn't let her go or walk away without a fight. Sarah had no idea what that might mean for Nate or for them both.

Chapter Thirty

Nate sat on a log near the campfire, staring into the flames, his face a mask of worry and frustration. The day had been grueling, with the perilous crossing of the landslide area testing everyone's nerves, but Nate's mind was clearly elsewhere. Beside him, Mary noticed his distant gaze and the tight set of his jaw.

"Are ye all right, Nate?" she asked.

Her concerned eyes searched his face, clearly seeing the turmoil beneath his stoic exterior.

Nate glanced at her, forcing a strained smile before it faded. "It was a tough crossing today," he began, his voice low. "But I was distracted, Mary. Sarah's screaming... I took every bit of self-control not to jump from my wagon and go to her. I felt so helpless, hearing her in pain and unable to do anything."

Mary nodded slowly, her expression sympathetic. "And what do you think that means for ye, Nate?"

He sighed heavily, the weight of his thoughts burdening him. "I've been struggling with the idea of giving up being a Wagon Master," Nate confessed, his green eyes reflecting the fire's glow. "But today, when I heard Sarah in pain, I realized... I realized I'd rather be by her side than leading the train."

Mary reached out, placing a comforting hand on his arm. "Being a Wagon Master has meant a lot to ye all these years," she acknowledged, her voice gentle. "It was a way for ye to channel all yer grief over losing yer parents into something meaningful. But that doesn't mean ye were meant to do it for the rest of yer life."

Her eyes held a knowing look, warm and wise in the firelight. "Sometimes God brings people together, and things change for the better. It's not just about what we lose; it's also about what we gain."

Nate looked at Mary, her words sinking in, a mixture of relief and resolve beginning to form in his heart. "Maybe it's time for a new chapter," he said. "One where I can be there for Sarah, for the baby, instead of always looking ahead to the next stretch of the road."

Mary smiled, squeezing his arm reassuringly. "Aye, and it's a chapter I believe will bring ye more joy than ye can imagine. Ye've been a leader to many, Nate. Now it might be time to lead a different kind of life—one with love and family at the center."

As Nate contemplated her words, a sense of peace replaced the tension coiled tight within him all day.

"I need to speak with her," Nate said. "Tell her that I want a life with her."

"Aye," Mary agreed.

"If only I could get a moment alone with her," Nate sighed.

Mary pressed her lips together thoughtfully. "Why dinnae ye leave it to me," she said wryly.

The following day, after breakfast, they were packing up camp when Nate spotted Mary signaling him over. Nate let go of the wagon harness and walked over to her.

"What is it?" he asked.

Mary smiled as she gestured with her head, and Nate followed her down the wagon line and toward the river, where a clump of willow trees grew on the bank.

"Mary—"

Just then, Sarah emerged from the trees and smiled softly at him. As he met her blue eyes, his heart skipped a beat.

"Jacob thinks she's with Emma," Mary said. "But you don't have much time."

"Thank you, Mary," Nate said.

Mary nodded and then turned to go, leaving Nate and Sarah alone.

For a moment, neither spoke as they stood beneath the dappled shade of willow trees near the river, the sound of water flowing softly.

"How are you feeling?" Nate asked, his voice laced with concern as he watched her closely, searching for any sign of discomfort.

"Better," Sarah reassured him, a gentle smile gracing her lips. "I haven't had any more pain since yesterday."

Nate's expression visibly relaxed at her words, a sigh of relief escaping him.

He took a step toward her, closing the small distance between them.

"I've been desperate, not being able to be with you," he confessed, his eyes locked on hers, conveying the depth of his feelings.

Sarah looked up at him, her own eyes mirroring the tenderness in his gaze as Nate reached for her hand, his touch warm and firm.

"I never imagined I would want anything more than being out here, leading the wagons," he said, his voice soft yet earnest. "But then you stepped into my life, and everything changed."

He paused, squeezing her hand slightly.

"You've made me think about a different life, dream about a different future," he continued. "I want to know that simple happiness again, like waking up on a Sunday morning to coffee and pancakes before church."

Nate reached across with his other hand and rested it gently on Sarah's stomach.

"I want this to be our baby," he said, his voice softening. "For us to raise him or her together, and for them to know what it means to have two parents who love them."

Sarah's eyes glistened as Nate painted a picture of the life he envisioned for them.

"When we get to California, I want us to settle down, to put down roots and be a family," he declared, his voice wavering slightly as he searched hers for any hint of hesitation.

"Are you sure?" she asked, her eyes searching his face.

Nate took another step closer, his gaze unwavering. "I've never been more sure of anything in my life," he affirmed strongly.

Sarah touched his face, gently tracing his jawline with her fingers. Nate leaned into her touch, and then, drawn by a force stronger than he'd ever faced, he leaned down and brushed his lips against hers. Sarah inhaled as he kissed her, breathing in her smell and feeling the warmth of her skin beneath his.

For a moment, Nate was lost in Sarah and the future they envisioned together. Then, all at once, the sudden sound of footsteps disturbed the quiet around them. Nate pulled away, turning toward the noise, expecting to see Mary. Instead, it was Jacob, his presence like a shadow falling over their newfound light. His expression was unreadable, but the intensity in his eyes was unmistakable. Nate's body tensed, protective instincts flaring as he instinctively moved slightly in front of Sarah.

“Jacob—” Sarah began.

“Shut up,” Jacob barked.

“Jacob,” Nate warned.

“I told you to stay away from her,” Jacob snapped, his eyes gleaming with hatred. “I told you that bad things would happen if you didn’t leave her alone.”

Nate took a step forward. “We will be arriving in Gray's Station tomorrow morning.”

“So?” Jacob spat.

“That will be the end of your journey with this train,” Nate said firmly.

“You can’t do that!” Jacob said, his voice rising in anger. “I paid my way, just like everyone else.”

“As the Wagon Master, I can and will leave you behind,” Nate said.

Jacob took a step forward, his hands balled into fists at his sides. “I have friends,” he said, his eyes flashing. “They won’t let you do this.”

“Well, your friends are more than welcome to stay behind with you in Gray’s Station,” Nate said.

Jacob said nothing for a moment, a muscle in his jaw tensing. Nate half expected him to pull out a gun.

"I am not goin' anywhere without her," Jacob growled as he looked at Sarah. "She's mine."

"No, Jacob," Nate said.

"She's agreed to marry me," Jacob spat. "We made an agreement."

"The agreement is over," Nate said.

Jacob took another step forward, but before either of them could say anything else, Elijah and Samuel appeared. They looked between the two men, their brows creasing.

"We're all set to go, boss," Samuel said.

"Good," Nate said. "Let's get going; the sooner we get to Gray's Station, the better."

Elijah and Samuel nodded as Nate reached for Sarah's hand. He walked past Jacob, holding her hand tightly; however, Jacob suddenly reached out and roughly grabbed Sarah's arms.

"Let her go," Nate said, his eyes flashing.

"She's mine," Jacob hissed.

Nate glared at him. "I won't ask you again."

Jacob's eyes darted across to Elijah and Sam, who were standing a few feet away, their arms folded across their chests, and after a moment, he let Sarah go.

"You are makin' a mistake," Jacob sneered.

"No," Nate said. "I'm not."

Nate guided Sarah back to his wagon and helped her onto the seat. "Nate, Jacob isn't just going to sit back and let this happen."

“I know,” Nate sighed. “But we just have to get through one more night, and then we will be free of him.”

Sarah pursed her lips.

“I won’t let anything happen to you,” he said, his expression softening. “You or the baby.”

***

The night was thick with darkness, the only light coming from the occasional flicker of lanterns scattered around the campsite. Nate sat on his wagon seat, eyes scanning the area intermittently while his mind churned with worry. Sarah was asleep inside, her gentle breathing occasionally audible in the quiet of the night. Despite the calm, Nate couldn’t shake the unease that clung to him like a second skin, the fear that Jacob might try something reckless.

As the hours ticked by, Nate's eyelids grew heavy, and despite his determination, he drifted off to sleep, lulled by the deceptive peace of the night.

He was jolted awake by the acrid smell of smoke and the distressed cries of oxen. His heart pounded as he leaped from the wagon, his eyes quickly adjusting to the darkness now sliced by the ominous orange glow of a fire near the corral.

“Fire! I need help here!” Nate yelled as he ran toward the corral, his voice cutting through the night, rousing the camp.

Thomas, Elijah, and Samuel quickly joined him, grabbing buckets of water and blankets as they fought to control the flames. Others from the train joined in to help, while others stood back, silently watching.

The fire was fierce, but together, they managed to get it under control before it could spread to the nearby wagons and supplies.

"How did it start?" Samuel asked as he wiped the sweat from his wrinkled brow.

"Dunno," Nate said, his voice hoarse.

He then turned, looking around the group. "Did anyone see anything?" he asked.

But no one came forward, and Nate frowned. How had the fire started? All of a sudden, his blood turned cold. He dropped his bucket and rushed back to his wagon, his heart in his throat. As he approached, he noticed the front flap of the wagon was open, flapping gently in the night breeze. A knot of fear tightened in his stomach.

"Sarah?" he called as he peered inside, but there was no answer, and the wagon was empty—Sarah was gone.

Panic surged through him as he searched the camp, calling out her name, his voice growing increasingly desperate. The camp quickly became alive with light and noise as others joined in the search, but there was no sign of her.

"Mary!" Nate cried as he hurried over to her. "Any signs of her?"

Mary's expression was grim as she slowly shook her head. "Jacob's gone too, laddie. And so is Peter's wagon," she added, her voice low.

Nate's stomach dropped to the ground, a cold dread washing over him. The pieces clicked together with a chilling clarity—Jacob had set the fire at the corral, a diversion to distract them, as he took Sarah away.

Without wasting another second, Nate turned to the men who had gathered around.

"Get the horses ready. They can't have got far," he declared, his voice ringing with fear and resolve.

His mind raced with scenarios, each more frightening than the last, but he pushed them aside. Right now, he needed to focus. He needed to find Sarah, whatever it took.

Chapter Thirty-One

In the darkness of the night, with only the faint moonlight illuminating the rough path, the tension in the air was palpable. Sarah sat rigidly on the wagon seat, sandwiched between Jacob and Pete. Her hands were bound tightly behind her with coarse rope, cutting into her wrists with every jolt of the wagon. Fear coursed through her veins, not just for her own safety but for the unborn child she carried.

Jacob, his face twisted in frustration and anger, kept glancing back as if expecting Nate and the others to appear at any moment. "Drive them faster!" he barked at Pete, who was struggling to control the nervous oxen.

"I can't see a thing, Jacob! It's pitch black out here," Pete shot back, his voice strained as he tried to navigate the uneven terrain.

Sarah's mind raced, desperate for a way to escape. Her options were limited; jumping from the wagon was too dangerous, especially in her condition. She knew any attempt could be fatal for both her and the baby. There was only one option: she needed to reason with Jacob, a feat she knew was near impossible, but she had to try.

"Jacob, what are you planning to do?" Sarah asked, trying her best to keep her voice steady despite the fear that gripped her.

Jacob's lips twisted into a grim smile as he met her gaze. "If we get to the supply depot before Nate and the others, we can get married."

A surge of defiance rose within her despite the precariousness of her situation.

“I won't marry you, Jacob. I never will,” she said firmly, her eyes locking with his in a silent challenge.

Jacob's face darkened at her words, his hand gripping the edge of the wagon seat tightly. “Then I'll drag you down the aisle if I have to,” he hissed, his voice low and menacing. “You're going to be my wife, Sarah, one way or another.”

Sarah recoiled at the venom in his voice, her heart pounding. The threat hung in the air between them, heavy and foreboding. With a sinking feeling, she realized Jacob was beyond reason, driven by obsession and wounded pride. His plan was not just about escaping Nate’s leadership or proving his worth but about possessing her, regardless of her wishes.

“Jacob, don't do this,” Sarah pleaded, her voice tinged with urgency. “You can't force someone to love you or marry you. What kind of life would we have together after this?”

But Jacob seemed deaf to her logic, his mind set on a course he believed would reclaim his dignity and control. “It doesn't matter,” he muttered, turning his gaze away from her and back to the dark road ahead. “You're *mine*, Sarah. It's too late to change anything now.”

As she grappled with her thoughts, the wagon suddenly lurched violently, hitting a large rock hidden in the shadows.

The oxen cried out in pain and stumbled forward, causing the wagon to come to a jarring halt. Unprepared for the sudden stop, Sarah was thrown forward against the wooden back of the bench in front of her. The impact knocked the wind out of her, and she groaned in pain.

“What the—” Jacob yelled in anger and frustration.

Pete quickly jumped down from the wagon, his lantern swinging wildly as he rushed to examine the oxen.

“Two of them are lame,” Pete said, his voice strained.

“Well, what are we supposed to do now?" Jacob yelled at Pete, his voice full of fury and panic.

Pete looked back at Jacob, frustration evident on his face. “We can't go any further with two lame oxen,” he argued, his tone firm despite Jacob's glaring.

“Well, we don't have a choice, do we?” Jacob barked. “That Wagon Master is probably already on our tail.”

“Well, maybe that's for the best,” Pete said.

Jacob stiffened. “What's that supposed to mean?”

“You know I didn't want to do this, Jacob,” Pete said.

“Well then, why did you, huh?” Jacob challenged.

“Because I thought we were friends,” Pete said, his voice strained. “But Jacob, this has all gone too far...”

“No one is makin' you stay,” Jacob spat.

Sarah was hardly listening as she edged toward the end of the wagon seat, her movements slow and deliberate to avoid drawing attention. Her heart pounded in her chest as she felt the coarse ropes around her wrists; the knot was tight but slightly loosened from the jolt. Using the edge of the wooden seat, she began to work at the ropes, her fingers numb but desperate.

Just then, Sarah heard a faint, eerie whistling sound, chilling her blood. Her eyes darted up in alarm, only to see an arrow arc gracefully yet menacingly through the night sky.

Before she could react, the arrow found its mark, embedding itself deep into Pete's chest. He gave a choked gasp, his eyes wide with shock, before collapsing heavily onto the ground. The wagon fell silent, Sarah and Jacob frozen in disbelief and horror.

"It's the Indians!" Jacob cried, his face twisted in panic.

Without a second thought, he grabbed Sarah, pulling her roughly from the wagon. "We need to find shelter, now!" he hissed.

"But what about Pete?" Sarah asked.

"Ain't nothin' we can do for him," Jacob said.

His grip was iron-tight around her arm as he dragged her away from the wagon and into the engulfing darkness.

"Where are we going?" Sarah cried, her voice high with fear as she stumbled alongside him, trying to keep pace with his frantic steps.

"Shut up!" Jacob snapped. "Unless you want us to both end up scalped."

Sarah clamped her mouth shut, her heart pounding against her ribs as they ran. The air around them was alive with the sounds of their heavy breathing and the distant noises of the night animals.

As they ran directionless, the ground beneath her feet was uneven, and several times, she nearly fell; only Jacob's harsh pull on her arm kept her upright.

After what felt like hours but could only have been minutes, Jacob spotted a small cave within a rocky outcrop. He pushed her toward it without slowing, practically throwing her inside the dark hollow. The sudden change from the cool night air to the damp atmosphere of the cave made Sarah cough, but she quickly stifled the sound with her fists, aware of the danger still lurking outside.

The darkness was almost complete inside the cave except for the faint moonlight filtering through the entrance. Jacob's heavy breathing was the only sound for a few long seconds as they both tried to gather their wits.

"Stay here; don't make a sound," Jacob whispered harshly, his eyes darting nervously toward the cave's entrance.

As Sarah huddled in the shallow cave, the rough stone pressed against her back. She could barely make out the entrance, a narrow slit that let in just enough light to cast eerie shadows on the walls. Her heart raced, each beat echoing in her ears like a drum. She didn't know if she was more afraid of being trapped here with Jacob or of the possibility that the Indians might find them.

The cave felt suffocating, the air heavy with the scent of earth and fear. Jacob stood near the entrance, his eyes darting nervously between the opening and her. His presence was a constant, looming threat, a reminder of the unpredictable danger she was in.

She closed her eyes, trying to steady herself and keep her wits about her. The baby was restless, moving in her stomach as if mirroring her anxiety. She placed her hands on her belly, hoping to calm the child and find some semblance of peace in this harrowing moment.

"It's okay," Sarah whispered to herself and her baby. "We're going to be okay."

Her breaths came shallow and fast, and she forced herself to take deeper, slower breaths, trying to quell the rising panic. She needed to stay strong, for herself and her baby. The thought of Nate somewhere out there searching for her gave her a flicker of hope. She couldn't let fear consume her, not now.

The rough texture of the cave wall bit into her back, grounding her in the present. She opened her eyes and glanced at Jacob. He was muttering to himself, his face twisted with anger and desperation. She couldn't trust him, but she needed to keep him calm, to avoid provoking him further.

The baby's movements grew more insistent, each kick a reminder of the life she was fighting for. She focused on the sensation, letting it center her. Her child needed her to be strong and to think clearly.

Sarah swallowed hard, her mouth dry as sandpaper.

"Please, God," Sarah prayed. "Please don't let anything happen to this baby."

As the minutes ticked by, Sarah kept her back pressed against the cold, damp cave wall, trying to think through her options. Her wrists ached from the tight ropes, and the close, musty air of the cave made it hard to breathe. Across the small space, Jacob stood guard at the entrance, his silhouette outlined by the faint moonlight. His gun was ready, a clear sign he was prepared for any threat—or any attempt from her to escape.

"Jacob, please," Sarah implored, trying to keep her voice calm despite the fear and desperation swirling inside her. "Take the rope off my wrists; it's hurting me."

Jacob didn't respond, focusing on the shadows beyond the cave mouth.

"It's not too late," she said softly, hoping to reach some part of the man hidden deep within. "We can return to the wagon train when the sun is up. You haven't done anything that can't be forgiven."

Jacob turned slightly, his profile catching the dim light. “We can't go back. Only forward," he responded, his voice low and firm. “Once we're married, everything will make sense. It'll all have been worth it.”

“How can you believe that?” Sarah asked, her voice a mix of disbelief and desperation.

To her surprise, Jacob's posture softened. He turned fully toward her, his eyes searching hers in the dim light.

”Can't you see how much I love you?” he asked, his voice breaking slightly. “All those years ago, when your father sold you to Robert, I begged him to let me marry you instead. I've watched you for years from afar, yearning for you. Robert knew that. He married you to spite me, to make me watch you two together all these years. Don't you realize how somethin' like that can twist a man out of shape?”

Sarah listened, a part of her heart aching. She'd always suspected Jacob had feelings for her, but she'd never realized how intense they were, at least not until after Robert died.

“But Jacob,” Sarah said gently yet firmly, her voice echoing slightly in the cave's confines. “Us gettin' married won't fix the past. It won't make you a better man.”

Jacob's face was a mask of pain and confusion, the moonlight casting shadows that made his features seem even more gaunt and haunted. “It has to,” he whispered, almost to himself. “It's all I have left.”

Despite everything, Sarah felt a deep sorrow for Jacob for the twisted journey his heart had taken.

“I'm sorry that things have turned out this way,” she said. “But you can't force someone to love you or to marry you and think it will erase all the hurts of the past. We both need to find peace, but not like this. Not based on more pain.”

"Don't you understand? All I've ever known in my life is pain. Pain from losing my mother and being blamed for it, pain from being hated by my father, and watching Robert get all the love I never had. My whole life, I've never known happiness... except when I look at you."

Sarah's heart ached at his words. She could hear the deep, festering wound in his voice, the lifelong scars he carried. She wanted to feel compassion but knew she had to be careful. "Jacob," she began gently, "I'm so sorry for everything you've been through, but I can't heal you."

"Yes, you can," he insisted, his eyes wild and pleading. "We can be happy, Sarah, if you'll just let me into your heart. You're the only thing that has ever made sense in my life."

She took a deep breath, choosing her words carefully. "Jacob, you need to understand that healing can't come from another person. It has to come from within you. I care about you, but I can't be the one to fix everything that's broken inside you."

Jacob's face contorted with a mixture of anger and desperation. "No, you don't get it! You're the only good thing in my life, the only thing that makes me feel like I'm not drowning. If you just give us a chance, we can be happy."

Sarah felt a pang of sorrow for the broken man before her. "I can't be that for you, Jacob," she said softly. "I can't be your salvation. You have to find a way to heal on your own. And I need to live my life, for me and for this baby."

Jacob's eyes flashed with frustration. "Why can't you see? I love you. We can make it work. Just let me in, Sarah. Just give me a chance."

Tears welled up in Sarah's eyes as she looked at him. "Jacob, I've tried to understand, and I've tried to help. But forcing this isn't the answer. You need to find peace with yourself first."

Jacob sighed, shaking his head. "It will all make sense when we are married. I promise."

A lump rose in Sarah's throat. He wouldn't listen; he was too far down this path to understand.

As the night wore on, exhaustion eventually overtook Sarah, and she fell into a fitful sleep. The rough ground was hardly comfortable, and her dreams were troubled by the sounds of the night and the looming presence of Jacob nearby.

She was jolted awake by Jacob shaking her shoulder, his grip firm and urgent. The first light of dawn filtered into the cave, casting a pale glow that did little to warm the chill air.

"Get up, we have to go," Jacob urged, his voice tense.

Sarah struggled to her feet, her body stiff and sore. As they left the cave, the morning air was cool against her skin, starkly contrasting with the heat that would soon bear upon them.

They walked for hours, the landscape barren and unyielding. Sarah could tell by Jacob's erratic path and frequent, confused glances around that he didn't know where they were going.

"Jacob, please, let's rest," Sarah pleaded after several hours, her throat parched and her legs trembling with fatigue.

But Jacob pushed on relentlessly, driven by a desperation that seemed to cloud his judgment.

By mid-morning, the sun continued its relentless climb across the sky, a fierce presence overhead that showed no mercy. Sarah's strength was waning dramatically, each step becoming more laborious than the last. Her clothes were dusty and soaked with sweat, clinging uncomfortably to her body and chafing her skin. She could feel the grit of the dust in her mouth and between her teeth, a constant, maddening irritation.

A dull cramp gnawed at her stomach, persistent and growing in intensity with each passing hour. It was a constant reminder of her condition, of the life inside her that she needed to protect. She placed a hand on her swollen belly, trying to offer comfort to both herself and the baby. But the pain was becoming unbearable, the weight of her fear pressing down on her, making it hard to breathe.

Her thoughts were a chaotic whirl of desperation and anxiety. Every now and then, a wave of panic would rise within her, threatening to drown her in despair. She couldn't help but think of Nate, wondering if he was out there searching for her, if he was worried about her and the baby. The thought of him gave her a small measure of comfort, a fragile thread of hope to cling to.

Jacob trudged ahead of her, his steps heavy and his shoulders slumped. He looked as exhausted as she felt, his face smeared with dirt and sweat. His eyes were hollow, filled with a mixture of anger and desperation. Sarah could see their journey's toll on him but knew she couldn't trust his intentions. His unpredictability was a constant threat, a danger that loomed over her like a dark cloud.

"Jacob, please, we need to rest," Sarah pleaded, her voice strained with pain and exhaustion.

"We can't stop," he snapped, not even turning to look at her. "We have to keep moving."

Sarah stumbled, her legs buckling beneath her. She managed to catch herself, but the effort left her gasping for breath. "I can't keep going like this," she said, tears of frustration and fear in her eyes. "The baby..."

Jacob finally turned, his expression a mix of irritation and concern. He looked at her, really looked at her, and for a moment, she thought she saw a flicker of the Jacob she used to know. "Fine," he said gruffly. "We'll rest for a bit. But not for long."

They found a small patch of shade under a scraggly tree, and Sarah sank to the ground, her entire body trembling with exhaustion. She leaned against the rough bark, closing her eyes and trying to steady her breathing. The pain in her stomach was relentless, each cramp a sharp reminder of the life she was fighting for.

Jacob paced restlessly nearby, his eyes scanning the horizon as if expecting someone to appear at any moment. His agitation was palpable, and Sarah knew he was barely holding it together. She needed to find a way to reach him, to make him see reason before it was too late.

"Jacob," she said softly, opening her eyes and looking up at him. "Please, we need to go back. This isn't going to work."

He stopped pacing and turned to face her, his jaw clenched. "I can't go back, Sarah. Not now. We have to keep moving."

"But where are we even going?" she asked, desperation creeping into her voice. "We're lost, and the baby... I don't know how much longer I can do this."

Jacob's face twisted with frustration. "We'll find a town, get married, and start over. You'll see. Everything will be better once we're away from them."

Sarah shook her head, tears spilling down her cheeks. "You don't understand. This isn't the way. We need help, Jacob. We can't do this alone."

He stepped closer, his expression softening for just a moment. "I love you, Sarah. I'm doing this for us, for the baby. Trust me."

She looked into his eyes, searching for any sign of the man she used to know. But all she saw was a broken, desperate man clinging to a dream that was tearing them both apart. "I want to believe you," she whispered. "But I'm scared. I'm so scared."

Jacob brushed a tear from her cheek, his touch surprisingly gentle. "We'll make it, Sarah. We have to."

As he pulled his hand away, she closed her eyes and leaned back against the tree, trying to find some measure of peace in the chaos surrounding them.

"Come on," Jacob pressed.

Sarah tried to take another step, but her body refused. She collapsed to the ground, the sand hot against her skin. As Jacob pulled her up once more, her eyes widened in horror. Beneath her, a small puddle had formed in the sand, water and blood, and she felt the dampness between her legs.

"Jacob," she managed to say, her voice tinged with panic. "The baby... it's coming."

Chapter Thirty-Two

As the midday sun beat down relentlessly, Nate, Elijah, and Samuel stood beside the abandoned wagon, a grim scene unfolding before them. Emma kneeled beside Pete's body with a somber expression.

"Is he alive?" Nate asked.

"Yes," Emma said. "But barely. Can you help me get him into the shade?"

Nate nodded as he and Samuel helped carry Pete into the wagon's shade. Emma fetched some water from her wagon, as well as a bottle of whiskey, a small sewing kit, and some clean cloth.

"He's lost a lot of blood," Emma said. "I need to remove the arrow and stitch up the wound."

"Here?" Elijah said.

"He's too weak to move," Emma said. "Nate, Sam, can you help me bring him down?"

Nate hesitated. They didn't have time for this; they had followed a false trail in the darkness, wasting precious hours, only to circle back to the wagon at dawn. The night's navigation had been a gamble, and now the stakes were even higher. He had to find Sarah, and the truth was that part of him did not wish to save the life of the man who'd helped kidnap her.

"Nate?" Emma pressed. "He doesn't have much time."

Nate gave her one stiff nod as he crouched down.

"Keep him as still as you can," Emma instructed as she prepared to remove the arrow.

Suddenly, Pete groaned, his face contorting in pain.

"This is going to hurt, Pete, but it's necessary," she warned, her voice soft but firm.

Then, she began to work the arrow free carefully. Pete's body tensed, and he stifled a yell, his hands clutching at the ground beneath him.

Once the arrow was removed, Emma reached for a bottle of whiskey and poured it generously over the wound to disinfect it. The sharp smell of alcohol mixed with the scent of dust and sweat.

Nate shifted toward Pete, gripping his chin with his left hand.

"Where did they go?" he asked, his voice hard.

Pete groaned.

"Tell me where they went, Pete," Nate pressed.

"Nate," Emma said, frowning.

Nate exhaled deeply as he got to his feet. He turned to Sam.

"You and Emma take the wagon back to camp with Pete once he's strong enough to travel," he said. "Elijah and I will carry on the search."

"No," Emma said suddenly. "I've done what I can for Pete, but Sarah might need me."

Nate hesitated.

"I am coming," Emma said, her jaw set in determination.

Nate nodded as he turned to Elijah, now crouched down, his fingers sifting through the sand. He was attempting to read the story told by the scant traces left behind.

"Anything?" he asked.

Elijah sighed. "With the wind last night, most of the tracks are covered," he reported, his voice tinged with frustration. "It's going to be difficult to pick up a trail."

Just then, Nate spotted a solitary figure on a distant hill, and his shoulders stiffened. The rider's silhouette was stark against the sky.

"Is that...?"

Emma's voice trailed off as Nate held his breath. The rider paused, surveying the scene, then let out a high, piercing call.

Within moments, more riders crested the hill, joining the first. The group began their descent toward Nate and the others, kicking up dust clouds as they approached.

Elijah stood, squinting toward the approaching riders.

"Looks like we're about to have company," he said, his hand resting on the handle of his gun, though his posture remained non-threatening.

Nate nodded, his mind racing. Encounters with Native American tribes could be unpredictable, and without knowing their intentions, every move had to be calculated.

"Let's keep calm," he instructed firmly. "We need their help, or at least their passage."

As the riders drew closer, their features became more distinct. The lead rider rode a powerful, dark chestnut horse that moved with a grace and authority mirroring that of its rider. He was a striking figure, taller than the others, with broad shoulders and an upright posture that commanded attention even from a distance. A long, feathered headdress cascaded down his back, the feathers predominantly golden eagle. His face was marked with red and black paint lines, accentuating his strong jawline and high cheekbones. A deep, jagged scar ran down the length of his face, and around his neck hung several strands of beads mixed with bear claws; his chest was bare except for a leather breechcloth adorned with intricate beadwork. Nate assumed that he was the chief by the way he carried himself.

Riding slightly behind him were his companions. One rider, a robust man with a stern face, wore a bandolier bag across his chest, richly decorated with symbols. Another younger rider, still a boy, had his hair tied back with a strip of leather, feathers tucked into it, and his face bore no markings.

Nate stepped forward, raising his hand in a gesture of peace. “We mean no harm,” he called out, his voice steady despite his heart pounding.

The chief’s gaze was intense and probing as he surveyed the scene before him. His expression was unreadable, giving nothing away of his thoughts or intentions.

“I am Chief White Eagle,” he stated, eyes locking onto Nate’s. “And this is Pawnee land.”

Nate took a deep breath, choosing his words carefully. “We don’t mean any harm,” he repeated. “My name is Nathaniel Jameson, and we are lookin’ for someone we care for. She is with a man who means her harm, and we aim to stop him before more wrong is done.”

Chief White Eagle said nothing for a long moment and then nodded slowly. “We will talk,” he said, signaling his men to lower their weapons.

"My son was patrolling last night," the chief said, nodding toward the boy. "He heard the sound of a wagon. Went to investigate."

Nate held his breath, waiting for the man to continue.

"He came upon a scene. Two men arguing fiercely," the chief continued, his gaze steady on Nate, ensuring the gravity of his words was understood. "He saw the woman, pregnant, her wrists tied. She struggled to free herself while the men fought."

Nate's fists clenched at his sides, his anxiety for Sarah growing with every word. Chief White Eagle paused, his expression solemn as he recounted the events that followed.

"My son, he wished to help her. He fired a warning shot, hoping to scare the men away." His voice held a hint of regret. "However, he misfired and struck one of the men. He panicked and returned to us."

The chief looked to his son, who shifted uncomfortably, clearly troubled by the outcome of his well-intentioned act.

"We went out to find the young woman after," he added. "But they had gone from the wagon. We searched but could not find them."

"Where did you search?" Nate asked quickly, his mind working through the possible routes Sarah and Jacob might have taken.

Chief White Eagle exchanged a brief look with his son, who nodded slightly before he turned back to Nate. "My boy, Running Wolf, will show you," he said. "There are places not many know, hidden from easy sight."

Nate nodded, his determination renewed by the offer of assistance. "Thank you," he said sincerely, the weight of their predicament settling heavily upon him.

"This wrong must be made right," the Chief said solemnly.

Nate's heart raced as Running Wolf guided them across the rugged landscape, the soil shifting underfoot, littered with scrub and the occasional twisted juniper. The terrain was harsh and unforgiving, a true test of their determination.

Elijah moved with the practiced ease of an experienced scout, his eyes sharp and focused, always alert for any signs of danger or clues that might lead them to Sarah. Emma, on the other hand, struggled slightly to keep up, her dress catching on the thorny bushes, but her face remained a mask of steely determination. Small clouds of dust rose with each step, lingering in the hot, dry air and catching the sunlight.

Nate's mind was a whirlwind of fear and anxiety. Sarah and the baby dominated his thoughts, and the unknowns gnawed at him relentlessly. Every step felt like an eternity, the uncertainty weighing heavily on his shoulders. He couldn't shake the image of Sarah in distress, her life and their unborn child's life hanging in the balance.

As they reached a small clearing, Nate's eyes swept the area, his gut sinking as he scanned the environment for any sign of Sarah. The clearing was eerily quiet, save for the distant calls of birds and the rustling of leaves in the wind. He searched desperately for anything—a scrap of fabric, footprints, or any other clue indicating Sarah had been there.

"Do you see anything?" Emma asked, her voice low but urgent. She was breathing heavily from the fast pace, sweat glistening on her forehead.

Nate shook his head, frustration and fear clawing at his insides. "No, nothing," he muttered, his voice tight with emotion. "She has to be here somewhere."

Elijah stepped forward, his eyes scanning the ground with practiced precision. "We need to stay calm and focused," he said, his tone steady. "Panicking won't help Sarah."

Running Wolf crouched down, examining the soil and the surrounding area. "Here we lost them."

Nate gritted his teeth, squinting slightly as he looked around.

"There is a small cave," Lone Wolf said suddenly. "Not far."

He pointed north, and without hesitation, Nate took off, his boots thudding against the hard-packed earth, the others trailing behind him.

"Nate?" Emma called after him.

However, Nate didn't stop. A cave would be the perfect place to hide, especially if Jacob believed Indians were after them.

The cave, a dark opening in the side of a low hill, loomed ahead, its entrance framed by boulders and dry brush. Nate's hope surged as they approached, but it quickly plummeted when they found the cave empty. The interior was cool and shadowed, a stark contrast to the blistering heat outside.

He turned as Emma and Elijah came inside. Elijah kneeled at the entrance, his fingers brushing over the ground.

"The earth is disturbed here," he noted, his voice echoing slightly off the stone walls. "They may have taken shelter here last night."

Nate, Elijah, and Emma left the cave. A short distance away, Nate spotted Running Wolf crouching in the dust. A moment later, he stood up and waved, and Nate hurried toward him.

"Here," he said, pointing to the ground.

Elijah kneeled. "He's right. They were here."

As they followed the trail, the sun climbed higher, its rays turning the air thick and oppressive. Nate wiped the sweat from his brow, his mind haunted by visions of Sarah in the heat, without water or shade. The thought of her and their unborn child in such peril was a constant gnawing in his stomach, fear and helplessness battling with his determination to find her.

Elijah pointed out signs as they went—here a broken branch, there a scuff in the dirt that might not mean much to an untrained eye but, to him, was a clear indication of their path. Running Wolf added his own knowledge of the area, identifying subtle signs of passage that blended almost seamlessly with the natural environment.

As the day wore on, Nate felt the weight of the desert sun pressing down on him like a physical force.

"We can't stop," Nate muttered to himself and anyone who might listen. "We have to find them." His voice was hoarse with dust and determination.

As they navigated through a sparse thicket dotted with sagebrush, the ground beneath them was a patchwork of dust and brittle leaves. The sun casts sharp shadows, making the terrain ahead challenging to discern in detail.

Suddenly, Running Wolf paused, signaling the group to stop. Ahead, a lone coyote was busily nosing the ground, oblivious to their presence. Its mottled gray coat blended almost seamlessly with the surrounding brush, and it seemed more interested in whatever scent it had picked up than the humans nearby.

Elijah instinctively reached for his gun, sliding it from its holster with a quiet snick. Nate tensed, ready to back up whatever decision Elijah made. However, Running Wolf shook his head sharply, a silent command to hold fire. Intrigued and confused, Nate watched as Running Wolf stepped forward, his movements deliberate but non-threatening.

The coyote paused, lifting its head to lock eyes with Running Wolf. The moment was charged, a silent exchange Nate could feel even from a distance. Running Wolf stood still, his presence neither menacing nor fearful. After a long, tense moment, the coyote blinked once, its amber eyes reflecting a wild intelligence, then turned and quietly trotted away, disappearing into the brush.

Running Wolf remained still for a moment longer, then bent to examine the spot where the coyote had been so intently sniffing. Nate felt a chill run down his spine. Something about Running Wolf's posture signaled concern. He glanced at Elijah and Emma, noting the same apprehension mirrored in their faces.

Nate hurried forward to join Running Wolf, his boots stirring small dust clouds. Reaching the spot, his heart sank as he caught sight of what had captured the coyote's interest: a small patch of ground stained darkly with blood. Fresh blood.

Running Wolf stood and faced Nate, his expression grave. "Blood is fresh," he said quietly, his voice carrying a weight that tightened Nate's chest. "Not coyote's doing."

The implication was clear, and Nate felt a wave of nausea mixed with fear. Sarah. Could it be Sarah's? He struggled to push the thought away, to focus on what needed to be done, but the possibility hung over him like a dark cloud.

Emma touched Nate's arm, a silent show of support.

Before anyone could say anything or do anything, they heard a scream in the distance.

Chapter Thirty-Three

The scream tore through Sarah's body, leaving her breathless, her throat raw. She leaned heavily against the trunk of an ancient juniper, its bark rough and unyielding beneath her palm.

Another wave crashed over her with relentless force, the pain sharp and all-consuming, radiating from her abdomen in tight, rhythmic spasms that seemed to squeeze the breath from her lungs. She gripped the tree tighter, her knuckles white, as the wave peaked. It felt as if a vice were clamped around her midsection, tightening with an intensity that left her dizzy and disoriented.

After what felt like forever, the pain ebbed, and she exhaled shakily; her long hair, which had shaken loose, now hung down her back, damp with sweat. Her skin was clammy.

From the corner of her eye, Sarah saw Jacob pacing back and forth, his movements erratic and unhelpful. He seemed disconnected from the urgency of the situation.

Then another wave of pain surged, and Sarah gasped, her body bending involuntarily as she tried to ride through the agony.

Breathless and frightened, Sarah looked down and saw the blood staining her skirts—a deep, ominous red that spread with each passing moment. Panic surged through her, cutting through the fog of pain.

"Jacob!" she cried out, her voice laced with fear and desperation. "Please, go get help. Something's wrong. Please!"

Jacob stopped pacing and looked at her, his face pale and drawn. For a moment, he just stared, seemingly frozen by indecision.

"Do something, Jacob! Please, you have to get help now!" Her voice broke on the last word, a sob catching in her throat as another wave of pain wracked her body, this one accompanied by a sharp, stabbing pain.

Still, Jacob did nothing.

As Sarah leaned heavily against the tree, her vision blurred by the intensity of her pain, a figure appeared in the distance. At first, it seemed like a mirage, a trick of her strained mind conjuring the person she most desperately wished to see. But then she heard it, her name being called out by a voice she recognized all too well—Nate's voice.

Her heart leaped in her chest, a surge of hope mingling with her pain. "Nate?" she whispered, her voice shaky, hardly daring to believe.

As he came closer, running toward her, she knew it was no illusion. "Sarah!" Nate called again, his face etched with worry as he closed the distance between them.

Just as he reached her, another wave of pain tore through her, more intense than before, bending her body with its power. She cried out, clutching the tree for support, her legs threatening to give way beneath her.

"Sarah, I'm here, I'm here," Nate said, reaching her side, his hands hovering over her, afraid to touch her for fear of hurting her further.

Emma immediately appeared beside him, her expression calm and focused amidst the chaos of emotion. She took Sarah gently with her hands, her touch reassuring. "Sarah, we need you to lie down," she instructed firmly, her eyes scanning the area for a suitable spot.

"Nate, give us your shirt," Emma said without looking away from Sarah. "We need something clean to put under her."

Without hesitation, Nate pulled off his shirt, handing it to Emma, who quickly folded it into a makeshift cushion. Together, they helped Sarah gently lie down on the ground, positioning Nate's shirt under her to provide some comfort against the hard, rocky earth.

Emma kneeled beside Sarah, examining her with a practiced eye. "Just focus on breathing, Sarah. I'm here, and I'm going to take care of you," she soothed, her voice steady in the tumult.

Nate kneeled on the other side, holding Sarah's hand tightly, trying to offer her strength through his touch.

"You're doing great, Sarah. Just hold on," Emma said. "I am just going to look and see how the baby is doing."

Sarah felt Emma's hands on her legs, and she exhaled.

"Nate," Sarah said, her voice trembling. "I'm scared."

"It's going to be okay," Nate said as he reached out to touch her face. "I am here."

"Sarah, the baby is the wrong way around," Emma said, her voice calm despite the urgency of the situation. "I'm going to have to try and turn her around."

"Her?" Sarah echoed, her voice trembling between bouts of pain. "It's a girl?"

Emma offered a small, reassuring smile. "Yes, it's a girl," she confirmed gently. "But this is going to hurt, Emma. I need you to stay awake and push when I tell you."

Sarah nodded, squeezing Nate's hands tighter, her knuckles white with exertion. Emma positioned her hands expertly and prepared to adjust the baby's position.

"Nate, talk to her," Emma instructed. "Keep her awake."

Nate leaned closer, his face lined with worry, but his eyes filled with love. “I’ve been thinkin’ about what we’ll do when we get to California,” he said, holding her hand tightly. “Maybe we get a little piece of land? Some chickens our little girl can chase around?”

Despite everything, Sarah managed a weak smile, momentarily uplifted by the image of them together as a family, but then a searing pain ripped through her, sharper than before. She screamed, the sound raw and harrowing, echoing off the surrounding trees. Then everything but the pain faded, her vision narrowing to pinpricks of light.

"Stay with me,” Nate said; his voice was like a rope, and she clung to it. “Stay with me.”

“The baby is turned around now,” Emma said. “Sarah. I need you to push when you feel the next urge.”

“I can’t do it,” Sarah gasped, tears streaming down her face, the pain overwhelming her resolve. “I can't.”

“Yes, you can,” Nate said. “You can do anything, Sarah. You are the strongest, bravest, most incredible woman I've ever known.”

Empowered by Nate's unwavering faith in her, Sarah felt a surge of strength from deep within. When the next urge to push came, she gathered all her energy and pushed with everything she had left. Her breaths were ragged, her body trembling, but she pushed again and again.

Then, suddenly, the pressure subsided. The world was still for a heartbeat—then filled with the sound of a baby’s cry, piercing the heavy air. Sarah lay back, exhausted and relieved, washing over her in waves. Nate’s lips pressed a kiss to her forehead.

“You did it, Sarah,” he said.

Tears of joy mixed with the remnants of pain on Sarah's face as Emma handed her

the tiny, squirming infant, gently placing her in Sarah's waiting arms. The baby was tiny, her skin slightly reddened from the effort of birth, with wisps of dark hair and a fierce little face that seemed to take in the world with surprising intensity.

As Sarah cradled her daughter for the first time, every ache, every moment of fear and pain, dissolved into insignificance. She looked down at the tiny face and delicate features and felt a connection so deep, so instinctual, that it seemed as though her heart grew to accommodate the surge of love that filled it.

Her daughter's eyes, wide and alert, met hers, and in that gaze, Sarah saw a reflection of her own hope and strength. The baby's small hand, with fingers so perfectly formed, grasped at Sarah's finger and held on with an unexpected strength. In that touch, every wrong in the world was righted; every shadow was illuminated by the pure, brilliant light of new life.

The weight of her daughter in her arms was the most grounding reality Sarah had ever known, and as she whispered words of love and welcome to the tiny ear, tears of joy and relief rolled down her cheeks, unheeded.

Sitting beside her, his eyes filled with tears, Nate watched over them with a protective warmth, his hand resting lightly on Sarah's shoulder, a silent vow of his presence, his support, and his unwavering commitment to their newly expanded family.

"We should get you both back to camp," Emma said.

In all the pain and joy, Sarah had forgotten all about Jacob.

"Where is he? Where's Jacob?"

"He ran off when we arrived," Nate explained. "Elliott, Sam, and Running Wolf went after him."

"Running Wolf?"

"I'll explain everything," Nate said. "But Emma's right, we need to get you back to camp."

***

Sarah stirred from her sleep, her eyelids fluttering open to the familiar surroundings of their camp. Confusion clouded her mind for a moment, the details of how she returned here hazy and disjointed in her memory. Panic surged through her as she abruptly sat up, scanning her immediate environment for any sign of her newborn daughter.

"Nate?" her voice was hoarse, tinged with urgency.

"I'm right here," Nate's reassuring voice came from beside her, and she turned to see him sitting on the bedroll, gently cradling their baby in his arms.

Relief washed over Sarah as she reached out to touch the baby, confirming that they were both safe and sound. The last fragments of her journey back to camp began to piece together—she remembered being carried through the wilderness, the jolting movements as they navigated back, and finally collapsing from exhaustion as soon as they reached safety.

"How are you feeling? Do you need anything?" Nate asked, his eyes scanning her face for any sign of discomfort.

"Water," Sarah murmured, her throat parched.

As Nate gently placed the baby into her arms and stood to fetch water, a warm wave of love washed over her. Holding her daughter, she felt an overwhelming sense of completeness and peace.

She gazed down at the tiny face, marveling at the quiet strength in her delicate features. The baby cooed softly, a sound so sweet and comforting that tears pricked at the corners of her eyes. She was a mother now, and despite their trials, the joy of this realization filled her with a fierce resolve.

The rustle of footsteps alerted her to someone's approach. Expecting Nate to return, Sarah looked up, a smile forming on her lips. But the smile froze as her eyes met not Nate's familiar gaze but the unexpected and unwelcome sight of Jacob standing there instead.

Jacob's appearance was disheveled, his eyes weary yet carrying a stubborn glint of determination. The sight of him sent a chill down Sarah's spine.

"Jacob," Sarah said, her voice tense. "What are you doing here?"

Her arms instinctively tightened around her daughter, protecting her even as she sat there, vulnerable on the bedroll.

Jacob's gaze flickered to the baby and then back to Sarah. His expression was hard to read, mixed with regret and something darker, unresolved. "I... I came to see if you were all right," he said, his voice low.

Sarah watched him warily. "Nate will be back any moment."

Jacob nodded but said nothing for a moment.

"Can I hold her?" he asked.

"No," Sarah said automatically.

Jake's expression hardened. "She is my niece," he insisted.

"We almost died because of you," Sarah said, her voice shaking.

"I am sorry," Jacob said. "I-I didn't know what to do. I was just trying..."

His voice trailed off, and Sarah stared at him, anger rising in her chest. But before she could say anything else, Nate returned. As soon as he saw Jacob, he froze.

The tension in the air was palpable, and Sarah watched as a range of emotions flickered across Nate's face—surprise, confusion, and then a hardening resolve.

"Nate—" Sarah's voice broke through the stillness, thick with anxiety. Nate's gaze snapped to hers, but only for a moment.

Then, without hesitating, Nate charged at Jacob, catching him in the stomach with his shoulder. Jacob grunted loudly, and suddenly, the two men were on the ground, grappling with each other, dust and shouts filling the air.

"Stop!" Sarah's voice rang out, desperate to end the violence, her heart pounding as she clutched her daughter closer.

The rest of the camp, alerted by the noise, began to gather around, forming a tight circle around the fighting men. After a moment, Thomas and Elijah managed to pull them apart.

Nate pushed himself off the ground but did not take his eyes off Jacob.

Then, Jacob, driven by a blind fury, drew a gun. The camp fell silent, every breath held, every movement stilled.

"I should put a piece of lead in you for stealing my family, the woman I love," Jacob shouted, his hand trembling as he aimed the gun at Nate.

Nate raised his hands in a gesture of peace. "Jacob," he said, his voice shaking. "Put the gun down."

"If anyone moves, I shoot him," Jacob threatened, his voice ragged.

Sarah felt a surge of something fierce and indomitable rise within her. She was tired of the fear and Jacob's claim over her life and happiness. Slowly, with the help of Emma at her side, she got to her feet. Emma handed her the baby and quietly retreated.

"We will never be together, Jacob," she said, her voice rising. "Even if Nate was gone, even if you were the last man on earth, I would never marry you."

"Shut up!" Jacob cried, putting his gun-free hand over his one ear.

But Sarah wouldn't shut up. She'd been silent for too long, and now she would be heard.

"I always thought you were better than Robert, but you're worse," she said, stepping forward. "You claim to love me, but you have hurt me as badly as he did."

"I am not like him," Jacob insisted.

"You are," Sarah said. "Right to your very core."

Jacob flinched as if struck, the gun in his hand wavering. Sarah saw the impact her words had on him, the realization of what he had become etching itself across his face. Part of her reveled in the power of her words, the ability to finally strike back at the man who had caused her so much pain.

"No," Jacob said, shaking his head. "I-I-I never meant to hurt you."

Sarah shook her head. How could he be so blind to the person he'd become? "But you are hurting me," she said. "This, right now, is hurting me. And I am not the only one you've hurt."

Jacob's bottom lip quivered.

"You blame who you are on the past, your pa, and Robert," Sarah continued. "But you are choosing to be this person, this monster."

"But I love you, Sarah," Jacob said, his voice cracking. "All I've ever wanted is for us to be together—"

Sara said nothing for a moment as she watched Jacob crumble, a broken man lost in his delusions and misdirected love.

Then she took a slow, measured step forward. "Jacob, if you truly care about me and my daughter," she said, her gaze unwavering as she locked eyes with him. "You will stop all of this. Stop the violence."

"Sarah—" Nate said.

"It's all right, Nate," she said, not turning to look at him.

She took another step toward Jacob, her movements deliberate. "You say you are not like Robert? Then prove it, Jacob. Let me finally have my life and the chance to find peace and happiness. If you love me, like you say you do, then let me be free."

Jacob said nothing as his Adam's apple bobbed up and down. Sarah hesitated only momentarily before raising her hand slowly and placing it over the top of the pistol. She felt Nate tense beside her, ready to intervene at the slightest hint of danger, but she did not take her eyes off Jacob. She met his blue eyes—so much like Robert's, yet filled now with a turmoil and regret that Robert had never shown.

In that moment, something shifted in Jacob's gaze. The hardness, the resolve that had driven him to this point, seemed to disappear, overtaken by the undeniable truth in Sarah's words.

With a heavy, almost imperceptible sigh, Jacob allowed her to push the gun down gently. The tension in his arm eased, and the fight seemed to drain out of him.

As soon as the gun was lowered, Elijah and Thomas moved in quickly. They grabbed Jacob, who, surprisingly, did not struggle. His resistance had left him, his fight deflated by Sarah's heartfelt words and the realization of the pain he had caused.

The camp remained silent, the only sounds being the soft murmur of the wind through the trees and the distant calls of wildlife. Sarah felt a mixture of relief and sorrow—relief that the threat was over and sorrow for the path Jacob had chosen that led him here.

Nate stepped closer to her, his presence a reassuring strength at her side. He said nothing, but his hand found hers, squeezing it gently, a silent communication of his support and love.

As Jacob was led away, his head bowed in defeat as Sarah watched him go.

"You all right?" Nate asked.

Sarah nodded, unable to find the words to say how she truly felt. She was finally free.

Chapter Thirty-Four

Nate stood outside Sam's wagon, his mind heavy with the day's events. He could hear the muffled movements inside the wagon where Jacob was being held. Taking a deep breath, he climbed up and peered inside, finding Jacob solemn and quiet, his hands bound, his eyes staring vacantly at the wagon's wooden floor.

Nate opened his mouth as if to say something and then closed it again. What was there to say?

He turned as he heard stones crunch underfoot and found Mary holding two cups of coffee. Her warm smile was a welcome sight after the day's tensions.

"Thought ye might need this," Mary said, handing him a steaming cup.

Nate accepted the coffee gratefully. "Thanks," he said. " It's been a day, hasn't it?"

"Aye, that it has," Mary replied, leaning against the wagon. "How's he doin'?"

Mary tilted her head toward the wagon, but Nate said nothing, taking a few steps away as Mary followed him.

"He hasn't spoken a word since earlier..." Nate said.

Mary nodded, pressing her lips together.

"I actually feel a bit sorry for Jacob," he admitted. "Which is mad, considering everything he's done."

Mary placed a comforting hand on his arm. "Ye're a good man, Nate," she said softly. "But I ken how you feel. It's no' easy, being in love with someone who doesn't love ye back."

"No," Nate agreed.

They fell silent for a moment, and in truth, Nate would never understand how Jacob felt or how love, unrequited love, could drive you so far. The only person he'd ever been in love with was Sarah, and she loved him too.

"I must say, I am glad and relieved Sarah's wee one arrived safely," Mary said. "After all her hardships, she deserves a bit of happiness."

Nate nodded, sipping the hot coffee, its bitterness a stark contrast to the sweetness of Mary's words. "She does. But there's still a long road ahead before we arrive in California."

Mary sighed, a knowing look in her eyes. "Aye, that's true, but after all ye've been through already, I'm certain ye can handle anything."

As the sun dipped low on the horizon, casting a warm, golden glow over the camp, the sudden appearance of several figures on horseback caused a ripple of tension among the settlers. Nate, who had been deep in conversation with Mary, paused mid-sentence, his gaze shifting toward the newcomers. The camp fell into an uneasy silence, the only sounds being the soft nickering of horses and the campfire crackle.

The chief led the group of men, his presence commanding even from a distance. Beside him rode Running Wolf, whose earlier actions had helped save Sarah's and her child's lives.

As they approached, Nate set his coffee cup down and stepped forward, his expression a mix of caution and respect. The settlers around him mirrored his actions, their bodies tense, eyes fixed on the visitors. Children peeked curiously from behind wagons, and a few men half-reached for weapons they hoped not to use.

The chief raised a hand in greeting, a universal sign of peace, and dismounted with a grace that belied his age. Running Wolf followed suit, his eyes scanning the camp with an alertness that spoke of his deep connection to the land and its nuances.

"Good evening," the chief began, his voice deep and resonant, carrying across the clearing. "We come in peace to see how the man my son harmed is healing."

Nate stepped closer. "Pete is recovering. We're grateful for your concern."

The chief nodded but did not accept Nate's handshake, so Nate let his arm fall by his side.

Then, Chief White Eagle glanced over his shoulder and nodded. One of his men stepped forward with a small leather bag, which he handed to the Chief.

"Where is the woman?" he asked. "The one who bore the child? I have something I wish to give her."

"She's resting—"

"Nate?"

He turned to see Sarah a few feet behind him, and Nate smiled at her, gesturing her forward. She walked slowly, coming to a stop beside Nate. She was carrying the baby in her left arm, her face nuzzled into the crook of Sarah's elbow.

Chief White Bear reached into the leather ball and removed another smaller bag; its top had a sturdy drawstring closure made from braided leather. The drawstring was adorned with small beads and a couple of tiny feathers. Attached to the bag was a small loop from which a tiny carved stone hung.

"For your child," he said, handing her the bag.

Sarah hesitated a moment and then reached out to take it. "Thank you."

"In the eyes of our people, the birth of a child in the wilderness speaks to the enduring strength of life itself," Chief White Bear said. "This child, born amidst the elements, carries the spirit of the earth in her breath and the resilience of the wild in her heart. Mother and daughter have shown a formidable strength that is revered and respected."

Nate glanced at Sarah's eyes, which were glistening with tears.

"The wilderness does not bestow its gifts lightly," the chief continued. "It tests us, challenges us, and in doing so, teaches us the profound truths of our own endurance and spirit. You have embraced the might of the natural world and, in return, it has bestowed upon her a child who will walk with the fortitude of the great trees and the wisdom of the flowing rivers."

Sarah looked down at the baby, a tear rolling down her cheek.

"Let this amulet serve as a guardian for her journey," he said, gesturing to the small stone hanging from the loop on the bag. "May it guide her steps under the watchful eyes of the stars—the same stars under which our ancestors walked and understood the deeper currents of the universe. As she grows, may she hold the strength of her birth story as a beacon, and may it remind her of the courage that runs in her veins, gifted by her mother's love and the blessing of the wilderness."

"Thank you," Sarah said again, her voice thick. "I will treasure it always."

Chief White Bear nodded as Nate turned to Running Wolf.

"Without your son, we may never have found Sarah," he said. "We owe you a debt."

"You owe us nothing," Chief White Bear said.

Nate nodded.

"We wish you well on the rest of your journey," he said.

With a final nod, the chief mounted his horse, and the men turned back toward the trail, leaving the camp quieter in their wake.

***

The campfire crackled softly as a thin veil of white smoke rose into the air, disappearing before it reached the stars. Nate and Sarah sat quietly by the glowing embers. The rest of the camp had long since retired, leaving the world around them peaceful except for the occasional pop and hiss of the firewood. The night was cool, and Sarah cradled the baby in her arms, the little one's breathing even and peaceful in sleep.

"Did Jacob have supper?" Sarah's voice broke the silence, her tone soft yet carrying a weight of concern.

Nate looked at her, his admiration for her compassion deepening. "Yes, Mary took him something earlier," he replied.

The warmth from the fire played across Sarah's soft features.

"We're going to arrive at Gray's Station tomorrow morning," Nate said. "A doctor there can check on you and the baby."

Sarah chuckled lightly, a sound that warmed Nate's heart. "Best not let Emma hear you say that," she teased, her dark eyes twinkling with humor in the firelight.

Nate smiled wryly, and they fell into a comfortable silence, watching the flames dance and flicker.

"I wonder what Jacob will do now," Sarah said thoughtfully.

"Do you care?" Nate asked gently, turning to look at her.

Sarah sighed, her gaze fixed on the flames. "I want to forgive him, Nate. Not so much for him but for myself. Especially now, with her." She glanced down at the baby. "I don't want her life to be shadowed by the past."

Nate's heart swelled with affection as he reached out, his fingers lightly touching Sarah's cheek, a gesture tender and full of understanding. The baby cooed softly in her sleep, a slight, contented sound that seemed to echo in the quiet night.

Nate looked down at the little bundle in Sarah's arms, feeling a surge of emotions he'd never anticipated. "I never thought I'd look at a baby and feel this much love, this fierce need to protect," he murmured.

The fire crackled, and a log shifted, sending a shower of sparks into the air. Sarah looked up at Nate, her eyes reflecting the fire's glow. "I've been thinking about it, and if it's okay with you, I'd like to name her Rose," she said hesitantly. "After your mother."

A lump formed in Nate's throat, emotions flooding in. He was touched beyond words, honored that she would think to connect their daughter to his own past, his own heart. He managed a nod.

"Little Rosie," he whispered, gently touching the soft hair on the baby's head.

Sarah smiled. "Little Rosie," she murmured.

They sat there a while longer, the world around them still and serene, wrapped in the comfort of each other's presence. As the fire dwindled to glowing embers, the night wrapped around them like a cloak.

"Nate," Sarah said.

He turned to her.

"I need to speak with Jacob."

Nate hesitated. "I don't think it's a good idea," he said after a moment.

"You don't have to leave me alone with him," Sarah said. "But I need to speak with him."

Nate sighed. "All right."

He got up and offered Sarah his hands, helped her to her feet, and together, they walked over to the wagon. As they approached, Nate turned to her.

"I'll be right by the door," he said. "If you need anything."

Sarah nodded as she handed the sleeping baby to Nate. He smiled at her as she turned and climbed up into the wagon, pushing the canvas flap aside.

Nate stood just outside the wagon, his back pressed against the wooden frame, as he listened to the conversation between Sarah and Jacob.

"Jacob, I've come to tell you that I forgive you," Sarah said, calm but firm.

There was a moment of silence, and Nate imagined Jacob's surprise.

"You... forgive me?" Jacob's voice was incredulous, tinged with disbelief.

"Yes," Sarah continued, her tone steady. "I need to forgive you for myself to finally move on."

Jacob let out a bitter laugh. "I don't deserve your forgiveness, Sarah. I shouldn't have done what I did, taking you from the camp. I blame the drink, but that's no excuse."

Nate could hear the regret in Jacob's voice, a raw edge of vulnerability that hadn't been there before.

"I know you're sorry," Sarah said gently. "But you need to understand that I'm moving on, and you need to do the same."

"I can't just let you go, Sarah," his voice was strained. "I made a terrible mistake, but if you give me another chance, I can make it right. I'll give up the drink, I promise."

"Jacob, you're the last Turner left," Sarah said, her voice softening. "If you continue down this road, drinking yourself to death, it won't make me happy. It won't change anything. You must choose to do something with your life, to be better than Robert."

A lump rose in Nate's throat at her words. She was offering Jacob a lifeline, a chance to redeem himself and find a better path. He hoped Jacob would take it.

There was a long pause, and Nate could almost hear the wheels turning in Jacob's mind.

"I don't know if I can," Jacob said, his voice barely above a whisper. "I don't know if I can be better."

"You can," Sarah insisted. "I know you can. But you have to want it. You have to choose it for yourself, not for anyone else."

Nate leaned closer, his heart pounding. He could feel the weight of the moment, the possibility of change hanging in the air.

Jacob sighed deeply. “I don’t know where to start.”

“Start by letting go of the past,” Sarah said softly. “And of me.”

“I can’t,” Jacob said.

“You have to,” Sarah said.

“But I love you,” Jacob said. “I’ve always loved you.”

“I know,” Sarah said. “But you need to let me go.”

The wagon fell silent for a long moment, and then Nate heard the creak of the wood. A moment later, the canvas flapped open, and Sarah climbed out. He reached for her hand, their fingers intertwining. She looked up at him, her eyes filled with relief and a hint of sadness.

“Are you all right?” he asked softly, searching her face.

Sarah nodded as she took Rosie from him.

“Come on,” Nate said.

As Nate and Sarah walked back to their wagon, Nate couldn’t help but glance over his shoulder. Jacob's figure was silhouetted against the wagon's white canvas, motionless, as if frozen in time. Nate wondered if Jacob truly had the strength to do as Sarah had urged—to move forward and find a better path.

***

As dawn broke over the horizon, Nate led the wagon train along the dusty trail toward Gray’s Station. The morning was brisk, the air tinged with the crisp scent of autumn approaching, signaling a change in season and a reminder of the urgency of their journey.

Gray's Station was a bustling outpost on the frontier's edge, a critical hub for pioneers traveling westward. The settlement consisted of a series of low, sturdy buildings made of wood and adobe huddled around a central trading post. The trading post, operated by the Gray family, served as a general store and a gathering point for travelers seeking to exchange goods, stories, and news from the Trail.

As they approached, the sounds of life at the station grew louder—the creak of wagons, the lowing of oxen, and the calls of traders hawking their wares. Smoke curled up from chimneys, carrying the smell of cooking fires and fresh hay. Despite its rough appearance, Gray's Station was a welcome sight for weary travelers, offering supplies, minor repairs, and a brief respite from the relentless wilderness.

Nate guided the wagon train into a designated area for travelers to set up camp. The area was well-used, with patches of bare earth where countless fires had burned and wagons had circled. As they came to a stop, Nate climbed down from his wagon and gathered the group for a quick meeting.

"Listen up," Nate began, his voice carrying clearly over the buzz of activity. "We'll only be here for one night, so I need everyone to focus on restocking your wagons. Check your supplies to see what you need, but make it quick. We can't afford to waste time here."

He scanned the faces of the settlers, noting the fatigue that marked their features.

“I know everyone's tired, but we need to keep moving. Winter's on our heels, and we must be well into the mountains before the first snows.”

Around them, the station buzzed with activity. Pioneers from other trains milled about, bartering with traders who had set up temporary stalls offering everything from fresh produce and meat to spare parts for wagons and handmade goods. Children ran between the wagons, their laughter a brief respite from the arduous journey.

Nate walked over to the trading post, its front porch cluttered with barrels of salted meats and sacks of flour. Inside, the shelves were stocked with goods, and the air smelled of leather, tobacco, and spices. He greeted Mr. Gray, the proprietor, a grizzled man with a friendly demeanor and a keen eye for business.

As he arranged for the necessary supplies, Nate’s thoughts drifted back to Sarah and little Rosie, now safely nestled in their wagon with Emma watching over them. The brief stop at Gray’s Station was a necessary pause in their journey, a moment to gather strength and resources for the challenges ahead.

As the day wore on, Nate was immersed in the bustle of activity, assisting where he could and ensuring their brief stay was as productive as possible. He watched Thomas and the local blacksmith animatedly discuss the alignment of an axle on one of the wagons, their voices merging with the clanging of metal and the occasional snort from an impatient ox.

Then, out of the corner of his eye, Nate spotted Jacob standing isolated a few hundred feet away, his belongings gathered into a worn bag at his feet. His shoulders were hunched as he absentmindedly kicked at the ground with the toe of his boot. As Nate watched him, he recalled Sarah's words from the night before about forgiveness and moving forward.

After a moment of hesitation, Nate turned and walked over to him.

Jacob heard his footsteps and turned. Nate half-expected to see the usual hardness in his eyes, the anger or defiance. Instead, Jacob looked resigned, tired, and somehow smaller than he had been.

"What will you do next?" Nate asked, breaking the strained silence that fell between them.

Jacob shrugged slightly, his gaze drifting over the busy station. "I don't know," he admitted, his voice hollow.

There was another pause, filled with the distant sound of bargaining voices and the occasional whinny of a horse.

"I never expected any of this when my brother convinced me to leave Kansas," he confessed suddenly, breaking the silence between them. "I've lost everything. The only family I ever knew."

Nate listened quietly, sensing the shift in Jacob. There was no blame in his tone now, just a sad recognition of his own failings.

"I'm sorry," Jacob said, his eyes meeting Nate's squarely. "For everything. I let my jealousy consume me."

Nate nodded, acknowledging the apology with a silent gravity. He could hear in Jacob's voice a genuine remorse and a painful self-awareness. Yet, it did not change what had happened. It was good that Jacob was finally taking responsibility for his actions. But Nate couldn't trust him.

"I just left Pete out there," Jacob said, his voice turning thick with emotion. "He was the only friend I had, and I just left him to die..."

Jacob's voice trailed off as he shook his head. After a moment, he looked up, sniffing as he stared into the distance. "When did I lose control of my life?" he muttered, more to himself than to Nate.

"The Trail has a way of revealing our true characters," Nate said after a moment. "Maybe you should take this as a second chance. To be a better man."

Jacob nodded slowly, the suggestion resonating with him in a way that might once have seemed impossible.

They fell silent again.

"Well, goodbye, Jacob," Nate said. "And good luck."

Jacob said nothing as Nate turned to leave

"Look after her," Jacob called out to him.

Nate paused, then continued walking without looking back, the weight of Jacob's words settling on him. As he moved away, his thoughts lingered on their final exchange. They were not friends, but neither were they enemies.

***

Nate felt relief and anticipation as the wagon train rolled away from Gray's Station. With all its hustle and bustle, the station had faded into the distance, leaving behind the open expanse of the Great Plains stretching out before them. Sarah was beside him on the wagon seat, her presence a constant comfort. Nestled contentedly in a basket between them, Rosie was a tangible symbol of the new life they were forging together.

The wagon creaked and rocked gently over the uneven terrain, a rhythmic motion that Rosie seemed to find soothing. Nate had expressed his concerns about Sarah sitting up front with him, especially so soon after her ordeal, but she had insisted.

"We need the fresh air," she said with a smile that brooked no argument. "And surprisingly, Rosie likes the rock of the wagon."

As they traversed the vast, open prairie, Nate's mind wandered back to the first time Sarah had ridden alongside him. So much had changed since then, and it seemed almost impossible to believe that so much had happened in just a few months.

Nate glanced over at Sarah, catching her smiling at him—a smile that reached her eyes and warmed him to his core.

"Do you think you'll miss all of this when we get to California?" she asked, her voice carrying a note of curiosity and a hint of nostalgia.

Nate took a moment before answering, his eyes scanning the horizon where the earth met the sky in a perfect line. "Part of me will," he admitted. "There's something about the Trail—the way it's both relentless and freeing. But, I'm ready for a new trail—"

He reached over, his hand finding hers, squeezing it gently. "One I no longer have to navigate alone."

Sarah smiled.

"With you and Rosie, the journey ahead isn't just a path through the wilderness—it's a path home," he said, his voice sure and steady. "A journey to a place where we can set down roots and build a life not just about survival but about living."

Sarah's smile deepened, her eyes sparkling with tears of happiness. “That sounds like the best kind of trail to me.”

Nate nodded, a profound sense of peace settling over him. The road ahead would indeed bring new challenges, but with Sarah and Rosie by his side, he felt equipped to face anything. The vastness of the plains around them no longer seemed daunting but inviting, a canvas on which they would paint their future.

As the wagon continued its steady progress, the sound of the wheels blending with the whispers of the prairie wind, Nate felt a deep gratitude for the journey that had brought him to this moment. The Trail had revealed character, forged bonds, and transformed challenges into opportunities for growth. Looking ahead, the Trail to California no longer represented an ending for Nate but rather a beautiful new beginning.

Epilogue

Sunset Hills, California, Fall, 1864

Sarah sat on the porch of their small ranch, the gentle creak of the old rocking chair providing a comforting rhythm as she read the letter in her hands. For a moment, she looked up, the late afternoon sun warm on her face, casting a golden hue over the sprawling landscape that stretched before her.

Sarah looked back down at the letter, her eyes skimming the words penned by Charlotte Turner, Jacob's wife.

Dear Sarah, Nate, and Family,

I hope this letter finds you well and in good spirits. It has been some time since we last corresponded, and I am pleased to share that we are expecting our second child come spring. The news brings joy to our home, and I wanted to share this happiness with you.

Jacob is doing better these days, though he continues to wrestle with the demons of his past. The guilt from what transpired five years ago on the Trail still haunts him, and though time has helped, I am starting to wonder if there are wounds that words can never truly heal.

Jacob wishes to write to you, but he holds back for fear you do not wish to hear from him. That said, he's asked me to please wish dearest Rose a happy birthday.

With warm regards and hopes for your continued happiness,

Charlotte

Sarah sighed softly as she finished reading the letter, folding it carefully and setting it aside. Her eyes wandered over their ranch, taking in the rows of crops, the contented animals, and the home they had built together. It was hard to believe that so many years had passed since those tumultuous days on the Trail. Sometimes, it felt like a different life altogether.

The months after they had left Jacob at Gray's Station were a blur of movement and adaptation. For over three years, there had been no word from him, a silence that had brought both relief and unanswered questions. Then, out of the blue, a letter had arrived from his bride, Charlotte Turner, telling them of Jacob's new life in Arizona.

Sarah could still remember the surprise when Charlotte's first letter arrived. She vividly remembered the unexpected arrival, the careful opening of the envelope, and the emotions that surged as she read Charlotte's words.

Charlotte had written of Jacob, of how he had told her everything that had happened on the Trail, how he had unburdened himself of the guilt and shame that had haunted him. She had described him as a man seeking redemption, battling his inner demons but determined to change.

In the end, Sarah was glad for that letter. As much as she wanted to put Robert and Jacob in the past, to move forward and forget them, she realized it was impossible. They would always be a part of her past, and knowing them had made her into the woman she was.

As Sarah sat, she heard the porch creak behind her. Before she could turn around, strong arms wrapped around her shoulders as Nate gently kissed her head. She closed her eyes, savoring the moment, breathing in the familiar scent of dust and sweat—his scent, one she would never tire of.

"Hey there," Nate murmured.

She opened her eyes and met his, the warmth of his gaze filling her with contentment. Nate leaned down to kiss her, his nose brushing softly against hers.

However, their stolen moment of tenderness was suddenly interrupted by the sound of small feet pattering across the front yard. Almost five-year-old Rose appeared first, followed closely by three-year-old Noah, who was crying and clutching his finger.

"Mama, Noah got stung by a paper wasp!" Rosie announced, her blue eyes wide with concern.

Sarah immediately kneeled, taking Noah's hand in hers and examining the little finger, which was already red and swollen. "Oh, sweetheart," she cooed, kissing the injured finger. Noah looked up at her with big green eyes, so much like his father's, the tears slowly abating.

Nate crouched beside them. "How about I take you to see the new foals, Noah?" he asked, his voice gentle. "Would that cheer you up?"

Noah's eyes lit up at the mention of the foals; his pain and the incident with the paper wasp were instantly forgotten. "Yes, Papa!"

Nate chuckled as he scooped him up, and the two of them headed off toward the stables.

"Rosie?" Sarah said as she turned to her daughter. "Don't you want to go and see the foals too?"

Rosie, however, hung back, her bottom lip quivering. She looked so much like Sarah, with her wild brown hair and tall frame, but her eyes were the same piercing blue as Robert's.

"Is everything all right? Are you worried about your birthday party tomorrow?" Sarah asked gently.

Rosie shook her head, her eyes filling with unshed tears. "No, Mama," she whispered. "It's something else."

Sarah's heart ached as she sat back down in the rocker and patted her lap, inviting Rosie to sit. "Come here, sweetheart."

Rosie climbed onto her mother's lap, wrapping her arms around Sarah's neck. Sarah looked into her daughter's eyes. Despite being only five years old, she was a sensitive child who felt things deeply. Nate always called her his "old soul" because she always seemed so much wiser than her years.

"Tell me what's wrong," Sarah said.

Rosie exhaled shakily. "At school yesterday, Abigail Collins said that her mama said papa isn't my real papa. Is that true?" she asked, her voice trembling.

Sarah frowned as a lump rose in Sarah's throat. The Collins family had been on the Trail with them, and although Sarah did not know them well, they had also settled in Sunset Hills. So, of course, they knew their history.

Sarah took a deep breath.

"Rosie, Papa is your papa in all the ways that truly count."

Rosie's eyes searched her mother's face for answers. "But what happened to my real papa?"

Sarah sighed softly, hugging Rosie closer. "Your real papa, Robert, died on the California Trail just after we left Kansas," she explained gently. "The same trail where you were born."

Rosie said nothing for a moment, but Sarah could see her mind working furiously behind her big, blue eyes.

"But does that mean Noah isn't my brother?" she asked.

"Of course he is," Sarah said. "And your papa is your papa, no matter what else anyone says."

Rosie pressed her lips together tightly.

"Rose," Sarah said. "If there's one thing I've learned in my life, it's that family doesn't always mean blood."

"Then what does it mean?" Rosie asked.

"It means love," Sarah said simply. "Your papa loves you like his own daughter. He's been there for you from the very beginning, loving and caring for you every single day. Family is about who's there for you, who loves you, and takes care of you. Like Grandma Mary. She's not your grandmother by blood, but we love her just the same, don't we?"

Rosie nodded slowly as she absorbed her mother's words. "Yes, Mama."

Sarah kissed Rosie's forehead. "Then you understand, sweetheart. Papa is your papa in every way that matters."

Rosie smiled, the uncertainty in her eyes replaced by a newfound understanding. She hugged Sarah tightly before hopping off her lap. "I'm going to find Papa and Noah!" she called as she raced off the porch.

Sarah watched Rose run off, her heart swelling with pride and love. She would never forget what Chief White Eagle had said about her daughter being born in the wilderness. She carried the spirit of the earth in her breath and the resilience of the wild in her heart. Rosie embodied the best parts of both her and Nate—kindness, compassion, strength, and resilience.

***

The small ranch was bustling with excitement as preparations for Rosie's fifth birthday party began. The garden had been transformed into a magical setting, with wildflowers and garlands of greenery adorning the trees and fences. Simple homemade decorations—paper butterflies, flower crowns, and colorful ribbons—fluttered gently in the breeze.

A long table covered with a checkered cloth was set with delicious homemade treats: fruit pies, sugar cookies shaped like flowers, and pitchers of lemonade. Freshly picked flowers were arranged in small vases, adding a touch of natural beauty to the spread.

Children from the nearby homesteads and the local school arrived, their faces lighting up with joy as they saw the garden transformed into a whimsical wonderland. Games were set up around the yard—sack races, a scavenger hunt, and a small area where they could make flower crowns and corn husk dolls.

Sarah stood near the entrance, welcoming the guests with a warm smile. Nate helped organize the games, and Noah followed him around. "Your little shadow," Sarah always teased Nate.

Rosie, dressed in a simple but pretty dress adorned with tiny embroidered flowers, ran around excitedly with her friends, her wild brown hair bouncing as she moved.

Sarah glanced over at Mary, who was carefully arranging the table's centerpiece: a beautiful birthday cake. Mary's meticulous attention to detail was evident, and the cake, adorned with fresh flowers and delicate icing, looked almost too beautiful to eat.

"You've outdone yourself again, Mary," Sarah said, approaching her friend and admiring the cake. "Rosie will be over the moon."

Mary smiled, a twinkle in her eye. "Aye, well, it's a special day, isn't it? Our wee lass is growing up so fast."

"Sometimes I still can't believe it," Sarah said, smiling.

They fell silent for a moment, and as Sarah glanced at Mary, she felt a rush of gratitude toward her. After Sarah and Nate had stayed in California, Mary joined another wagon train but only stayed with it for a year or so before finally deciding she was done. She'd settled in the town near them, becoming a huge part of their lives. She made birthday cakes for the children for every birthday and often fetched them from school. Sarah could not imagine their lives without her.

"I got a letter from Emma the other day," Sarah said.

Mary's eyes lit up with interest. "Aye, is that so? How is she doing?"

"She's doing well," Sarah replied, her voice filled with pride. "She's been taken under the wing of a mine doctor teaching her surgical skills. Can you believe it? Our Emma, becoming a surgeon."

Mary's smile widened, pride evident in her expression. "Aye, I always knew she had it in her. She's got a heart of gold and a mind sharper than a new blade."

Sarah nodded, smiling softly as she thought of the friends they had made on the wagon trail. They didn't see them as much as they would have liked to, but they made a conscious effort to keep in touch and be abreast of all the news. Elijah was still out there on the Trail, working as a scout, and came to visit whenever he found himself in California. Old veteran Samuel settled in the next town over, and they saw him every few months until he passed away last year. Thomas still wrote to Nate. He worked as a blacksmith for the mines and was married with a child on the way. Sarah missed them all, her chosen family, and sometimes she wondered if they'd ever all be in the same place again. After all, they'd been through so much together.

Sarah sighed softly as she put a comforting hand on her arm.

"Like the wheels of a wagon, life moves on," she said as if she could hear Sarah's thoughts. "We cannae stop it, and we shouldn't want tae. But we carry the memories with us and the people we've met along the way."

Sarah nodded, her gaze drifting over the lively garden party, the joy and laughter filling the air. She would never forget the Trail and the people who had forged their paths alongside hers. It was a journey that shaped her, that had changed her entire life.

Just then, Rosie came running up, her face alight with excitement. She grabbed Mary's hand, tugging at it insistently.

"Grandma Mary, can you tell us the story of the Loch Ness Monster?" Rosie pleaded, her eyes wide with anticipation.

Mary chuckled wryly, shaking her head. "Ach, lass, yer parents won't thank me for sendin' all ye wee friends home shiverin' in their trousers."

Rosie pouted, her bottom lip jutting out in a practiced expression of irresistible charm. "But it's my birthday, Grandma Mary! Please?"

Mary laughed, unable to resist the pleading look in Rosie's blue eyes. "Aye, all right then."

Rosie beamed as she pulled Mary away to a patch of shade where the children were all already gathered, sitting cross-legged on the grass.

Mary cleared her throat as she folded her hands behind her back. "Aye, I'll tell ye the tale of the Loch Ness Monster," she said. "But only if ye promise not tae have nightmares!"

The children cheered, their faces filled with eager anticipation.

"Now, in the misty hills of bonnie Scotland, there lies a deep, dark loch called Loch Ness. It's a place o' mystery and legend, where the waters are said tae hide a creature unlike any other..."

The children leaned in closer, their eyes wide with fascination. Mary's voice was soothing and thrilling, weaving the story with suspense and charm.

"Those who have seen her say she is a fearsome sight to behold," Mary continued. "She's got a long, serpentine neck, rising high above the water like the mast of a ghostly ship. Her skin is dark and glistening, like the scales of a giant fish, and it shimmers in the moonlight. But it's her eyes that will send shivers down yer spine—glowing like fiery coals, watching yer every move from beneath the waves."

Mary paused for dramatic effects as she looked around the group of children, her eyes twinkling with mischief.

"Many a brave soul has tried tae find the monster, but she's a clever beastie, always slippin' away just when ye think ye've got a glimpse of her. Some say she's as old as the loch itself, a guardian o' the deep..."

Sarah smiled to herself, and a moment later, Nate slipped his arm around Sarah's waist, pulling her close.

"She's always been a good storyteller," Nate said, his voice full of amusement.

"She has," Sarah agreed.

She looked up at him, and he smiled, his green eyes twinkling with warmth and love.

"She's growing up so quickly, isn't she?" Nate said softly, nodding toward Rosie, who listened intently to Mary's story.

Sarah smiled, her heart swelling with pride. "Mary and I were just saying the same thing. And before we know it, Noah will be right behind her," she said, glancing over at their son, who was also listening intently.

"All the more reason to hold tightly to these moments," Nate said.

Sarah leaned her head against his arm, feeling the warmth of his skin beneath the thin cotton on his shirt. Nate was right; Sarah wanted to cling to them every second and hold onto them for as long as possible before they slipped away. Someone once told her that the days were long, but the years were short, which hadn't felt truer than it did at the moment.

As they watched their children, Sarah sighed contently. Her life was so full; it was simple and happy. It almost felt surreal to think how things had been before she left Kansas. She would never forget that part of her life, but it was a past that no longer held any power over her. She finally had everything she could ever wish for and knew she owed it all to Nate. He had saved her in every way a person could be saved. He was her other half, who had stood by her through every trial and triumph.

Nate looked down at her and smiled. For a long time after they'd left the Trail, Sarah had worried Nate would miss it and pine for his old life. But if he did miss it, he never said anything. Instead, he embraced the life they'd built together, and in as many ways as Nate had given Sarah a new life and a family, she'd given him those things, too.

As the sun began to dip below the tree line, the children's laughter filled the air, mingling with the soft rustling of the leaves and the distant lowing of the cattle.

Sarah and Nate stood together, hands entwined, their hearts beating in perfect harmony. They were surrounded by the people they loved and the life they had built together. With Nate, Sarah could be her true self, more in control of her life and her own happiness. She had no idea where their path would take them next, but she didn't care. As long as she had her family and friends, they could overcome anything.

THE END

Also by Sally M. Ross

Thank you for reading "**The Wagon Master's Promise to a New Life**"!

I hope you enjoyed it! If you did, here are some of my other books!

Also, if you liked this book, you can also check out **my full Amazon Book Catalogue at:** **https://go.sallymross.com/bc-authorpage**

Thank you for allowing me to keep doing what I love! ❤